Spellbound IN A KILT

Other Books by Anna Durand

Lachlan in a Kilt (The Ballachulish Trilogy, Book One)
Aidan in a Kilt (The Ballachulish Trilogy, Book Two)
Rory in a Kilt (The Ballachulish Trilogy, Book Three)
The American Wives Club (A Hot Brits/Hot Scots/Au Naturel Crossover Book)
Brit vs. Scot (A Hot Brits/Hot Scots/Au Naturel Crossover Book)
Dangerous in a Kilt (Hot Scots, Book One)
Wicked in a Kilt (Hot Scots, Book Two)
Scandalous in a Kilt (Hot Scots, Book Three)
The MacTaggart Brothers Trilogy (Hot Scots, Books 1-3)
Gift-Wrapped in a Kilt (Hot Scots, Book Four)
Notorious in a Kilt (Hot Scots, Book Five)
Insatiable in a Kilt (Hot Scots, Book Six)
Lethal in a Kilt (Hot Scots, Book Seven)
Irresistible in a Kilt (Hot Scots, Book Eight)
Devastating in a Kilt (Hot Scots, Book Nine)
Relentless in a Kilt (Hot Scots, Book Eleven)
One Hot Chance (Hot Brits, Book One)
One Hot Roomie (Hot Brits, Book Two)
One Hot Crush (Hot Brits, Book Three)
The Dixon Brothers Trilogy (Hot Brits, Books 1-3)
One Hot Escape (Hot Brits, Book Four)
One Hot Rumor (Hot Brits, Book Five)
One Hot Christmas (Hot Brits, Book Six)
Natural Passion (Au Naturel Trilogy, Book One)
Natural Impulse (Au Naturel Trilogy, Book Two)
Natural Satisfaction (Au Naturel Trilogy, Book Three)
Fired Up (standalone romance)
Echo Power (Echo Power Trilogy, Book One)
The Mortal Falls (Undercover Elementals, Book One)
The Mortal Fires (Undercover Elementals, Book Two)
The Mortal Tempest (Undercover Elementals, Book Three)
The Janusite Trilogy (Undercover Elementals, Books 1-3)
Obsidian Hunger (Undercover Elementals, Book Four)
Unbidden Hunger (Undercover Elementals, Book Five)
Willpower (Psychic Crossroads, Book One)
Intuition (Psychic Crossroads, Book Two)
Kinetic (Psychic Crossroads, Book Three)
Passion Never Dies: The Complete Reborn Series

Spellbound IN A KILT

Hot Scots, Book Ten

ANNA DURAND

JACOBSVILLE BOOKS JB MARIETTA, OHIO

SPELLBOUND IN A KILT

ISBN: 978-1-949406-71-9 (paperback)
ISBN: 978-1-949406-72-6 (ebook)
ISBN:978-1-949406-73-3 (audiobook)

Manufactured in the United States.

Jacobsville Books
www.JacobsvilleBooks.com

Publisher's Cataloging-in-Publication Data
provided by Five Rainbows Cataloging Services

Names: Durand, Anna, author.
Title: Spellbound in a kilt / Anna Durand.
Description: Marietta, OH : Jacobsville Books, 2021. | Series: Hot Scots, bk. 10.
Identifiers: ISBN 978-1-949406-71-9 (paperback) | ISBN 978-1-949406-72-6 (ebook) | ISBN 978-1-949406-73-3 (audiobook)
Subjects: LCSH: Witchcraft--Fiction. | Man-woman relationships--Fiction. | Scots--Fiction. | Americans--Fiction. | Highlands (Scotland)--Fiction. | Romance fiction. | BISAC: FICTION / Romance / Contemporary. | FICTION / Romance / Romantic Comedy. | GSAFD: Love stories.
Classification: LCC PS3604.U724 S64 2021 (print) | LCC PS3604.U724 (ebook) | DDC 813/.6--dc23.

Chapter One

Kirsty

When a lass gets dumped by the only man she's ever loved, and he calls her insane when he ends things, she has a right to expect never to see that scunner again. For years, that's what I have believed. I will never see Luke Turner again, not even when I die and go to heaven. He must be going to someplace hotter and much further south.

But I won't think about *him* anymore.

Today, my cousin Jack is getting married. My entire family, including cousins and honorary members, have gathered on the green behind my cousin Rory's castle, where the wedding of Jack and Autumn will take place. The ceremony is beautiful. I cry, of course. Weddings always do that to me. But when Jack throws an arm around Autumn and drags her into him for a passionate kiss, I get a strange pang in my chest.

Luke used to kiss me that way.

Not that I still think about him. That's only happened once—today. Well, maybe I've thought of him on occasion. That means nothing. I think of him only so I can do a blessing to ward off any sentimental rubbish I might feel otherwise.

After the ceremony, guests don't have to walk far to get to the reception. It's happening on the green too. I chat to my sisters for a while, but Isla and Elspeth decide to introduce themselves to Jack's in-laws while I want to talk to Autumn. We've had lovely chats since I met her a few weeks ago, and we've become friends.

I wander over to the table where Jack and Autumn are sitting. "May I sit with you?"

"Absolutely," Autumn says.

I still think it's odd that most of my cousins and my brother have all married Americans. Logan fell in love with Serena, an older woman, last year. I'd been a bridesmaid at their wedding. Jack met Autumn in Las Vegas two years ago, though they got married and divorced so quickly no one even met her. They couldn't get along back then, or right after they were reunited recently, but they soon realized they still love each other. Jack suggested the other day that maybe Luke and I might not hate each other as much as we think. I assured him that's nonsense.

Luke is a horrible man. Very sexy, but still an erse. He can be charming too, but aye, he is always an erse. An enormous one.

Autumn and I chat to each other for a few minutes, and she wants to know more about the metaphysical shop I own in Loch Fairbairn, the village where we both live.

"Come by the shop anytime," I say. "I'll be happy to teach you about Wicca."

Jack still thinks Wicca is bollocks, but Autumn is more open-minded. My brother, Logan, agrees with Jack. But then, he used to be an MI6 agent and got used to relying on facts instead of things he can't see or touch.

"Thanks for the offer," Autumn says. "That's so sweet of you, Kirsty."

I smile, but then movement across the green catches my attention, and I can't help glancing at the figure approaching us. My mouth falls open. I think my eyes go wide too, since they suddenly feel dry. What in the world is going on? Am I hallucinating? I must have gone off my head, because I cannot be seeing who I think I'm seeing.

No, it can't be Luke Turner.

"Hey there, Kirsty," he says, as he stops near our table.

But aye, it is the American ersehole.

I leap up so quickly my chair topples over backward. "Luke? What are you doing here?"

He's wearing a charcoal suit with no tie, but I've never seen him in that sort of clothes before. Luke always used to wear jeans and T-shirts, not posh suits. Why is he dressed like that? Why is he here?

Luke aims his grey eyes straight at me, hooking a thumb in his waistband and cocking one hip. "Nice to see you too, Kirsty. What, no hello kiss?"

A kiss? Is he cracked?

I shake my head, and I'm fair certain my mouth is gaping. "You cannae be here. Crashing a wedding is…rude."

"Crashing?" Luke says with a chuckle. "One of your pals invited me. He called yesterday. His British accent confused me for a minute, but then he said he's married to one of your cousins, and it suddenly made sense. Kind of."

"But I—You—" I stumble backward a few steps. "You hate me. Why would ye want to be at my cousin's wedding?"

"Alex Thorne told me you're in trouble and you need me. I should come right away, he said." Luke walks up to me, halting an arm's length away. "I might think you're insane, but I never turn my back on a woman in need. So, what's the problem?"

"Whuh—" I blink several times quickly but cannae make sense of any of this. "You flew here all the way from America because a stranger told you to?"

"Nah." He shrugs. "I've been living in the UK for three years. Joined a private research institute down in England."

Logan stalks over to us and stops beside me. My brother levels his deadly calm glare at Luke. "Who the bloody hell are you and what have you done to upset my sister?"

"I'm so sorry," Luke says. "I've been disrespectful, haven't I?"

"Aye, and you're one second away from being dead on the grass."

The American erse chuckles again. "I guess that's a Scottish saying? Well, anyway, I'm Luke Turner. Kirsty's ex-boyfriend."

Alex Thorne ambles up to us. "What's going on over here? Looks like quite the rammy."

I slowly rotate my gaze toward Alex. "You did this, didn't you?"

"What if I did? You lot meddled in my life, so I'm returning the favor. You'll thank me later."

Luke glances at the crowd of MacTaggarts gathering around us, then he looks at me. "Could we go somewhere more private to talk?"

"Aye."

Where can I take him? Someplace private? Maybe I should hit him over the head with a dinner plate and walk away.

I seize his arm and drag him through the doorway into the garden, out of sight of the rest of my family and friends. And I shut the garden door to keep my nosy relatives from peeking in here.

Facing Luke, I demand, "What are you doing here? And donnae give me that rubbish about Alex saying I need you."

Luke runs a hand through his dark-blond hair. "It's not 'rubbish,' Kirsty. He said that."

"Maybe he did, but that doesn't explain why you're here."

He tips his head to the side, almost smirking. "How about that hello kiss?"

"You really are off your head if you think I want to kiss you." I fold my arms over my chest. "You called me insane, and I know you're a bleeding ersehole."

"I probably am." He leans closer and speaks in a softer voice. "But I have a valid reason for coming here, and it has nothing to do with the fact you're still in love with me."

"What? I am not in love with you." I stab a finger into his chest. "You are the devil."

He chuckles. "That's not what you said when we were making love. As I recall, you told me I'm an angel with a dirty mind, a god in bed, and—"

"Haud yer wheesht!" I might have shouted that. Honestly, how much can a lass take? Maybe I did call him those things ages ago, but I don't want him anymore. Even if he does look even sexier now. Still, it's impolite for him to point out I said those things. "Well, now I understand the truth. You are the devil, and I know incantations to make you disappear."

"And you wonder why I think you're bonkers." He slings an arm around my waist and hauls me into his body. "But I'd still love to get naked with you. For old times' sake."

I knee him in the groin, though not as hard as I'd like to since I'm glued to his body and can't get leverage.

He gasps and staggers backward—while still holding onto me.

I give him my best evil glare, but I can't do that as well as Logan would. "Luke Turner, you are evil."

"Don't you want to know what my valid reason is?"

"No. I want you to bugger off."

"Can't do that."

I wriggle, trying to get away from him. "Let me go."

He shoves a hand into my hair and kisses me.

Chapter Two

Luke

Kirsty's lips feel as soft as I remembered during all the fantasies I've had of her over the years since I walked away from her. Yeah, okay, I admit I've thought about her a lot. Hard to forget the first girl I ever loved. I don't regret leaving her. No self-respecting scientist could get involved with a woman who seriously believes she has supernatural powers. I'm not thinking about that right now, though. Not thinking, period. Her lips have parted just enough that I could slip my tongue between them if I wanted, and though I shouldn't do it, I can't resist pushing inside her mouth so I can answer a question that has plagued me for years. Does she taste as good as I remember?

Oh yeah, she does.

I wrap my other arm around her too, pulling her body even closer while I thrust my tongue deeper, loving the way a soft moan whispers out of her and she relaxes against me. Kirsty wouldn't do that if she didn't have at least residual feelings for me. Maybe I have those too.

But it doesn't matter. I can't get too close to her.

When I peel my lips away from hers, she gazes at me with a dreamy expression.

No, I'm not looking at her that way. Only women get dreamy-eyed when an old flame kisses them. And that's all Kirsty is to me now—a girl I once dated more than a decade ago. Any stirrings of old feelings I might experience don't mean anything. I got over Kirsty a long time ago.

"Why did you do that?" she asks.

"Because I felt like it. Besides, you never gave me that hello kiss, and I think it's only right that we should greet each other that way. I mean, we dated for thirteen months."

"Aye, and thirteen is an unlucky number."

"I thought Wiccans believed it wasn't unlucky."

She puckers her lips, the dreamy expression disintegrating. "Maybe we do, but anything that involves you is cursed from the start."

"That's cute, Kirsty. You're so desperate to deny you're still in love with me that—"

"Haud yer wheesht, ye demon." She wriggles out of my arms and stumbles backward a few steps, blowing a lock of her brown hair away from her pale blue eyes. "Now, tell me what your valid reason is for being here."

"In a minute. First, I'd like to know why Alex Thorne thought you needed my help."

"Because he's an interfering erse, that's why."

"Come on, kitten, that's not an answer."

"Donnae be calling me pet names." She straightens her blouse, which got a little askew when we were kissing. "And I have no idea why Alex contacted you. I don't need help. All I need is for you to go away. Right now. Bugger off."

She waves her hands at me in a shooing gesture.

I chuckle. "Are you casting a spell on me? Damn, that makes me want to kiss you again."

"Well, I don't want to kiss you."

"Sure you do." I amble up to her and hook a finger under her chin. "You still want me, Kirsty. Wouldn't have kissed me the way you did a minute ago unless you've still got the hots for me big time."

"There is no heat. I'm feeling quite cool at the moment."

"Liar." I skim my thumb over her mouth. "Your lips are pinker, your cheeks too. Your body betrays your lie, kitten."

Her gaze flicks to the closed door that accesses the lawn outside the castle compound.

We're standing right beside that door, and I can hear the faint sounds of music and revelry going on out there. A heavy bass beat thumps, audible even through the stone wall. The wedding reception is in full swing.

I rub my thumb across her lips again. "One more kiss. For old times' sake."

"How many old-times kisses do you expect to get?"

"Just the right amount. When you're sagging against me and begging me for more, I'll know that's enough kissing—but not enough of other things."

Her pupils have dilated, and her breathing has grown labored. She does want me. And I want her, one last time before I tell her the real reason why I came here. Kirsty will never let me touch her again once she knows the truth.

I back her up to the wall and press my body into hers, our mouths almost touching. "We want the same thing. There's nothing wrong with scratching that itch."

"Are you suggesting we shag?" She says that in a surprised, almost breathless tone. Then she licks her lips, her gaze fixated on my mouth.

"Yes, I'm suggesting that." I palm her breast through her blouse. "If you don't want this, just knee me in the balls again. I won't try to kiss you after that."

"I…" She looks into my eyes. "*Bod an Donais*, I do want it."

That's all I need to know.

Pushing a hand into her hair, I seal my mouth over hers and plunge my tongue deep. She kisses me back, curling her tongue around mine and making hungry little noises that ensure my dick gets hard in record time. God, to feel her body again, pliant and willing and as starved for me as I am for her. Kirsty is the hottest girl on the planet. She seems like a sweet, innocent lass who would never get down-and-dirty with a guy like me, but she turns into a wild thing in the bedroom.

Who needs a bed? I'll be fucking her in a castle garden.

I shove a hand under her skirt and hike it up, thrusting my palm inside her panties so I can slide my fingers between her folds. Damn, she's wet and ready. Kirsty always was quick to get aroused, so I shouldn't be surprised now. But I am. In a good way. Though I'd love to feast on her, I don't think we have time for that. Her family is right outside that door, and I fully expect her murder-obsessed brother to storm in here anytime and drag me away from his sister.

So I rip her panties off and drop them on the ground.

Kirsty throws her arms around my neck and hoists one leg up to hook it around my hip.

I kiss her harder, deeper, groaning as I push a hand between our bodies to unzip my fly and free my dick. I should stop and make sure she's on the pill, since I don't have a condom, but I can't hold on to that thought for more than a millisecond. I have Kirsty in my arms, devouring me with her tongue, and she has her leg strapped around me, all but begging me to fuck her.

She rocks her hips forward, brushing my cock—and it throbs for her.

Christ, I can't stop myself. I grasp her hip with one hand and her ass with the other, and I thrust into her hard.

Her head falls back, her mouth open, as she clutches me with her leg.

I pound into her, over and over, grunting and pulling her hips into me with every inward lunge. Her cream dribbles down my cock and instigates a wet sucking noise, but I can't think about anything except how good it feels to be inside her again, watching her enraptured expression and driving her toward climax. She gasps and digs her nails into my shoulders. I pump harder and faster, the pressure in my dick escalating every second until I feel like my whole body might explode if we don't both come soon. Her tits bounce with every thrust, and she swings her other leg up to clutch me with both thighs.

"Ah, Kirsty," I growl.

She buries her face against my neck and sinks her teeth into my shoulder, stifling a cry. Her body convulses around me, her inner muscles gripping me so many times that I couldn't count them even if I tried.

I grit my teeth as fire scorches down my spine, straight into my cock, and machine-gun spasms force me to unleash everything inside her. My strangled shout echoes off the castle wall.

Kirsty sags against me, her legs still strapped around my hips.

I'm breathing too hard to speak, but I drop soft kisses along her throat until I reach her ear. For a moment, we just stay like that. Entangled. Joined. Too stunned to speak or move. Then I push her legs away and set her down on her feet.

Zipping up my slacks, I clear my throat. "Damn, I needed that."

She blinks several times quickly. "What?"

I kiss her cheek. "Thanks for that."

"Thank—" Her gaze narrows, and her lips pucker. "Ye bleeding ersehole. Did you do that just to prove you could seduce me?"

"No. I did it for old times' sake."

"Stop saying that bloody phrase." She slams her palms into my chest, making me stumble backward half a step. "You really are evil."

"Admit it, kitten. You enjoyed that as much as I did." I chuck her under the chin. "You came hard, that's for sure."

The she-devil swings her knee up, clearly intending to nail me in the balls again.

I catch her knee in my palm. "Uh-uh-uh. That's no way to treat the guy who just screwed you so good you bit me."

She sidles away from me and straightens her clothes. Then she tries to fix her hair but gives up. "Go away and never come back. Leave Scotland. If you ever cross the border again, I will—"

"What? Sic your brother on me?" Before she can snarl at me again, I change the subject. "About time I told you why I came here. Don't you think?"

Kirsty scowls. "Fine. Tell me, if you must."

"I want to study you."

"What?"

"You heard me. I want to study you and your Wiccan ways, to understand why people like you feel the need to indulge in all that nonsense. This will be an objective effort to uncover the delusions behind these folk beliefs."

"That's rubbish. You are not objective."

"What have you got to lose? Let me study you, Kirsty."

"Didnae I just say I never want to see you again?"

I shrug. "This is science, not romance. You can feel free to try to prove I'm wrong. Might be fun."

"No." She stomps over to the door and grasps the knob. "Sod off, Luke. I will not be your experiment."

She tries to open the door, but it doesn't budge. While she keeps yanking on it, she gets the cutest look of frustration on her face.

I come up behind her, push her hand off the knob, and pull the door open. "There. You can thank me with a kiss."

"Go to hell."

Kirsty stalks out onto the lawn.

I can't resist calling out to her. "We can talk about the study later."

Yeah, we can talk later. Because I am not leaving Scotland. I can't leave without accomplishing my goal, though I can never tell her the real reasons why. I might've fudged a bit when I explained my study to her, but I have no choice. All she needs to know is that I'm staying so I can stage an experiment. I'm hanging around in the name of science. Not for Kirsty MacTaggart.

But if we accidentally have sex again…

Well, a man only has so much willpower.

Chapter Three

Kirsty

I wander around the periphery of the green, avoiding everyone because I still can't think straight. I had sex with Luke. In the garden. Up against the castle wall. While my entire extended family was out here. I've gone off my head in the worst way, haven't I? Now that I'm a stark-raving bampot, maybe I should tell Jack to get me a room at a psychiatric clinic. He's a psychologist, after all.

But no, I can't tell anyone what just happened.

My sisters, Isla and Elspeth, notice me and start to move this way.

I hurry over to the first person I see who isn't related to me and who won't demand I explain why I look like I've just been shagged in the garden. I tried to straighten my clothes, but they still look…rumpled. Autumn, Jack's bride, has just said goodbye to my cousin Evan and his wife, Keely, so I head for Autumn. We've only known each other for a few weeks, but I already love her like a sister. She's one of the kindest people on earth, and I know she won't glare and threaten murder like Logan would, or cast a disenchantment spell like my sisters might.

Autumn smiles when I approach her. "Hey Kirsty, how'd it go with Luke?"

Everything inside me freezes. I can't speak or think or move.

"What's wrong?" she asks. "You don't look so good."

"Donnae feel so good." A few minutes ago, I felt incredible. Luke had been shagging me, and I'd loved every second of it. Until I remembered he's a flaming ersehole. "Think I might go home."

Autumn studies me for a moment. "Something happened in the garden, right? Did Luke get nasty with you?"

Not in the way she means. But aye, we both got "nasty" in the garden. Should I tell Autumn that? She's a good friend, and I do need to talk to someone about what happened.

So I move closer and speak in a soft voice. "Luke and I had sex in the garden."

"What?" Autumn speaks softly too, despite the shock in her voice. "Seriously?"

I nod. "It just sort of happened."

"Are you okay with that?"

"Donnae know. He thinks I'm insane because I'm a Wiccan, but then he kissed me and—" I make a pained face. "That thing happened. After that, he said he wants to study me, like I'm an experiment."

"Study you?"

"Luke is a scientist."

"What kind?"

I shrug. "At university, he was studying physics, but I cannae see what that has to do with me. I'm not defying the laws of gravity."

"He didn't explain."

"I sort of ran away before he could say anything else. Well, first he thanked me for having sex with him, but in an arrogant and completely evil way. He is the devil."

Autumn smiles. "The devil? Wow, he pushed your buttons big time. Are you sure you don't still have feelings for him?"

"Yes, I am positive." I sigh and rub my forehead. "Think I just want to go home. Would ye mind if I left early?"

"Of course not."

I groan pitifully as I realize one important fact. "But I came with Isla and Elspeth, in Isla's car."

"Your sisters will understand if you want to leave, and Evan and Keely are heading out soon. You could catch a ride with them, I'm sure."

"Thank you, Autumn. You are an angel."

She grins. "If you knew the things I did with Jack in Vegas, you wouldn't call me an angel anymore."

"Please never tell me. Donnae need to know what you and my cousin do together."

"You assume I'm talking about sex."

I raise my brows.

She laughs. "Okay, yeah, it was sex."

As I scan my gaze over the crowd, I finally spot Evan and Keely. Evan is another of my cousins who married an American and finally found happiness after years of living as a virtual recluse. I don't care how many of my cousins found love with Americans, and I don't care that my brother did too. I will never love Luke again. He is a horrible person.

But Serena did swear she hated Logan when they first met. Now, they're happily married.

No, that has zero bearing on my life. Luke is an erse. As for his experiment…

Autumn waves her arms and shouts, "Evan! Keely! Get over here, please."

"Did ye have to shout that?" I ask.

"Nobody cares. MacTaggarts are always hollering at each other."

"Maybe I don't want everyone in the world to know I'm sneaking away with my cousin and his wife."

"Stop worrying, Kirsty." Autumn swivels her gaze to something past my shoulder—and she winces. "Logan is coming this way."

"What? No, I cannae talk to my brother right now. He'll want to know what Luke and I talked about in the garden."

"So tell him. Just leave out the part where you and Luke banged each other."

I shut my eyes.

"Oh, this isn't good," Autumn says.

My eyes fly open.

No, no, no, this can't be happening. Luke is walking toward us from the opposite direction from where Logan is walking toward us. When my brother and my ex-boyfriend collide, it will be a nuclear explosion.

I could run away, but that would make me a coward. No, I will not run. I'll stand and face the imminent apocalypse.

Logan reaches us first, and he's wearing his deadly calm expression, the one that makes most people cringe. I don't cringe, though. I've known Logan all my life, since before he joined the military and then MI6. I know what he was like as a wee laddie, and I saw him dressed as Superman for Halloween when he was ten. So aye, Logan can give me that I-was-a-tough-spy look, but it willnae intimidate me.

"What did that *cacan* do to you?" Logan asks, both demanding an answer and expressing concern in his unique way. "You came running out of the garden seeming very upset."

"How would you know? You and Serena were on the other side of the green where you couldn't see me."

"Lachlan told me."

I roll my eyes. Why does everyone in my family have to interfere in everything? Aye, their meddling has helped some people, but I don't need any interference in my life.

Luke reaches us and hooks a thumb inside the waistband of his trousers. "Hey Kirsty, we didn't finish that conversation."

"Aye, we did. I said no."

My brother squints at my ex-boyfriend, his deadly calm stare turning into a lethal glare. "What did you do to my sister, ye *bod ceann*?"

First, he calls Luke a wee shit, now a dickhead. But I'm sure Luke has no idea Logan is insulting him.

"It's between me and Kirsty," Luke says.

"No, it's between you and my fist that I'll be skiting across your face in two seconds if you donnae explain why my sister was upset after she spoke to you."

"Ahmno upset," I say, but no one is listening to me.

"Take it easy," Luke tells my brother. "I was discussing a proposition with Kirsty, that's all."

"You propositioned my sister?" Logan takes one menacing step toward Luke. "Ahm going to skite—"

"Yeah-yeah, I got the whole 'skite' thing. I dated Kirsty for a year, so I learned some of the Scottish sayings. You're threatening to beat me up. And hey, that's cool. Go ahead and do it."

Logan's brows knit together. "What did you say?"

"Go on and beat the shit out of me. If it'll make you feel better." His voice remains calm, almost nonchalant.

Does he honestly want Logan to beat him up?

Evan and Keely amble up to us, seeming a wee bit confused by the situation. Logan still wears that deadly calm look, but he also has his eyebrows scrunched up. Meanwhile, Luke just gazes at my brother as if Logan is an interesting experiment he's running in his lab.

If he has a lab. Donnae know, donnae care.

"What's going on over here?" Evan asks.

"Nothing that concerns anyone but me and the *cacan*," Logan says in a voice that matches his expression.

"Autumn called us over here," Evan says. "Not sure why, though."

"Kirsty needs a ride home," Autumn says. "Can you two drop her off?"

"Of course." Evan eyes Logan and Luke. "If you're sure it's safe to leave these two alone."

Logan steps backward. "I think this one understands me."

"Sure," Luke says. "I get you."

"I'd better not hear you two brawled on the green after I left," I say. "Behave like adults, please."

"Are you ready to go?" Evan asks.

I nod.

My cousin and his wife lead me away from the two men in my life who seem determined to drive me as insane as Luke thinks I am. As I climb into the backseat of Evan's car, I can't help wondering.

What experiment does Luke want to conduct? On me?

Chapter Four

Luke

Logan MacTaggart did not beat me up. I wouldn't have let him, anyway, if I'd believed for one second that he meant to do it. Maybe I'm not an ex-spy or whatever, but I am not a wimp. After Kirsty left with those other two people, who I assume are her relatives, I went back to my hotel. When I'd been dating Kirsty back in college, she talked about her large extended family, but I'd kind of assumed she was exaggerating when she mentioned how many MacTaggarts live in this area.

Nope. The Highlands are overrun with them.

And I'm staying in a hotel in the town where a lot of those people live. Loch Fairbairn isn't much to look at, kind of a bump-in-the-road village, but at least I could find a room here. The hotel doesn't offer five-star luxury, but it's clean and pleasant. Since I've never stayed in a five-star hotel, I don't notice the difference.

Just as I'm dropping onto the bed, stretched out on my back, my cell phone rings. The caller ID tells me who's harassing me, and I groan. Can't I get even a few minutes to myself? The flight from England had been crowded, then I inserted myself into the throng of MacTaggarts at cousin whoever's wedding. No solitude to be found.

The phone rings for the second time.

Groaning again, I sit up and answer. "Hey, I'm here."

"In Scotland? Good." My boss is British, of course. His name is Dr. Melvin Prickett, and he keeps tabs on me like I'm a toddler. "Have you begun the experiment?"

"No. I just got here."

"Hours ago. What is taking so long?"

"It was a wedding reception. There were lots of people, which made it hard to get Kirsty alone and talk her into the idea."

"But you've convinced her?"

"Uh, no. Not quite yet." I rub the back of my neck, grimacing while Melvin makes annoyed breathing noises. "It's not my fault. Her brother got mad at me for… Well, I think for existing. Anyway, I lost my window of opportunity, for the moment."

No, I'm not going to tell my boss that I screwed Kirsty and that's why I lost my window. Maybe I should've let her brother assault me. Being hospitalized with severe internal injuries would've given me a great excuse for not getting the job done.

"We have a strict time line," Melvin says. "You know what's at stake."

"Yeah, I know. And I'll get Kirsty on board—soon."

"I will hold you to that, Luke."

Melvin hangs up on me.

Why did I promise I could get Kirsty on board soon? She seemed less than thrilled with the idea of me studying her. But if I don't get this machine running pronto, I'll be in big trouble.

I go to a cafe down the street for dinner, but everyone there looks at me funny, like I have big fangs and I'm drooling and growling. While I wait for my food to arrive, I wonder what on earth is wrong with the people in this town. Do they hate all outsiders? Or all Americans? Then I find out the real reason for their behavior. A different waitress delivers my meal, one who is not shy about expressing her opinions.

She sets my plate on the table, or rather, smacks it down. And she gives me a big phony smile. "Here ye are, ye *cacan*. I should dump this food on your head after the way you upset Kirsty, but that would be unprofessional."

"And telling me you wanted to do that isn't unprofessional?"

The woman leans in until her nose almost touches mine. "Kirsty is my cousin."

Oh, now I get it. This town is full of MacTaggarts, so of course, I ran into one of Kirsty's multitude of cousins. The entire family must hate me, and I imagine I'll have trouble finding any establishment that doesn't harbor at least one of her relatives. I'd better get used to it.

Because I am not leaving.

I offer my hand to the waitress. "I'm Luke Turner. And you are?"

"Annag Beattie." She narrows her eyes, which I guess she thinks will intimidate me. "My husband is strong and very macho. He could batter you with one finger."

"Fascinating. May I eat my food now?"

She puckers her lips, then spins around and walks away.

I guess all MacTaggarts, even the women, plan to threaten me with violence. Maybe I should worry about that, but I have bigger problems. I doubt they actually will assault me, anyway. Even Kirsty's brother didn't do anything except glower and bluster.

When I notice other customers giving me dirty looks, I decide to take my meal to go and head back to the Loch Fairbairn Arms, where I eat alone in my room. At least the woman at the front desk didn't give me the evil eye. Maybe she'll wait until I'm asleep and sneak into my room to put a poisonous snake in my bed.

It's possible I've watched too many movies.

Despite the hostility of everyone in this town, I survive the night. Sleeping wasn't an option last night, and this time, I order room service instead of going to the cafe. The guy manning the front desk this morning told me there's only one restaurant in town. That means I'll need to find another means of feeding myself. Sure, room service food is okay. But they have a pretty limited menu, so I'll need to visit one of the nearby villages to get something else.

Assuming Kirsty doesn't have relatives everywhere.

Why am I starting to feel like Burt Reynolds in *Deliverance*? Wish I'd never watched that damn movie. If I hear bagpipes playing that banjo-battle song, I'll run for the hills. Literally. There are mountains everywhere.

Now I've become a scaredy-cat who can't handle some Scottish people glaring at me. Oh come on, I haven't sunk that far. Have I? No, absolutely not. Maybe I have let my boss manipulate me, but it's my own damn fault he can do that.

I decide to go for a walk since it seems kind of early to go talk to Kirsty. I don't know where she lives, anyway. Yeah, I had a concrete plan when I came to this country. As I wander down the sidewalk aimlessly, not paying attention to my surroundings, I keep thinking about Kirsty and how I wound up here in Scotland. A stranger called me, and I came running because he said Kirsty needed help. Sounds like Alex Thorne enjoys butting his nose into other people's lives, but that does not explain why I'm here.

The girl I'd loved a long time ago needed me, so I came.

Except Kirsty knew nothing about that British guy's phone call. Why had I paid attention to what Alex Thorne said? No, it's not a mystery. I listened because he told me what I wanted to hear—that the girl I'd loved a long time ago needed me again. Maybe it had felt like fate or something, except that I don't believe in garbage like that. Fate? Bullshit. A nosy Brit orchestrated our reunion, not angels in heaven or whatever.

I amble past the cafe and keep going. Even if that Annag woman isn't working today, I don't feel like testing my luck. I also amble past the law offices of Rory MacTaggart. Oh great. More of Kirsty's blood-thirsty relatives. Her lawyer cousin, or whatever relationship he has to her, will probably barrel out of his office any second to glare at me and growl vague threats.

Oddly, I'm getting kind of used to that.

What I can't wrap my head around is the fact that Kirsty and I had sex in a castle garden yesterday. She talks like she hates me, but then she lets me hike up her skirt and fuck her. Women are great at sending mixed signals, but Kirsty's are so tangled up I don't even want to try to understand them. We did the deed one more time. It meant nothing more than that. Sort of like an overdue goodbye fuck.

A man I don't recognize walks by and gives me a friendly smile and a nod.

He must not be a MacTaggart.

I smile back at him, then continue on my way to wherever the heck I'm going. Turning off the main drag, I head down a side street that houses shops and other stuff that I barely pay attention to—until one store makes me stop dead. A sign above the entrance features the standard pagan designs, like a pentacle and the moon, but it's the shop's name that has me staring up at the sign, frozen in my tracks.

Da-Shealladh, A Metaphysical Sanctuary & Shop. Kirsty MacTaggart, proprietor.

Kirsty owns a store? I don't know what I'd expected her to be doing these days, but the idea that she runs a "metaphysical sanctuary and shop" surprises me. I've always known she had the brains to do anything she wanted, so I don't know why seeing her business stuns me. It can't be because I assumed she spent the last twelve years pining for me and living with her parents while she waited for me to come back for her. No, I wasn't pining for her either. I got on with my life, so of course, she got on with hers.

Does she have a boyfriend?

Not that the answer matters to me. I still think she's insane, and nothing will ever change my mind about that. Kirsty is a sweet, passionate, smart lunatic.

Should I go into the shop? I do need to talk to her, to convince her that participating in my study will be good for her. That could be a lie since I have no clue how this plan will affect her. Maybe she'll finally give up her silly idea that she has supernatural powers and also give up her silly obsession with Wicca. I won't tell her that's what I'm hoping for, though, because she'll need time to realize her beliefs are bogus.

Yeah, I'm kind of an arrogant ass. At least I'm self-aware enough to realize that.

I walk up to the shop's doors, where a sign announces the place is open for business. As I pull the door open, a bell above it chimes. The scent of potpourri or incense or something like that wafts around me, and I can't deny the aroma is rather pleasant. Walking further into the store, I notice shelves and racks filled with all sorts of hocus-pocus hooey, like amulets and books about Wicca and other metaphysical junk. The merchandise looks like high-quality stuff, and the decor goes along with the metaphysical theme without screaming in my face that this is a Wiccan establishment. Are there enough witches and sorcerers and whatever else here in the Highlands to support a store like this one?

Kirsty stands behind the counter at the rear of the store, shuffling through what looks like mail. She lifts her head, noticing me, and her lips pucker. "What are you doing here?"

"Enjoying the village. Just happened by your shop."

"Well, you can happen away from it too."

"Come on, at least let me explain about the study." I approach the counter, resting one elbow on it. "Unless you're afraid you'll beg me to screw you again."

"No, I will not."

"Okay, then listen to what I have to say." I lean closer. "What have you got to lose?"

Chapter Five

Kirsty

What have I got to lose? My sanity, for one. My self-control seems in jeopardy as well, but I won't tell him that. Luke used to be so sweet and considerate, always asking my permission before he kissed me or made love to me. But he revealed his true self on the day when I informed him that I'm a Wiccan, and he called me insane. Then he disappeared from my life. Now, he's back—and the erse won't leave me alone.

A study? To prove my beliefs are rubbish? I donnae see how anyone with half a brain could think I would agree to become a test subject in an experiment with such a slanted mission statement or whatever scientists call it when they do bollocks like that. Maybe I'm slightly biased too, but I don't feel bad about that. My bias has never involved calling another person a bampot. Well, Luke had said "insane" and "lunatic," but he never used the Scottish word for either term.

"You'll be compensated," Luke says. "Fifty pounds per session."

"Session? I willnae be letting you lock me up in a cage like a chimpanzee."

"No cage. We can conduct the sessions anywhere you like."

"Mm-hm." I drum my fingers on the counter. "You believe science explains everything, while I believe the universe is full of mysteries. Your bloody stupid experiment won't change my mind or yours."

"Give it a try before you condemn science. And like I said, you'll be compensated."

"Donnae need your money. I do quite well with my store, thank you very much."

He surveys the interior, swiveling his head slowly. "It's a nice place, if you like this kind of stuff. What does the name mean? Duh-shee-lad?"

Aye, he mangled the Gaelic phrase, but tourists never get it right. Many locals don't know the language either. Maybe I shouldn't have given my store a Gaelic name, but it had seemed appropriate at the time. Besides, explaining what it means and how to pronounce it helps me interact with my customers.

"*Da-shealladh*," I say. "It means the second sight. The ability to see this world and the spirit realm."

"You seriously believe you can do that."

"My brother Logan was skeptical too, until my prediction for him came true."

"What exactly did you predict?" he asks carefully.

"I told him the answer would be yes."

Luke twists his mouth into a half-smirk. "That's your great prediction? It could mean anything."

"But I also knew Serena had broken up with Logan before he'd told anyone. Then, when he proposed, she said yes."

He snorts. "Oh please. You'll have to do better than that to convince me, kitten."

"Stop calling me that."

"You used to love it."

"Aye, and I used to love you." I pick up a stapler, then realize I have no ruddy idea what I meant to do with the thing. I smack it down on the counter. "Things change, Luke. We are not dating anymore, and I don't like being called 'kitten' anymore."

"Calm down, hey? I'm trying to be nice."

"Well, you're bloody awful at it."

He sighs. "Maybe I am. But I won't give up until you agree to participate in my experiment. I might be a jackass these days, but I'm also persistent."

"Aye, ye always were bloody-minded."

Luke leans over the counter, though he can't reach me that way. "Remember that Gaelic thing you used to say when we were making love? I'd love to hear you say it again."

"Donnae remember." I do remember, of course. How could I forget all the times I'd whispered those words into his ear? But I will not recite them now.

"We had sex, Kirsty. Yesterday."

"Does your experiment involve shagging?"

"No." He grins. "But I could work that into it if you want."

"I do not want that. Rather have a poke with a bug-eyed alien from Mars."

He pulls back, though he keeps his elbow on the counter. "Please don't tell me you believe in aliens too."

"Please don't tell me you're an enormous *bod ceann* and a hypocrite. You were the one who used to love watching documentaries about UFOs."

"It was a phase. I outgrew it."

The doorbell chimes, and a middle-aged couple enters the store.

"Excuse me," I say to Luke. "I have customers."

While I talk to the couple and help them choose gifts for their grown children, Luke remains at the counter watching me. I wish he wouldn't do that. His attention makes me uncomfortable, probably because we had sex yesterday. Now Luke wants to "study" me like I'm a lab rat. My beliefs don't make me insane, but his determination to convince me everything I believe in is nonsense seems like a mental imbalance to me. I can't reconcile the Luke I knew at university with the man he became once I told him about my beliefs—and I absolutely can't reconcile the boy I loved with the man standing in my shop today.

Most of my extended family doesn't believe in Wicca or psychic abilities, though my two sisters do. No one ridicules us, though. They call us the Witches of Ballachulish, but it's an affectionate nickname inspired by the fact we grew up in the village of Ballachulish. MacTaggarts are tolerant of each other's differences. Luke could learn a thing or two from my family.

When I escort the couple to the counter so I can ring up their purchases, Luke moves to stand near the closest row of shelves. And he keeps watching me out of the corner of his eye. *Stop doing that.* Though I try very hard to beam that thought into his mind, I don't think it works. Even I don't believe I can influence someone's thoughts, which probably explains why my attempt fails.

I wish I could control his mind. Then I'd have the power to make him go home.

As my customers leave, I say, "Thank you for visiting *Da-Shealladh*, and blessed be."

The bell chimes as the door swings shut.

And I'm alone with Luke. Again.

He ambles up to the counter and leans against it. "You're very good with your customers."

"Are you giving me a compliment?"

"Yes." He skims his gaze up and down my body, the half of it he can see. "You're even sexier now than you were back in college."

"Donnae be getting any ideas. I will not have a poke with you ever again."

"Is that what your second sight tells you?"

"No. It's what *I'm* telling *you*."

He smirks. "You're so cute when you try to deny you want me."

I open up my laptop computer and try to focus on bookkeeping. "Go home, Luke. I will never take part in your barmy, insulting experiment."

"Hmm." He folds his arms over his chest and gazes into space as if he's thinking. "Why did you give your shop an unpronounceable name?"

"*Da-shealladh* is not unpronounceable."

"Nobody who doesn't speak Gaelic would be able to enunciate those weird syllables."

Enunciate? Not many men his age would use that word, so he shouldn't criticize what I call my shop. I decide to ignore him. No matter what else he says or does, I will pretend Luke Turner does not exist. That means I pay no attention when he starts to explore the aisles of merchandise and squints at the decorations on the walls. Aye, I ignore him. I only see what he's doing because this is a small shop, so there isn't much room for him to disappear into a corner.

After twelve minutes, I can't take it anymore. "Are you ever going to leave?"

"Nope." With his hands lodged in his trouser pockets, he gives me a snarky smile. "Not leaving until you agree to take part in my experiment. What have you got to lose? If you're one hundred percent sure nothing can shake your faith in Wicca, then you might as well go along with my study just so you can prove me wrong."

That is a good point. But I know he's suggesting it only as a means of talking me into giving him what he wants.

"What do you get out of this experiment?" I ask.

"Science is its own reward."

"That's bollocks. You're after something, but I cannae figure out what it is."

"Maybe I'm still madly in love with you."

I roll my eyes.

He turns away and starts rummaging through a wooden box filled with polished stones.

And I go back to my bookkeeping. For a minute, two at most. "What would your experiment involve? Needles stuck into my brain?"

Luke faces me and smiles, shaking his head. "No needles. Electrodes. You know, little sensors that have wires attached to them."

"Aye, I know what electrodes are."

"Does this mean you're thinking about it?"

"Possibly."

Why am I considering his offer? It's rot. But it might be interesting to see how he reacts when he can't talk me out of my beliefs. Besides, life has been rather monotonous lately. I come to work, I go home, I come to work,

I go home. Attending Jack and Autumn's wedding had been the most excit-ing thing I'd done in months. That's pathetic, isn't it? I haven't had a date in even longer. The pool of eligible men in this area is limited. And none of them makes me feel the way Luke does.

The way he *did* make me feel. Ages ago. I don't want him anymore.

A wee bit of extra money wouldn't hurt, though.

No, I shouldn't do it. My family will think I've lost my mind. But maybe no one needs to know what I'm doing with Luke. They can assume whatever they like because I donnae care what anyone thinks of me. The fact that a shiver of excitement tingles over my skin at the thought of participating in Luke's experiment means nothing. I like a challenge, that's all.

I roll my shoulders back and set my palms on the counter. "All right."

His brows hike up. "You're saying yes?"

"Aye."

"You want to be my test subject?"

"How many times do I have to say yes? You should be smugly pleased with yourself for talking me into this barmy experiment."

Instead of seeming pleased with himself, though, he acts as if he's relieved.

"Thank you, Kirsty," Luke says. "I appreciate this."

He sounded sincere. What in the world? First, he calls me insane, then he kisses me and…other things. He follows that up by stalking me to my place of business and insulting me some more. Now, when I finally agree to participate in his experiment, he seems genuinely grateful. I will never understand him.

"I have a business to run," I say. "So you'll have to work your experiments in around my schedule."

"No problem."

He wanders back to the wooden boxes filled with stones.

Another customer enters the store, and as I help the woman find the right necklace for her sister, I keep glancing at Luke. Whatever his real agenda is, I will need to be careful with him. He hasn't told me everything about his experiment. Of that, I'm certain. But when he thanked me for agreeing to participate, he had seemed almost like the old Luke, the one I'd fallen for so many years ago.

No, I will not fall for him again.

Chapter Six

Luke

I leave Kirsty's shop a little while later and head back to my hotel so I can prepare for the experiments. I need to find an appropriate venue for them too. Maybe I could rent an office space. Sure, no problem. MacTaggarts probably own half the buildings in the Highlands, and I'd bet a year's salary that they know the owners of the other half. So yeah, I expect to stumble into lots of roadblocks. Well, since Kirsty agreed to participate, maybe I can enlist her help in finding a quiet place where I can conduct the tests.

Melvin calls me while I'm considering my options.

"Have you gotten started yet?" he demands.

"You asked me that this morning, and the answer hasn't changed. Kirsty did agree to participate, but I haven't gotten the tests going yet. I'm working out the logistics."

"You don't need to be as rigorous as usual. We need a good result. That is the paramount goal."

Is he telling me, in a sideways manner, that I should fudge things to make the results come out the way he wants? Melvin's not above doing that, and maybe some other scientists would do it too, but I pride myself on being rigorous and ethical. Sure, because screwing my ex-girlfriend right before I talked her into being my test subject isn't unethical at all.

Christ, what's happened to me?

"We both know what's at stake for you," Melvin says. "But my arse is on the line too, Mr. Turner. Do not let me down."

I know damn well what he means. Melvin loves to remind me of the guillotine he has hanging over my head. How did I get to this point? Letting a jackass order me around when all I want to do is explore the scientific possibilities. Instead, I'm using my ex-girlfriend as a means of keeping my job. Yeah, it's entirely possible I act like an ass around Kirsty because I feel…guilty or something.

But I don't have the luxury of guilt anymore.

"Don't worry," I tell Melvin. "Nothing will go wrong. I'll get it done, but I can't rush this, or she might back out."

"Remember the keyword. Dee—"

"Yeah, I know. Now, say goodbye so I can get back to work."

As soon as we hang up, I dig around in my suitcase until I find my bottle of antacids. I swallow four of them. Working at the British Institute for Psychophysics had seemed like a great opportunity two years ago. Now, I wish I'd never met Dr. Melvin Prickett. But it's too late to back out. I've got no choice but to see this through to the end.

I haven't even set up the parameters for my experiment, and I briefly wonder why. Procrastination isn't my thing. The fact I've delayed for this long has nothing to do with Kirsty. I get my computer and start a new document—"Psychophysics and the Belief in Wicca and Other Metaphysical Constructs." Okay, that's not a half-bad title. Kind of wordy, but then, scientists aren't known for being concise or crystal clear. We love our jargon. Hovering my fingers over the keyboard, I consider how to phrase my testable question.

Is Kirsty insane? No, that won't do.

Can an individual steeped in the metaphysical be convinced to give up those beliefs? That's a little better, but still not good enough. It sounds too biased.

Is belief in the metaphysical a sign of mental illness?

Maybe I should skip the question and come back to it later. I'll work on my hypothesis instead. *The application of logic to the metaphysical will cause the subject to renounce their beliefs.* Not sure that's any better than my questions. What I should be contemplating is whether I want to talk Kirsty out of her beliefs. Maybe I don't share them, but trying to make her doubt something that clearly means a lot to her seems like a mean thing to do. But this is my job. I have to do it. I'm a scientist. Why do I care if shattering her beliefs hurts? She'll be better off once she accepts that none of that garbage exists. Facts matter. Wicca doesn't.

Acid creeps up my throat, burning and souring my tongue. Not enough antacids in the world to cure what's wrong with me.

I give up on formulating my experiment and head for the lobby to ask the young guy behind the front desk where I can find an office to rent.

"Nothing like that in Loch Fairbairn," he says. "Evan MacTaggart owns most of the buildings in the village, so you could speak to him, I suppose."

Perfect. Another MacTaggart. Maybe I should pin a sign to my back saying, "Kick my ass, please. Let's get it over with." I'm just lucky the MacTaggart syndicate didn't prevent me from booking a hotel room in town.

Since I can't think of anything else to do, I go back to Kirsty's shop.

Two women who look a lot like her stand on this side of the counter while Kirsty stands behind it. They're talking and laughing, though I think they must be speaking Gaelic. It sounds like gibberish to me. I do like the cadence of the language, though, and the words can sound sort of elegant.

When Kirsty spots me, she bites her lip and glances at the other two women, almost as if she's anxious.

The other two turn to look at me.

"Kirsty, you have a customer," one of the women says.

"No, he's not a customer." Kirsty manages to sound annoyed and nervous at the same time. "That's Luke Turner."

The pleasant expressions on the faces of the other two women disintegrate. The one who seems a little older puckers her lips. "That's the *cacan*?"

"I prefer *bod ceann*," I say. While I have no idea what the phrase means, I got the gist of it when Logan called me that. It's an insult.

"You know what *bod ceann* means?" The woman sounds surprised and almost offended.

Maybe Scots don't like outsiders using their secret language.

"Luke has no idea what it means," Kirsty says. "He is American, after all."

"Oh, aye," the other women agree, as if that explains everything.

"Prejudiced against Americans?" I say. "Thought you MacTaggarts loved to marry our kind, probably for the sex. The men in your family that I've met all seemed like they wouldn't know how to make a woman—"

Kirsty smacks her palm down on the counter. "Stop talking, Luke. These are my sisters, Isla and Elspeth. They donnae need to hear your arrogant rubbish."

"We love rubbish," declares the woman who seems younger than the one who spoke earlier. "It's very entertaining, which explains why we love Logie so much. He's full of rubbish."

Logie? I need to work really hard to stop myself from chuckling. They must call their brother Logan by that nickname, but I'd bet every cent I have that he hates it.

Kirsty shuts her eyes briefly and shakes her head just a touch. "Might as well introduce yourselves."

The one who seems older approaches me, offering her hand. "I'm Isla MacTaggart, the oldest sibling in our family. Logan is the second oldest, and Kirsty is third. Elspeth is the baby."

"I am not a baby," Elspeth says, almost pouting.

"You're the youngest. That's what I meant."

Since Isla is still holding out her hand, I shake it. "Nice to meet you."

"Oh, it willnae be nice if you hurt our Kirsty. Logie doesn't take kindly to men who make his sisters unhappy." Isla leans in and whispers, "He was an MI6 agent, which means Logie knows all the most painful ways to kill someone."

"I'll keep that in mind."

But yeah, it's kind of hard to be intimidated by what she said when she keeps calling her brother Logie. *Ooh, Logie's going to thrash me.* No, that doesn't quite work.

"Are you ready to start your experiments already?" Elspeth asks.

I stare at her. "Experiments?"

Kirsty clears her throat and hunches her shoulders. "I didn't think it was a secret."

Well, I guess I hadn't told her not to share the news. I should have, and Melvin will rip me a new one if he finds out, but it's too late to worry about it. "Would you three mind if we keep this between us? I'd rather not have the whole village gossiping about it. Might, ah, interfere with the integrity of the experiment."

That almost sounded plausible.

"Of course," Isla says. "Our lips are sealed."

She makes a zipper motion across her mouth, and Elspeth does the same.

Kirsty squeezes her eyes shut and makes a pained face.

"Now," Isla says, "tell us what you mean to do with our sister."

"I, uh… It's just a scientific study of metaphysical beliefs."

"Oh, you mean that you want to know why people like us feel the need to indulge in all that nonsense."

That's almost verbatim what I told Kirsty yesterday.

And now she's peeking out at me through her half-closed eyes while her face cinches up even more.

"That doesn't sound very objective or scientific," Isla says. "Are you sure you're a real scientist? Maybe you meant you're a Scientologist."

Her cheerful tone and pleasant smile make it hard for me to take offense. I'm beginning to think Kirsty's sister is teasing me.

Elspeth giggles. "Maybe you want to abduct Kirsty and take her to your cult so you can perform naughty sex rituals with her."

"Aye, he probably does," Isla says. "He looks like the wicked sort who—"

"Haud yer wheesht!" Kirsty shouts. She takes a deep breath that lifts her tits and exhales it slowly while the tension relaxes out of her. She sounds like her usual self when she speaks again. "Luke and I need to discuss the experiment in private. Please."

Isla smirks. "She means 'bugger off, ye eejits.' Aye, Elspeth?"

"Aye." The youngest sister smirks at me too. "But I think he's the sort of man who makes sure a woman enjoys it when he shags her. My third eye tells me so."

Third eye? Kirsty mentioned second sight. But now Elspeth thinks she's got three eyes? That must mean something else in the Wiccan world.

"Do not tell anyone about the experiment," Kirsty says, and I've never heard her sound so commanding before. It's hot.

Isla rolls her eyes. "Come on, Elspeth, you've scared the laddie enough."

The two sisters leave the shop, laughing and chattering in what must be Gaelic.

Kirsty pretends to be obsessed with the wood grain on the countertop. "I'm sorry about that. My sisters can be…overly enthusiastic. And I honestly didn't think it would matter if I told them what you want to do with me."

What I want to do? Screw her, that's what. But I can't do it. She means the experiment, and a scientist must remain objective—even when he's fantasizing about his test subject's tits.

"It's okay," I tell her. "But if we could keep it between you, me, and your sisters, that would be good."

"When MacTaggarts make a promise, they keep it."

"I'll take your word for it." Shoving my hands into my pants pockets, I hesitate, suddenly having no idea what to say. Then I remember. "I need a quiet place to conduct the experiment. Do you know of any offices for rent or—"

"Oh no, you don't want an office. That won't be quiet enough." She picks up the phone that sits on the counter beside her computer. "I'll take care of it. Donnae worry."

No, I don't worry at all about what kind of place Kirsty will find for me. She hates me, and I called her insane more than once. But hey, she'll be reasonable about this. It's not like she'll book a super-expensive venue just to bankrupt me.

I listen while she makes her call. Not because I'm eavesdropping. I can't help overhearing her part of the conversation since she's standing six feet away from me.

"Rory," she says cheerfully, "it's Kirsty. Aye, I need a favor."

I watch her facial expressions while she talks to Rory, who I assume is the solicitor whose law office I saw during my meanderings in the village. Maybe he's going to lend us his office. No, I kind of doubt that. But maybe he's rich and owns a house nearby that he never uses.

Kirsty grins. "That would be perfect, Rory. Thank you so much. Emery is right, you are a teddy bear in disguise."

I have no idea who Emery is. But I doubt any MacTaggart man is a teddy bear.

She hangs up the phone and gives me a closed-mouth smile with her cheeks dimpled.

"You found a venue," I say. "And you're very pleased with yourself for doing that."

"Aye, because I found the perfect place."

"Where is it?" I'm getting a sinking feeling in my stomach, like she's about to tell me something I don't want to hear.

Kirsty grins again. "My cousin Rory's castle."

Chapter Seven

Kirsty

Maybe I am enjoying this a bit too much, but after the way Luke has behaved, I think I've earned the right to feel pleased with myself. I found a venue, all right. But I doubt Luke will appreciate it since he seems to dislike every member of my family—the ones he's met, at least. Well, he didn't dislike my sisters as far as I could tell, though he made no effort to disguise the fact he thinks we're all insane for being Wiccans.

If he wants to disabuse me of my beliefs, why can't I do the same to him?

That's a silly idea, I know. Why should I care if he looks down his nose at me? I don't want to date him, never again. But turning his experiment back on him might be fun and illuminating.

"Your cousin's what?" Luke asks, sounding genuinely baffled. "Is that the same castle where the wedding reception was held?"

"Aye. It's called Dùndubhan, and it is the most secluded place you could hope for, if you're serious about wanting to go through with this experiment."

"I am. Are you backing out?"

"No. I keep to my word, unlike some people."

He rests both elbows on the counter, his arms folded. "You're implying I lied to you at some point, but I didn't do that."

"You claimed you loved me, but as soon as I told you about my beliefs, you ran away."

"That's not lying. I changed my mind about you."

"If you had loved me, you would've accepted me as I am instead of trying to change me."

He studies me for a moment, one finger tapping on the counter. "I didn't try to change you, Kirsty. We weren't compatible anymore."

"You don't know that. You left before you could even find out if we would still work as a couple." Why am I saying that? I don't want to get back together with him, and I don't want him to think I might want that, so I shouldn't care about what he did ages ago.

"I'm a scientist," he says in a calm voice that annoys me for some reason. "You're a spiritualist. The two don't mesh."

"Spiritualist? I donnae contact the dead." I lean toward him. "I am a Wiccan. That's a completely different thing."

"How? It's all supernatural mumbo-jumbo."

I decide to try a different tactic. "Do you believe in string theory?"

"No, it's not a belief. I accept it as a valid hypothesis to explain the nature of the universe."

"But no one has ever seen a string, and nobody knows if they even exist. The hypothesis is nothing more than the fantasies of scientists who pray for a theory of everything. Aye?"

He goes perfectly still, staring at me without blinking.

I wave a hand in his face. "Are ye conscious? Should I call a doctor?"

Luke blinks twice, slowly. "You know what string theory is?"

"Aye, the wee Scots numpty understands things only a brilliant man like you is supposed to know about."

"That's not what I meant." He stares at me again, but this time he doesn't seem catatonic. "What else do you know about science?"

"More than you, I'd wager."

He snorts. "I seriously doubt that."

"Do ye now?" I straighten, squaring my shoulders. "Can you name all the constellations in the sky? Do you know who Paracelsus was and what he was famous for?"

"Well, ah…" Luke glances away. "No, can't say I do."

"Soooo, the great scientist doesn't know everything."

"That's not my field of study. I'm a psychophysicist."

I could make a sarcastic comment about that term, how it means he's a psycho, but since I don't know what it actually means, I hold off on that for the moment. "What is a psychophysicist?"

"Scientists like me study the intersection of matter and mind, though we usually refer to it as sensation these days. Fechner came up with the idea that we should study more than just stimulus, but also the sensation or response to it. Sensation, used in the context of psychophysics, is more of a hypothetical construct."

"I see." Though he probably thinks I don't, I'm not as ignorant as he assumes. "Essentially, you're studying nothing. If the concept of sensation is hypothetical, then you might as well be praying to the sun for divine inspiration."

"That's a ridiculous comparison."

"Can you measure what someone feels? With instruments or scans or what have you."

"No. It's a qualitative measure, not a quantitative one."

"You believe sensation exists, but you can't prove it or explain it. What an individual test subject describes as a particular sensation isn't a true, objective measurement."

He gawps at me again, though this time his jaw goes slack.

Aye, a silly Wiccan like me isn't supposed to know about science. I should be dancing naked in the woods while praying for a demon to ravish me. The demon would be Luke, when he ravished me in the garden, but I didn't pray for him to do that. It just happened.

"Let's talk about this later," I say. "Give me half an hour, and I'll be ready to go to Dùndubhan with you. Rory said we can stay there overnight, if you like, instead of driving back to Loch Fairbairn. The castle has four levels and lots of rooms to choose from."

"Sounds like a hotel."

"No, it's a museum. Well, parts of it are. My cousin Jamie and her husband, Gavin, run it for Rory and Emery, who own the castle."

"Emery?"

"Rory's wife."

"I see." Luke pushes away from the counter. "Earlier, you said we'd have to fit the experiments in around your work schedule. Now it sounds like you'll be blowing off work to help me."

"Not blowing off anything. I need to show you how to find Dùndubhan. And besides, my sister can fill in for me here."

"Okay. Guess I'll go back to the hotel. Where should we meet up?"

"At the Loch Fairbairn Arms. I'll be in the lobby in half an hour."

"Sounds good. Thanks, Kirsty."

He walks out the door.

And I call my sister Isla.

"Did that man do something to you?" she asks instead of saying hello.

"No. Why would you assume he did something?"

"Because I donnae trust him. His aura is clouded, which means he's probably keeping a secret."

"Luke doesn't believe in auras—or anything, as far as I can tell."

"Everyone believes in something, whether they realize it or not."

I'd love to hear her argue that point with Luke. He thinks he doesn't believe in anything, yet he accepts that a hypothetical thing called sensation exists despite the fact he can't measure or detect it. I don't plan to talk him into accepting Wicca, but it would be nice if he stopped insulting me simply because I have spiritual beliefs.

When I ask Isla to take over running the shop for a few days so I can help Luke with his experiment, she agrees. But she can't resist making sarcastic comments about what Luke and I will be doing all alone at Dùndubhan. The castle, according to Isla, has "gobs of places where two randy people can have fun." I tell her that's not why I'm going there with Luke, but she just laughs.

"I thought you hated him," I say.

"No, I don't trust him. I'll do a tarot reading and see what that tells me."

As the oldest sibling in our family, Isla thinks it's her duty to poke her nose into every aspect of our lives. Logan used to avoid meddling like the plague, until he married Serena. These days, I swear he enjoys getting involved in the interference antics of the American Wives Club. That's the informal group started by Emery, Erica, and Calli—the American wives of my cousins Rory, Lachlan, and Aidan. Gavin Douglas, who married my cousin Jamie, is an honorary member of the club since he's American too.

More of my cousins have married Americans since then, and even Logan married one. I love Serena like a sister, but I would never complain about who Logan chose to marry even if I didn't like her. Luke wants to interfere in my life, but he feels free to criticize my life choices. He could learn a few things from my brother.

When I meet Luke at the Loch Fairbairn Arms, he's carrying his suitcases. "I checked out, so somebody else can have the room if they need it. Though I might be homeless if you kick me out of the castle."

"Donnae worry, ye willnae be homeless." I pat his cheek. "I'll lock you in the dungeon if you get too cheeky."

His brows lift briefly, then he follows me out to the car.

I had stopped off at my house on the way here and packed a few bags. To my surprise, Luke does not comment on the fact I have luggage in the trunk. He just stows his suitcases in there and doesn't even smirk or lift an eyebrow. I guess he isn't assuming luggage means I want to sleep with him. Maybe I was the one assuming he would think that.

No, that doesn't mean I want to do it. Absolutely not.

The drive to Dùndubhan takes half an hour, and we gradually leave the main roads as the landscape becomes more rural and less populated. Aye,

Rory's castle is remote. I hadn't exaggerated when I told Luke it's the most secluded place available to us. Back before Rory met Emery, he had wanted seclusion and solitude. Now, he loves to spend time with our extended family. The Ogre of Loch Fairbairn has become a happy, settled man.

If Rory could change…

No, I will not finish that thought. I donnae care if Luke ever changes into a good person because I do not want him back. Not ever.

I steer the car onto the dirt driveway that leads to Dùndubhan. The forest forms a canopy over our heads, making it impossible to see what lies ahead of us, and the gloom also camouflages the metal gate that hangs open along the side of the drive. They must have opened it for us.

"How much farther is it?" Luke asks.

"Not far."

"A mile? Two miles? It didn't seem this far yesterday. But then, that Alex guy ordered a taxi for me, and I wasn't paying attention to the scenery. So, how far—"

"You sound like a bairn, asking 'are we there yet' over and over."

He huffs. "I was asking a question, that's all. I'm not a whiny kid."

"You've developed a thin skin, haven't you? I was teasing, Luke."

This time he grunts.

As the dirt drive transitions to gravel, the canopy of trees thins ahead of us. Little by little, the castle compound emerges from the forest like the ghost of Camelot rising from the ashes of history. Dùndubhan isn't a fairy-tale castle, though. The boxy design speaks to its original purpose as a medieval fortress and conjures thoughts of knights battling to protect their laird's domain. I don't know the full history of Dùndubhan, but I've always imagined it as the site of a great battle—won by the right side, of course.

"Looks smaller than I remember," Luke tells me, sounding less than impressed. "And I think somebody forgot to shave off the sharp edges."

He's trying to fash me, isn't he? By insulting my cousin's castle.

"Sharp edges are good for chasing away the enemy," I say, as if I know all about how medieval fortresses were built.

"Is there really a dungeon?"

"No. I don't think so, anyway."

The grey-stone structure looms over us as I drive through the massive wooden gates, which stand open, and into the courtyard. I lose sight of the square turrets. Luke glances around with a look of mild interest, though I suspect it's an affectation. He seems to feel that he needs to behave as if he doesn't give a toss about anything, and I can't help wondering if it's a defense mechanism.

Why does he need to disguise his feelings?

For the next few days, I will be alone with Luke in this castle in the back of beyond. Maybe that will give me time to figure out why he's so guarded and snarky. But that thought leaves me with more questions.

Should I try to figure him out? Or will I regret letting him into my life again, even for a few days?

Chapter Eight

Luke

It's possible I've downplayed my interest in this castle, just so Kirsty won't think I'm excited by the prospect of staying in a medieval fortress. Yeah, I can tell just by looking at this place that it served as a stronghold. The high wall that surrounds it and the massive gateway attest to that fact, not to mention the turrets that would've made it easier to spot the enemy and shoot arrows at them. I wonder if the castle was surrounded by trees back then, or if it occupied a clearing. I noticed a modern metal gate about halfway up the long, long driveway, so I guess they don't rely exclusively on medieval methods.

Why don't I want Kirsty to know this place fascinates me? Because she might take that as a sign of…something.

Christ, I can't even explain my feelings to myself in my head. Finding out Kirsty knows about string theory and other scientific topics threw me for a loop. A big, sloppy loop that got tangled around my vocal cords. Me, speechless? That's crazy. But I couldn't form a single syllable, much less a complete sentence, when she started talking about theoretical physics.

As we get out of the car, I notice things I hadn't paid attention to yesterday, like the shorter wall that encompasses three sides of the garden while the fourth side is part of the outer wall. The lawn where the wedding reception took place lies just outside that outer wall. I also notice a cottage attached to the garden wall, nestled close to the compound's exterior. There's another building off to the left of the garden, but I can't tell what purpose it serves, though I do see modern-looking metal doors attached to that structure that suggest it might be a large garage.

I tip my head back to study the square turrets, but the glare of the cloudy sky makes me squint.

When we get our luggage out of the trunk, Kirsty tries to carry her own bags. But I suddenly get a macho impulse and can't resist it, so I lug all our bags toward the castle with some of them jammed under my arms and others dangling from my hands. All this luggage is kind of heavy and definitely awkward, but I can't back out now. The macho psychophysicist idiot needs to impress the sexy Scottish girl.

What's gotten into me?

I give up trying to understand myself as Kirsty leads me up a walkway to a wooden door. She swings it open, gesturing for me to go inside. I lug our, uh, luggage across the threshold. Maybe that's where the term luggage came from—people lugging shit around.

My thoughts all fly away when I take in my surroundings. I drop the bags on the floor, and the sound echoes up the spiral staircase that stretches high above my head.

"This is the vestibule," Kirsty tells me. "The entryway, if you like. Rory insists everyone should use the proper term for it, though, so don't call it anything other than the vestibule when he's around."

"I thought we were going to be alone here."

"We are. I meant if you ever see Rory."

"Oh." I can't stop staring up at the three floors above us. "Do I need to carry our luggage all the way up there?"

Kirsty laughs. "Not unless you're wanting to develop a hernia. We can stay in the ground-floor guest wing. It has several bedrooms, and the kitchen is in that wing. Let me give you the grand tour before we worry about the luggage."

"Okay." Not sure I want to slog up those stairs just to get a tour of the place, but she's being nice. I don't want to annoy her again. She might back out of the experiment.

Kirsty leads me up to the first floor. She seems to expect me to be confused by the fact the ground floor is not the first floor, but I've worked in buildings that had a similar layout—only in that they had a ground floor and a first floor above that. I've never been in any other structure like Dùndubhan. Not sure I can pronounce that name right, but I give it a try so I can satisfy my curiosity.

"Is the name Dùndubhan a Gaelic thing?" I ask.

"Aye. It means fortress of the black water."

"Does that mean there's a lake or stream nearby?"

"A river. It's back in the woods, and you can't see it from the house."

"Are you calling this huge castle a house? That doesn't seem appropriate."

"People have always lived here. Even today, Jamie and Gavin stay here most of the time, and Mrs. Brody lives in the cottage attached to the garden wall."

"Mrs. Who?"

"Brody." Kirsty pauses at the first-floor landing. "Evelyn Brody has been the housekeeper at Dùndubhan since Rory first bought the castle. She was Mrs. Darroch back then. Her second husband, Tavish, is the groundskeeper."

"Uh-huh. I guess Rory and Emery lived here back then too."

"Oh no," Kirsty says with a laugh. "He was married to Una at the time. Emery is his fourth wife."

"Fourth?" I probably should've tried to squelch my surprise, but I've never met anyone who was married four times. That's almost as many wives as Henry VIII had.

Kirsty ushers me into the first floor where there's a huge empty space that doesn't seem like just a hallway, but she keeps talking about her family. "Lachlan was divorced once, and Jack divorced Autumn but then married her again. That's the wedding reception you crashed yesterday. Anyway, Jamie was engaged to a British erse before she married Gavin, and—Oh, I shouldn't be havering about this. I'm sorry."

I can't keep up with these Scottish people. Four wives? Divorced and remarried? Mrs. Darroch became Mrs. Brody, and… Damn, I don't think I want to hear all about everyone she knows. The MacTaggart clan is probably as enormous as this castle.

Why, then, do I keep asking her questions? My mouth has a mind of its own.

"How many cousins do you have?" I ask.

She stops us in the middle of the long hallway. "You want to know about my family? I assumed you'd be annoyed that I was havering about them."

"No, it's, ah…kind of interesting. I was an orphan, so I guess I sometimes wish I had a big family. Listening to you talk about yours makes me feel like I'm almost part of a family too."

Oh shit. Why did I tell her that? Being around Kirsty gives me verbal diarrhea.

She stares at me. "You were an orphan? Why did you never tell me that when we were together?"

I hunch my shoulders. "Don't know. You talked about your family so much that I guess I felt weird about admitting I don't have anybody."

"Did you grow up in an orphanage?"

"No, I bounced around from one foster home to another."

"Luke, I'm so sorry." She rushes up to me and wraps her arms around me. "I wish you'd told me years ago."

"Not the kind of thing I tell anybody." I twist out of her embrace, taking a step backward. "Could we not talk about that anymore? I'd rather listen to you talk about your family and this castle."

"All right. Let me show you around." She waves at the large space we're standing in. "This is the great hall. And over there, that doorway accesses the old library that's now Rory's office, when he's at Dùndubhan. Let's head up to the second floor."

While we trudge up the spiral staircase again, I can't help admiring her sexy ass. I'm glad she's walking in front, otherwise I wouldn't get such a nice view to keep me going during our epic journey through the castle. My legs are getting a workout for sure. On the second floor, Kirsty shows me the long gallery, which looks pretty much like a regular hallway that happens to be very long. There's a bedroom in the tower, she tells me, though I have to ask what that means.

"You saw the turrets outside," she says. "Those are on top of the tower, and the bedroom is inside there. It's actually between the second and third floors."

"Sure, I get it." I don't, but I doubt it matters if I understand the complicated layout of this place.

Kirsty shows me more rooms, but we don't go inside the master suite on the third floor. That's Rory and Emery's room when they're in residence here. Jamie and Gavin prefer to sleep in the bedroom at the opposite end of the hall.

If I lived here, I'd sleep on the ground floor. Those stairs are murder on my knees.

She takes me back down to the first floor and guides me through a dining room into another hallway. "This is the guest wing. You can choose whichever bedroom you like."

"Ladies first. I'll choose from whichever ones are left after you pick yours."

She blinks several times quickly. "*You* are being chivalrous?"

Is it really that shocking? Well, yeah, I suppose it is. I've acted like a jerk ever since I showed up at her cousin's wedding reception. Knowing what Melvin wants me to do has played a part in my behavior, but I can't explain that to Kirsty. She'll hate me if she finds out the truth.

Suddenly, I care what she thinks of me. No, I won't examine that too closely.

"Can we eat before we pick our rooms?" I ask. "I'm starving after that long drive and the exercise I got clomping up and down those stairs."

"Let's go into the kitchen."

She waves for me to follow her down the hall and through a swinging door. This castle has a modern kitchen with a granite island and a large refrigerator, not to mention a double oven and a microwave. I see a big stand mixer too. Had I expected to find a medieval oven with flames inside it? Not sure that's what medieval ovens looked like, but then, I'm no expert on ye olden days.

"Will a turkey sandwich do?" she asks as she swings the fridge door open.

"Sure, sounds good." I amble up to the island and lean against it. "Tell me, do you have a favorite cousin?"

Kirsty is bent over, rummaging through the fridge's contents, but she freezes and glances sideways at me. "Aye, I do have a favorite. I love all my cousins, all my family, but I have a special relationship with one in particular."

"A 'special' relationship?"

She puckers her lips and tosses packages of turkey and cheese onto the island, then slings a jar of mayo onto it too.

The jar barely misses me.

"Donnae like what your tone implies," she says. "I'm not shagging my cousin Magnus."

"I didn't suggest you were." But okay, maybe I'd thought that for about a second. But no, Kirsty isn't that kind of girl. "I take it you and Magnus are close."

She relaxes as she shuts the fridge door and grabs a loaf of bread off the counter. "Aye, Magnus has always been my favorite cousin. Everyone else thinks he's dangerous, but I know he's a sweetie."

"Dangerous? What's this guy done to make his own family think that about him?"

"Nothing we know of. It's his profession that unsettles them. Well, that and the way he presents himself."

"What do you mean?"

She points toward a drawer. "Could you please get out a knife? I need to slice the bread. Mrs. Brody baked it fresh this morning."

I snag a knife and grip it in my hand. "Want me to slice? I'm good at that."

"Donnae think being a skilled bread slicer is something worth bragging about."

"Maybe not." I notice a small breadboard on the counter and move it onto the island, then I begin slicing. "So, you haven't explained why everybody's afraid of this Magnus character."

"Because they don't understand him. Magnus isn't around much. First, he was in the army and got deployed to Iraq. Then, he became a bounty hunter."

"Seriously? A bounty hunter. That sounds cool. Will I get to meet him?"

"It's doubtful. He's not home often since he chases fugitives all over the world." She unscrews the cap on the mayo jar, thrusting a spoon inside. "Magnus is a good man, but I think I'm the only one who believes that. He likes to act as if he's a villain, and his tattoos reinforce that idea. I think he likes to have everyone feel that way about him. It's part of his mystique."

"When did you last see him?"

"About a year ago. He only stayed for a day, then he took off again." She spreads mayo onto the slices of bread I hand her. Without looking up, she says, "It's time you told me why you're really here."

Chapter Nine

Kirsty

When I glance up at Luke, without lifting my head, I see him staring down at the loaf of bread. He clearly knows what I meant when I said he needs to tell me why he's here. And he doesn't want to do that. If he expects me to participate in his so-called scientific experiment, he'd better tell me the truth. I haven't had any luck so far with convincing him to be honest with me—completely honest—but I keep hoping he will do that.

Aye, I'm a moron. I shouldn't care if he tells me the whole truth, but I do.

I still have trouble reconciling the way he is now with the sweet boy I met at university. Luke used to bring me flowers just to make me smile, and he would watch sentimental romance movies with me even though I knew he would rather be watching documentaries or action films. We talked too, about anything and everything, from funny stories to serious things. I even told Luke about Elspeth's battle with bacterial meningitis and how she'd almost died from the illness. I never got round to explaining how that experience changed our family, especially Logan.

My brother had joined the army as soon as Elspeth recovered. He never told any of us why he did that, but I know Logan well enough to realize he'd done it because of our baby sister's illness. Maybe someday he will tell me why, but I haven't asked him. His time in the military and MI6 changed him, that much I do know. But it changed our entire family, not just Logan. We worried for him when he was away, stationed in a combat zone. And we watched him become harder and more closed-off over the years. Serena has helped him become less closed-off, but I don't think Logan will ever shed all the scars, emotional and physical, that he acquired after he joined the army.

"What are you thinking about?" Luke asks, his voice gentler than I've heard him sound since he stormed back into my life yesterday. "You look serious and almost sad."

"I was thinking about the past."

"Not about me, since you weren't scowling."

He's trying to make me smile, I think. Why? The man who called me insane shouldn't care if I feel bad and definitely shouldn't want to make me feel better.

"I wasn't thinking about you," I say, trying to sound calm. "What I was thinking about is none of your business."

"Fair enough."

We take our meal into the sitting room and eat in silence. I gaze out the three tall windows, but every time I glance at Luke, he's watching me. Why? I'm not that fascinating. When we were a couple, he used to gaze at me with love and sweetness, but now he stares at me like he can't figure out what sort of creature I am. He probably wants to put me into a petri dish so he can examine every molecule of my body until he finds the answers he seems determined to ferret out. I don't have answers for him, though. I am what I am, nothing more, nothing less. He can examine me for the next decade, but I will always be the same. No mysteries here. I'm just a lass who owns a metaphysical shop.

"You never answered my question," I say after I've finished my sandwich. "Why are you really here?"

"In what sense? I'm here because I got into your car and you drove me to this castle."

"Ugh, Luke. You know what I mean. Your ruddy experiment is a cover, but I cannae figure out what you're trying to hide from me."

"What makes you think I'm hiding anything?"

"Ahmno stupid. And you're still a bloody awful liar."

He sags into the sofa and exhales a long sigh. "Maybe there are other reasons, but it's none of your business."

Mhac na galla. He loves to throw my own words back at me.

I stand up. "Fine. If you're not going to explain yourself, then we might as well get on with the experiment. Let's find a good space for that."

"You still want to do it? Even though I'm being a stubborn jerk and refusing to tell you what you want to know."

"Aye. I'm a tolerant person, unlike you."

He springs up off the sofa, suddenly standing inches away from me, and frowns. "I am not intolerant. Just because I prefer science over mysticism doesn't make me prejudiced."

"You called me insane because my beliefs don't line up with yours. That's the definition of intolerance."

Luke glares at me for a moment, then skirts around the coffee table to get past me. He flings the sitting room door open. "Come on. Let's find a room where we can conduct the experiment."

I follow him as he stalks down the hall toward the doorway to the dining room, not because I do whatever the erse orders me to do, but because I agreed to his barmy experiment. And I keep my word. We explore all the rooms downstairs, but he rejects every single one of them without offering a reason why. He just grunts and moves on.

When he finally speaks, he sounds slightly less irritated. "Are there any rooms that don't have windows? Besides the bathrooms, I mean."

"Only the wine cellar and the dressing room in the master suite. That's like a large walk-in closet. Why does it matter if there are windows?"

"I want to reduce the amount of electromagnetic interference as much as possible. But I'm sure you have no idea how much EM pollution there is way out here."

"You should stop making assumptions about me." I wave toward a large window, since we're standing in the long gallery on the second floor. "Mobile phones work out here since there's a transmission tower not far away in that direction. We also have Wi-Fi throughout the castle. I don't think you're likely to find a room other than the wine cellar that has no electromagnetic interference."

He stares at me with a blank expression.

"Will ye never learn?" I ask. "Making assumptions about me will only prove what an intolerant numpty you are."

"I'm not—" He throws his head back and blusters out a sigh. "Never mind. Maybe I can find some metal sheets to put up as a barrier to the EM interference."

"The tower bedroom only has one small window. And I think Tavish left some metal sheeting in the potting shed."

"Okay. Let's go check that out."

I lead him back downstairs and out the vestibule door. As we cross the gravel drive, I veer away from the arched entrance to the garden and head for the outside of the garden wall where the potting shed lies.

"Are we the only ones here?" Luke asks. "In the whole compound or whatever you call it."

"We are alone. Mrs. Brody is taking the week off so she and Tavish can have a holiday. They're going to Wales."

"For a vacation? Wales?"

"Donnae sound so disgusted. It's a beautiful region."

"But vacations are supposed to be fun. What's there to do in Wales?"

I stop at the door to the shed. "Have you ever been there?"

"Well, no, but—"

"Then ye best haud yer wheesht. Aye?"

He twists his mouth into an annoyed expression, but then flattens it out. "Yeah, sure, you're right. I'll keep my mouth shut about Wales."

But not about anything else. That's what he implied.

I open the shed's door and flick the light switch inside. "There. I see the metal sheeting."

"This place smells like—" Luke clears his throat and shoves his hands into his jeans pockets. "Never mind. Let's just get the metal sheets and go."

I have no doubt he was about to say something derogatory about the shed, like that it smells dank. But he stopped short of doing that. Maybe he is trainable after all.

The metal sheets are rather narrow, so he has no trouble carrying them under his arm. I offered to help, but he grunted and did it himself anyway. Even when we start climbing the vestibule stairs, he refuses my repeated offers of help. The bloody-minded man needs to prove his manliness by lugging metal sheeting all the way to the second floor. There, we head through the long gallery to the doorway that leads into the tower bedroom. I open the door for Luke, but he still insists on carrying the sheets by himself. When he tries to navigate the stairs that access the bedroom, he stops at the third step.

"Is there a problem?" I ask.

"That's an awful long ways to haul these things."

"Would you like a wee bit of help? From an insane lass?"

Luke flashes me a scowl over his shoulder. "Can you please stop reminding me I called you that?"

"Do ye want the help or not?"

He sighs, and his shoulders slump. "Fine, okay. You can help."

Aye, he says that as if he's doing me a favor by letting me carry metal sheets for him. I suppose his manly pride won't allow him to ask for help. He needs to make it sound like the idea isn't his and he doesn't approve of it.

Despite his attitude, I grab one end of the stack of metal sheets he has under his arm. "Better?"

"Let's just get this done."

Needing a woman's help makes him testy. Luke has changed, for sure, and I can't decide if it's for the better—or if he even likes the way he is now.

Without too much trouble, we make it up the stairs and into the bedroom. It's larger than it looks from the outside, when you're standing in the driveway while gazing up at the tower. Still, this room is on the smaller side. But it should offer enough space for whatever Luke has in mind. How much equipment can he need for his experiment? He wants to talk me out of my beliefs, and it seems to me that doesn't require any sort of equipment except his mouth and his snarky attitude.

Luke sets the metal sheets on the floor. "I don't want to damage the walls. Do you have any duct tape?"

"Aye, right here in my bra. What do you think?"

"Where can I get some?"

"In the kitchen."

Luke's brows draw together. "The kitchen? Why would anyone keep duct tape there?"

"Because it's handy for a lot of things, not just taping metal sheets to the wall."

He looks at the doorway and the stairs visible beyond it, then he bows his head and sighs. "Where in the kitchen can I find the duct tape?"

"The pantry. Third shelf."

"Okay."

He trudges down the stairs.

Well, since he didn't ask me to go with him, I don't suppose I need to do that. He hasn't been entirely pleasant to me, with the odd exception, and I don't care to listen to him complaining and grunting while he hunts for duct tape. I wander over to the window and look out at the trees and the grey sky. Someday soon, I will get Luke to tell me why he's here. Not just why he's at Dùndubhan, but the reason he came to Scotland in the first place and crashed the wedding reception.

Aye, he will tell me.

Chapter Ten

Luke

Finding the duct tape doesn't take as long as I'd expected, but I need to lean against the kitchen island for a minute or two so I can catch my breath. How many frigging stairs does this place have? The vestibule staircase goes up to the third floor, but there are steps in the tower too and who knows where else. If all castles are designed like this one, I never want to become a handyman in old fortresses in Scotland. I'd die of a heart attack after two days. I'm in good shape, but this place is crazy, with all its rooms and doors and the screwy layout.

We walked through the dining room to get to the guest wing. I saw a doorway in the guest wing hall that seemed to lead outside, but apparently, there is no way to get into that part of the building from inside the house except to go through the dining room. What in the world? Who designed this nutso building?

Don't even get me started on the tower bedroom.

No, I don't think I'll ever buy a castle, even if I could afford it. How much does one of these medieval fortresses cost, anyway? More money than I'll ever see, that's for sure. Kirsty's cousin Rory must be stinking rich.

I still wonder about her mysterious cousin Magnus. No, I don't think she has a sexual relationship with him, but he sounds…strange. A bounty hunter? I've never met one of those in person or heard of anyone I know meeting one, so I guess I assumed nobody actually does that for a living. But Kirsty's cousin does. She clearly adores him, though she made it sound like nobody else in the family even likes him. They think he's "dangerous," she said.

Great. I hope I never meet that guy. He'd probably murder me on sight.

Now that I can breathe again without wheezing, I grab the duct tape and go back upstairs. When I walk into the tower bedroom, Kirsty is leaning against the window frame, gazing out at the trees or the clouds or who-knows-what. Her lips are curved into a slight smile. She looks so beautiful and serene, like she doesn't have a care in the world. I can tell she does have cares, though. Everybody's got those, right? But Kirsty had seemed sad earlier when she was thinking about whatever it was that she didn't want to talk about, not with me.

I clear my throat to get her attention. "Got the duct tape."

She turns toward me, pushing away from the window. "Good. I'll help you get the metal sheeting up."

"Thanks." I approach her and hand over the big roll of tape. "I'll hold up the sheets, and you secure them. Okay?"

"Aye."

With both of us working together, it only takes us about five minutes to get the window covered up. The room is darker now, obviously, but the chandelier above our heads offers soft illumination. Kirsty shuts the door to the stairs that wind upward to the top floor, then I shut the door we'd come through earlier. The golden glow from the chandelier lends Kirsty the look of a fairy princess. What kind of garbage is that? I'm turning into a moron with romantic mush for brains. Yes, okay, she looks pretty in this light. But that doesn't mean anything. I can't get involved with her again. She believes in Wicca and all that metaphysical nonsense.

And she believes string theory is on par with all her silly beliefs.

Still, she is beautiful and smart. Her arguments for the irrationality of theoretical physics might not be complete hooey. No, of course they are. Physics is science, not supernatural claptrap.

I glance around the room. "Shit. I forgot my equipment. Stay here, I'll go get it."

Kirsty shrugs. "Go on, then."

Though I only need a few minutes to get downstairs and grab the case I keep my equipment in, I pause at the bottom of the vestibule staircase to do some pre-breathing before I head up to the second floor. Yeah, I feel a lot like a deep-sea diver, needing to fill my lungs with oxygen before I dive in, though I don't think I can get the bends from going up and down these stairs. At least, I hope not.

Kirsty is sitting on the bed when I get back to the tower bedroom. "Took ye long enough. Did ye go the long way round?"

"There's a route that's longer than the usual one?"

"I was joking, Luke. Goodness, you are so uptight these days."

Uptight? Me? She really is nuts. "I wasn't uptight when I fucked you in the garden yesterday."

"No, but you are the rest of the time. Just like Rory used to be, but without the 'science is my religion' rubbish."

"It's not a religion. It's just science. Facts, not made-up bullshit."

Kirsty laughs, and heaven help me, I still love it when she does that. "What about string theory? There are no facts to—"

"Can we stop talking about science? Just for now. I need to get set up for the experiment."

"Aye, do what you need to do. I'll just relax over here." She lays her body across the bed with her head on one of the pillows and shuts her eyes. "Maybe I'll take a wee nap."

"Sure, whatever."

Kirsty stretches her arms above her head and arches her back, moaning and smiling.

While I unzip my hard-sided suitcase, I try very hard not to look at her. But my peripheral vision didn't get the memo, and I can't help noticing the way she keeps moving her body, almost like she's having sex with a ghost. For Christ's sake, why does she have to do that? It's making my dick wake up. Screwing her in this room would not be a smart way to start off this experiment.

But it would feel so damn good.

No, that's the lust talking. My body will always want her, but I need to remain objective, or this experiment will crash and burn before I even get started.

"We need a couple chairs," I say. "And a table. I could use that long one by the window, but I don't see any chairs in here."

She sits up. "You can get those from the long gallery."

Fantastic. More stair climbing. Well, at least I don't have to go all the way down to the ground level since the long gallery is on the second floor. I think.

I find two chairs and haul them up the stairs into the bedroom. Kirsty offers to carry one of the chairs, but I grunt in response, which is my way of telling her I don't need help. Maybe I kind of do, but I can't make myself ask a woman to lug a chair for me. Kirsty seems to think it's funny that I insist on moving furniture on my own.

Once I get both chairs into the bedroom, she smiles and laughs softly. "You are so cute when you act macho and grumpy. But honestly, accepting a little help isn't a sign you're losing your masculinity."

"I know I'm not losing—Never mind." I drag the table into the middle of the room, halfway between the foot of the bed and the wall. "Give me a few minutes to finish setting up."

The table that had been by the window is longer than the nightstand, but narrower too. My legs are longer than Kirsty's, which means my knees will probably bump into hers if I set the table lengthwise. So instead, I put the chairs at either end with the table's length between them.

Kirsty sits at the foot of the bed, watching me, her feet swinging. The bed is tall, so her shoes dangle six inches off the floor.

I wish she weren't wearing a skirt. It reminds me of yesterday in the garden when I—*Don't think about that, idiot.*

After getting the furniture positioned, I pull items out of my large suitcase and lay them on the table. My portable partition is wider than the table, so I use more duct tape to hold it in place. The partition stands two feet tall, so Kirsty won't be able to see what I'm doing on my side of the table. Maybe I should blindfold her too, just to make sure she can't cheat.

Would she do that? For some reason, I can't believe she might. Kirsty isn't a cheater.

Once I've got everything I need set up on the table, I wave for Kirsty to come over here. "Have a seat. It's time for the first test."

"Test?" She ambles over to the table and settles her shapely ass onto the chair. "What sort of experiment is this?"

"I'm testing your hoodoo."

"My what?" she says with a laugh. "That doesn't sound like a scientific term."

"Would you rather I call it bullshit?"

"No, I'd rather you behave like a rational adult. But that doesn't seem likely."

Am I acting irrational and immature? Maybe. Not sure. Ever since I saw Kirsty again for the first time in twelve years, I haven't been thinking like a mature adult, or like a rational scientist.

I take my seat and pull my chair up to the table, laying my arms on the surface. "We'll start with cards. Each one has a single symbol on it—circle, square, triangle, or wavy lines. Understand?"

"Aye, I'm not an eejit."

"You can't see the cards, which makes this a single-blind experiment."

She gives me a sexy little smile. "I love it when a man explains his experimental methodology to me."

Is Kirsty flirting? I can't understand why she would do that, considering how hostile she's been since the moment we saw each other again. But the way she said "experimental methodology" made me want to repeat the mistake I made yesterday. This time, I'll toss her onto that bed and—No, I will do nothing of the sort.

Shuffling the cards, I focus on the task to avoid looking at her. "I'm about to lay down the first card. Are you ready?"

"Aye. All my hoodoo is on the highest setting."

"Cute. But this is a scientific experiment, so please concentrate." I pick up the top card on the deck and flip it over so I can see the image on it. "What do you see?"

Kirsty shuts her eyes.

For a moment, silence fills the room. I wait for her to respond and try my damnedest not to look at her.

"Square," she says.

The card shows a circle. *Hah.* Not psychic after all. That's what my irrational male brain tells me, but my scientist side demands I continue the experiment because one data point is not enough. I put a check mark in the appropriate column on the spreadsheet I have open on my computer screen.

I flip over another card. "What about now?"

"Wavy lines."

Another wrong answer. While I put another check mark in my spreadsheet, I do my best not to seem pompous because I still don't have enough data to reach a valid conclusion. I flip a third card. "Tell me what you see."

"Circle."

I stare down at the card. It does show a circle. Well, that doesn't mean anything because I still don't have enough data. I keep flipping cards and asking what she sees until I have one hundred responses—one hundred data points. Then I pause to examine the data I've amassed so far.

"Did you cheat somehow?" I ask, sounding annoyed and confused because, dammit, I am annoyed and confused. "This isn't possible. The results are evenly split between correct and incorrect responses."

She smiles at me, her cheeks dimpled, and seems awfully pleased with herself, though in an adorably smug way that makes me want to kiss her hard and deep. And do other things hard and deep too. Why her smugness makes me hot for her, I have no idea.

"Well?" I demand. "Did you cheat?"

"If you think I might have, maybe you should blindfold me and do the test again."

She hasn't admitted to cheating, and honestly, I can't believe she would do that. But the results make no sense. A fifty-fifty split? That's statistically improbable at best and completely insane at worst. Maybe I gave her visual cues without intending to do that, like a subconscious tell. Her idea about using a blindfold makes sense and will ensure I'm not telegraphing anything to her without meaning to reveal too much.

I look around for something I can use as a blindfold. Don't see anything. Which means I'll have to slog down all those stairs again to find a scarf or a towel or something.

Kirsty nods toward the other doorway, the one that leads up to the top floor. "Go upstairs. I'm sure Emery left a scarf or two in the master suite."

"How do you know I'm looking for a scarf?"

She smiles. "Because you don't believe the results and you need to prove it's an error. Go on, find something to blindfold me with."

"Don't you think Emery will mind that a stranger rummaged through her belongings?"

"Tosh. Emery won't care." Kirsty pushes her chair back. "But I can go find something if you're afraid to set foot in a woman's bedroom."

"I'm not afraid, but it would be…inappropriate for me to do that. You should go."

Kirsty heads for the door but pauses as she walks past me. "You should thank me for not skelping you for suggesting I'm cheating on your little test."

"Maybe I would thank you, but I have no idea what you're threatening to do to me."

She leans down, our eyes inches apart. "I said you should thank me for not smacking you around."

Kirsty gives me a smug, but somehow hot, smile and sashays out of the room.

And I wait.

Chapter Eleven

Kirsty

Emery didn't leave a scarf in the master suite, but I do find one of Rory's neckties. That will do. If Luke insists on moving forward with his "study," I'll keep doing anything I can to make him doubt his mantra that science is the answer to every question. Do I have psychic abilities? Well, only I know the answer, and I don't feel like sharing it with Luke. Not yet.

Honestly, I have no idea if what I believe is true. That's why it's called faith. But I don't like Luke's insistence that I cannot possibly have any witchy powers. He needs to have his arrogant certainty shaken. No one can declare without any doubt that anything is or is not true. Most of what we experience in life can't be measured or fully explained.

When I return to the tower bedroom, I hand Luke the necktie. "This will do, aye?"

He accepts the item and eyes it with a strange expression. "You want me to blindfold you with this."

"That's what you wanted. Isn't it?"

"Yeah, sure." He stands. "Sit down and I'll tie it around your head."

"Whatever you say."

I walk past him and settle into my chair again.

Luke comes up behind me and secures the necktie around my head, covering my eyes. I can't see a thing, and that's the point. He'll know I didn't cheat. How would I do that, anyway? I couldn't see his cards, not with the barrier he set up between us. I'm not a magician.

I hear his footsteps as he goes back to his chair.

"All right," he says. "Let's try this again. Literally blind this time. Are you sure you can't see anything?"

"Positive. I don't have x-ray vision."

"How many fingers am I holding up?"

I can't help laughing. "You've gotten so paranoid. I cannae see your fingers, Luke."

"Take a wild guess."

"Fine. Six."

"I wasn't holding up any fingers."

Sighing, I shake my head. "Satisfied now?"

"Yes. We'll begin the experiment now."

I hear cards being shuffled, then rustling sounds as if he's moving around, though it doesn't sound like he's gotten up from his chair.

"Let's begin," he says. "First card."

"Triangle."

We continue the experiment with card after card. Luke makes little huffing noises now and then, but otherwise, we don't speak to each other except as part of the "literally blind" study he insists on undertaking. I lose count of how many cards he's flipped. But at last, he announces we've reached the end of this round.

"You can take off the blindfold," he says, and he sounds almost defeated.

I remove the necktie. "Are you all right?"

"Yeah, I'm terrific. You've got to be cheating, somehow, but I can't figure out what you're doing."

"Let me guess. You got another fifty-fifty split."

"It's statistically impossible." He shoves a hand into his hair, head bowed. "Or at least extremely improbable."

"Why don't you try a different test? I'll do whatever you want."

He jerks his head up, staring at me with wide eyes. "Why would you do anything I want? You think my study is bullshit."

"No, I think you are not objective when it comes to witchy powers. Maybe you're the one cocking up the test, subconsciously."

Luke scratches his cheek. "I suppose that's possible."

"Did you just admit you might be wrong?"

"Who said anything about being wrong? I'm admitting I might have accidentally contaminated the test."

"Because you desperately want to prove the metaphysical doesn't exist."

"No. Because science tells me it's impossible."

I lean back in my chair, regarding Luke with a new understanding. "Science is your religion. You can't believe any of the principles drilled into you might not be one hundred percent accurate."

"Stop trying to convince me that science is baloney. The precepts are—"

"Dogma. That's what too many of them are. String theory? Well, we've already had that discussion." It was more of an argument, but I won't mention that. It would be rude.

"You can't talk me out of believing in facts."

I spring forward in my chair. "You just admitted it's a belief, not an irrefutable law of nature."

He scowls. "You tricked me. And I meant you can't convince me to ignore the facts, not that I need to believe in them."

"Then how do you explain the results of your wee study?"

"My wee study? You make it sound silly." He slumps against his chair's back, rubbing his forehead. "I need another participant. It's not a genuine experiment with only one person."

"I can help you find another test subject."

He squints at me. "Let me guess. That person will have the last name MacTaggart."

"Well, I do know other people who aren't related to me. But my brother Logan is almost as skeptical as you are, so he could be an excellent candidate. He was in the army, then MI6. No one is tougher or less willing to believe in witchy powers than my brother."

Luke lays a hand on the table and taps one finger. "That's not a half-bad idea. Though Logan is your brother, so he might help you cheat."

It's my turn to huff and frown. "Do you not realize how insulting it is every time you accuse me of cheating?"

"Sorry. I didn't mean it that way."

"What other way could you possibly mean that statement?"

He slumps forward, both arms on the table, and bows his head. "I don't know."

"Let me ring Logan. He'll be happy to help out."

Luke lifts his head, one corner of his mouth slanted upward. "Sure. He'll be happy to show you how to skelp me good."

"Only if you accuse us of cheating on your test."

"Fine. Call Logan."

I hurry to where I'd left my purse on the floor and dig out my mobile. Logan answers on the second ring. "What is that *cacan* doing to you now?"

"Which *cacan* would that be, Logie?"

"The one who's dragged you off to a remote castle in the woods. And donnae be calling me that name."

I laugh. "Donnae ye get tired of telling me that? I rang you because I need a favor."

"What is it?" he asks, sounding a wee bit suspicious.

That's Logan. He's suspicious of essentially everything and everyone, until he gets to know a person. He knows me, but I have no doubt he can guess that whatever I ask of him won't be something he wants to do.

"Luke is trying to do a study," I say, "to determine whether witchy powers exist. But he only has one test subject—me. We need another participant."

"Are you asking me to be that *cacan*'s guinea pig?"

"That's right. Maybe you can prove scientifically that your sisters do not have supernatural abilities."

Logan says nothing for a moment, which always means he's thinking. "I'll do it, but only to protect you from whatever that *cacan* is trying to do to you."

"Aye, you do that, Logie. Come to Dùndubhan right away."

"Be there in one hour." He pauses, then adds, "Good thing Serena and I decided to stay in Scotland for a while instead of going home to Utah. I need to protect my sister from an American fiend."

I can't help laughing. "See you soon, Logie."

As I end the call, I turn toward Luke.

His brows are crinkled. "He's coming?"

"Of course. Logan always comes whenever a family member needs his help."

"I guess it'll take at least an hour for him to get here."

"Aye. In the meantime, we can go downstairs and have a piece. I saw some donuts in the kitchen."

"Donuts aren't very Scottish."

I roll my eyes. "Not everything I eat needs to be authentically Scottish. We had sandwiches earlier."

"True." He pushes up out of his chair and stretches, groaning. "I'm not looking forward to going down those stairs again. This castle needs an elevator."

"Do ye need a wee lie-down first?" I point toward the bed. "Go on. I don't mind."

He eyes the bed, then looks at me and licks his lips. "Only if you lie down with me."

The husky tone of his voice suggests he doesn't want to take a nap.

"No sex," I announce.

"Did I say anything about sex?"

"You were thinking it."

He walks up to me, halting so close I can smell his aftershave. "Maybe I am thinking about it. What we did yesterday wasn't my finest moment. Can't let you go on thinking all I can manage is a quickie in the garden."

"I'm sure you can manage a lot more than that." My voice has turned huskier too, though I don't want to sound that way. He might get the wrong idea. Which would be the same idea I'm considering.

But no, it's a horrible idea.

Even if it would feel bloody wonderful.

Luke combs his fingers through my hair. "We have an hour to waste. And I'm not hungry—for food."

"We shouldn't. You and I are not a couple."

"I know. But we can be…fuck buddies."

"Cannae believe you just spoke those words. No one actually does that."

He moves closer, grasping my nape and tipping my head back. "Let's stop pretending we don't want each other. Maybe we'll never be a couple again, but that doesn't mean we have to ignore our lust. Two consenting adults can do whatever we want."

Fuck buddies? He's lost his mind.

I must have done too, since I'm considering his proposition. "Would this be another scientific experiment?"

"No. It's just for the hell of it."

"Won't sex cock up your impartial study?"

He slides his free arm around my waist and tugs me into his body. "Only if we let it, which we won't. Casual sex, that's all. No strings, no messy emotions, just a way to get off."

My breathing has become heavier, and try as I might, I can't make it calm down. My pulse refuses to calm either. And the way I can feel his erection pressed into my belly does not make it any easier to think rationally about his suggestion.

I want him. Cannae deny that. Maybe…

No, no, no. This will only lead to more complications. But I will never fall in love with him again, and it's been too long since I had a lover. Why not blow off steam with Luke? Casual sex. Aye, that sounds reasonable. To a numpty.

But I want to do it.

"All right," I say. "Let's have sex."

<h1 style="text-align:center">Chapter Twelve</h1>

Luke

Kirsty said yes. I didn't suffer an auditory hallucination. She just told me she wants to be fuck buddies with me. My dick twitches against her belly, announcing its approval of this cockamamie plan I dreamed up a minute ago strictly because I can't stand *not* to screw her again. Will doing the deed with my ex-girlfriend invalidate the study we're trying to complete? No. We'll both be more relaxed and ready to resume the experiment after we've gotten rid of this sexual tension.

And if it comes back, we'll get rid of it again. And again. And again.

No, I haven't gone completely insane. Maybe I've tipped a little off-kilter, but that's all. I can handle this. Banging my ex, the only girl I ever loved, will not result in disaster because I don't love her anymore. The fact that I have her body hugged to mine does not influence my decision at all. Watching Kirsty during our experiment, and seeing that bed out of the corner of my eye, I couldn't help getting turned on. It's an autonomic response. Man sees woman. Man gets hard. Man fucks woman and feels much better and saner afterward.

I finger the top button on her blouse. "Let's get to it."

"Aye."

While I unbutton her blouse, I slide my arm down so I can palm her ass. She exhales a shaky breath. I'm not breathing normally either, but that's only because of my autonomic, and therefore uncontrollable, reaction to a desirable woman who agreed to have sex with me. Her shirt falls open as I free the last button, revealing her lacy white bra. I push my hand under her skirt and feel the lace of her panties. She unbuttons my shirt much faster than I'd opened hers and spreads her palms on my chest, the warmth of her skin and the smoothness of her palms turning me on even more.

Can't wait. No more slow undressing.

I get rid of my clothes as fast as humanly possible, and my shoes clunk on the floor when I toss them away.

Kirsty shimmies out of her blouse and skirt, now dressed in only her lace underwear.

And I suddenly realize one vital fact. "I don't have a condom."

"Didnae worry about that yesterday."

"I know. Sorry. But I—"

"Relax. I'm on birth control."

Thank goodness for that. I can't wait one second longer.

Especially when Kirsty removes her bra and panties.

I suck in a ragged breath, fisting my hands and clenching my teeth. I'm not angry. I'm so damn hot for her that I feel like a sex-crazed animal. Her tits are even more mouth-watering than I remembered, just the right size to fit in my hands, and their tips point at me like her body is begging me to taste her flesh. Her flat belly draws my attention down to her navel, then lower to the hairs on her mound. I want my face between those thighs. Right now.

She glances at my hard-on and drags her tongue over her bottom lip.

I lean around her body to grasp the covers and yank them off. "Get on the bed, kitten. Right now."

"What if I don't?"

"Then I'll take you on the wood floor. You'll be more comfortable on the bed, so get your ass on there." I bend my head to whisper in her ear, "You've got five seconds before I drag you down to the floor. Five, four—"

She wraps her fingers around my cock.

"Three," I gasp. "Two—"

Kirsty hops onto the foot of the bed, then crawls backward. "I'm ready."

I climb onto the bed and crawl across it too, until I'm positioned over her body on all fours, gazing down at her. She's beautiful, yes, and I want her so badly I can't think straight. But I don't love her anymore. I can't. Everything she believes in goes against all the scientific facts I've learned and memorized. Right now, though, the only thing I want to memorize is her body.

Screw the past. This is sex and nothing else.

I lunge my head down, about to kiss her, until I realize casual sex partners shouldn't do that. I don't want Kirsty to get the wrong idea. So I divert my mouth to her throat and drag my tongue up it until I can latch on to her earlobe. I wrap my tongue around her stud earring and suck. She exhales a breathy moan. Why am I taking it slow? I don't need to do that since we're not a couple. I only need to screw her, but I can't stop myself from skidding my lips back down her throat and across her collarbone so I can kiss a path down her chest between her tits until I reach her belly button. I swirl my tongue inside it, then move my mouth to her breast. The sight of her rosy nipple makes my dick ache, and I press my open mouth to that little peak so I can lick and suckle it.

She arches her back, moaning louder.

Every sound she makes, every little movement, drives me crazy.

I struggle to catch my breath, and though my eyes want to look at her, I know I shouldn't do that. I remember the expression she gets on her face whenever we're having sex. Not the way she'd looked yesterday when I screwed her like a maniac. I remember that expression from when we used to make love, but I can't give her that today. Sex only. Can I pull that off? No emotion, nothing but gratification. I've never tried, but I need to do it now.

Skimming my lips down her belly, I nuzzle the hairs on her mound and flick my tongue out to tease her folds. She's already so wet. I can smell it and taste it. When she spreads her thighs for me, I dive my head down to seal my mouth around her clit and suckle it. She lets out a sharp cry, which only cranks up my lust and makes my dick throb harder. I can't wait much longer, not after twelve years of imagining what it would be like to feel her body around my cock again, so I slip two fingers into her folds to stroke her slick flesh while I keep tormenting her clit, licking and sucking and grating my teeth over it until she cries out again, the sound echoing off the high ceiling.

Kirsty thrusts her fingers into my hair, her nails scraping my scalp. "Luke, yes, oh God."

I rasp my fingers up and down her folds, then push my thumb inside her opening while I keep petting her flesh. Her back bows up, lifting off the mattress, while she gasps and whimpers and grips my head with both hands. She writhes, and I pump my thumb in and out, faster and faster, as I keep sucking on her nub, latching on to the hard, erect core of it.

Then I nip that rigid bud.

And she comes, her body tightening around my thumb while her cries reverberate off the stone walls and she clutches my head so tightly it hurts, but I don't care. As the last wave of her climax subsides, I rise to my knees at her feet. Lifting my hand, I slowly lick her cream off my fingers one by one until I get to my thumb. Then I lick that even more slowly, sliding my tongue around its entire length and circumference.

"Damn," I growl, "you taste so good."

"Luke, please, I need you inside me."

"I love hearing you beg, but it's unnecessary. Nothing will stop me from fucking you, kitten, not even if a tornado rips the roof off this castle."

She spreads her legs wider and bends her knees, her heels flat on the mattress.

Only a coma patient would fail to understand that gesture. I might be an idiot at times, but I'm not so brain-dead I don't get the message.

I plant my palms at either side of her body and thrust inside her hot, smooth channel. Christ, she feels even better than I remember. Her body molds to my cock in a way I've never experienced before, not with her or any other woman, because I've never had sex without a condom. Not until yesterday. That had been quick and dirty, no time to enjoy the sensation of her flesh on mine. But today, I can revel in it for as long as I want. Even if her brother bursts through the door and starts shouting Gaelic curses at me, I won't stop screwing his sister. I've waited too long for this moment.

Kirsty grips my biceps while I pull out and plunge into her, over and over, and the sound of our bodies colliding bounces off the walls. I thrust harder, faster, grunting every time I punch into her. The pressure inside me mounts second by second, the need to come so fierce that I grit my teeth in a desperate effort to stave off my climax until she goes off first. I grasp her hips and lift them off the bed, then sink inside her even deeper with every thrust. Her wetness glistens on my cock, but I barely notice that with my focus locked on Kirsty's face. I swore I wouldn't look at her while I took her body, but I can't stop myself. I gaze into her eyes, those pale blue pools mesmerizing me until I couldn't tear my focus away from her if I tried.

"Come for me, kitten," I growl. "Come for me now."

I shift one hand so I can scrape my thumb across her clit.

Her entire body goes stiff, and she seems to stop breathing in the second before her orgasm hits. Her mouth falls open. She fists her hands in the sheets and screams, "Luke!"

As her inner muscles pulsate around my cock, I grit my teeth so hard my jaw aches. But I don't need to hold back anymore. She's coming, and I can't wait any longer. I throw my head back and pound into her, letting go of my self-control while spasms fire through my cock like machine gun rounds, hard and hot and unstoppable. I go off while buried deep inside her, punching into her twice more without withdrawing, letting out half-strangled shouts.

Once it's over, I can't move. I just sit here, on my knees and still grasping her hips, breathing so hard I'm starting to see black spots in my vision.

That has never happened to me before.

Sex with Kirsty can't be so incredible that I almost pass out from it. That's crazy. But in the moment, with her flesh surrounding me, I'd kept thinking vaguely romantic thoughts. I looked into her eyes while we both came, though I swore I wouldn't do that. It doesn't mean anything. I got caught up in the intense pleasure of being inside her, that's all. The last thing I should ever do is fall for her all over again. Once she finds out what I intend to do to her, she won't want me within ten miles of her ever again.

I don't want to do it, but I have no choice.

Why haven't I pulled out of her body yet? Gazing down at the place where our bodies remain joined, I can't figure out why I haven't moved. We're done. I screwed her, we both came, end of story. But I love the way it feels to have her wrapped around me, and I love the dreamy look on her face. She always gets that way after sex, and it always makes me want to pull her into my arms and kiss her.

But I can't do that. Not anymore. Not considering what lies ahead for both of us.

Kirsty stretches her arms out to me. "Come here, Luke. Hold me, please."

Shit. How am I supposed to resist that? But I can't give her what she wants.

I pull out of her body and caress her thighs. "I have a better idea. Let's do that again."

Chapter Thirteen

Kirsty

Again?" I say, gazing up at him with what must look like a dazed expression. I feel sort of dazed, or maybe I'm just extremely relaxed. I haven't had sex this good in years. Aye, I've been with other men since Luke threw me over all those years ago. But no one else has ever made me feel the way Luke does. I know I shouldn't get attached to him again, but I can't help it. Sex with anyone makes me feel closer to the man in question, but sex with Luke affects me in a much more intimate way.

Oh no, ye bloody eejit, don't go falling for him again.

I won't do that. Never again. Earth-shattering sex does not mean I still love him. But I did beg him to hold me. Maybe I am an eejit after all.

Why did he suggest we have sex again when I asked him to hold me? I don't expect Luke will answer that question if I ask him, so I won't bother. Aye, that probably means I'm a coward.

"Can we talk instead?" I ask.

He sinks back on his heels, still kneeling between my legs, and groans. "Why do women have to get all 'let's cuddle and talk' after sex? It was hot, but we don't need to discuss what happened."

"I don't want to talk about sex. I want you to answer the question I've asked you before. Why are you here? What is your so-called valid reason?"

He groans again, wiping a hand over his mouth. "I don't know."

"What?" I push up onto my elbows. "But you said—"

"I know what I said, and I did have a valid reason yesterday. Today, I don't know."

"That's rubbish, Luke. You know why you're here."

"Yeah, to do you again and again until our hour is up."

I frown at him. "That won't work. I know you're hiding something, so tell me what it is. I agreed to do your silly experiment, so the least you can do is be honest with me."

"Have you been honest with me? I mean, totally honest?"

Though I open my mouth, intending to say yes, I freeze. Have I been completely transparent with him? I'm not sure about the answer. I should never have given in to my desires and let Luke make love to me. My mind and my heart are even more confused now, which means I cannot do that again with him. I shouldn't still have feelings for him, but I…think I might.

As my brother would say, bloody fucking hell.

Luke smirks and kisses my knee, which is still bent. "Come on, let's do that again. For old times' sake."

"It's not old times' sake if you keep doing it repeatedly. You are so full of rubbish, Luke."

"Maybe I am." He skates his hand down my inner thigh, triggering an involuntary shiver from me. "But you can't deny I give you incredible orgasms."

I hate that he's right, and I hate that he can still arouse me so easily. I know only one thing for certain. Luke Turner will shatter my heart all over again, and I'm not sure I can stop it from happening.

"No more sex," I tell him as I shimmy backward to get some space from him. Then I sit up and wrap my arms around myself in a pathetic attempt to hide my breasts from him. As if the man hasn't seen them already, many times. "We can continue the experiment, but no more fuck buddies. Understand?"

"Are you reneging on a deal? We agreed to—"

"I've changed my mind."

"Women are so fickle." He slides off the foot of the bed and starts picking up the clothes we'd left on the floor. He tosses mine to me. "Better get dressed. I need a snack before your brother gets here."

I hop off the bed and shimmy into my knickers. "We will not tell Logan we're having sex."

Luke pauses in the middle of zipping up his trousers. "We won't tell him we're having sex? That implies we'll be doing it again. And again. And again."

"No, I—It was a slip of the tongue."

"Sure. Whatever you say, kitten." He slaps my erse. "I'll wait for you to beg me for sex."

"That will never happen."

"Uh-huh." He finishes zipping up, then slings an arm around my waist to tug me into him. "We both know neither of us can control our lust for each other. It's a force of nature."

"*Magairlean. Falbh a ghabhail do ghnùis airson cac.*"

Luke's face goes blank, and his jaw goes slack. "What did you just say?"

"It's Gaelic. I said 'bollocks,' then I told you 'away and take your face for a shit.' "

He bursts out laughing. "That's hilarious. I love all the kooky things you Scots say. How do I take my face for a shit, anyway? That stuff comes out of my ass, not my head."

"And ye've got yer head up yer erse, donnae ye? Aye, so you know exactly where to put the *cac*."

He chuckles. "I love it when you speak Gaelic nonsense. It's cute."

I wrestle free of his grasp and put my bra on. "My *da-shealladh* tells me you will not be getting your *slat* inside my *péiteag* ever again."

"Your what?" he says with a slight laugh. "I know what *da-shealladh* means, but the rest is gibberish."

"No, it's not. *Slat* means penis, and *péiteag* means vagina. Can your scientific brain grasp the meaning?"

"Uh-huh. You're claiming you'll never have sex with me again, but we both know that's baloney. You want me too much to abstain for more than a few hours, a day at most." He pulls his shirt on. "You'll be dragging me into the nearest room, with or without a bed, before the day is done."

"No, I will not. Logan will be here soon, which means ye willnae have any more chances to seduce me."

He slaps my erse again. "Sure, kitten, you lie to yourself all you want."

"Thank you. I will." The second I realize what I said, I start furiously struggling to get my clothes back on while avoiding his gaze. "I meant I'll do whatever I like, not that I'll be lying to myself."

And he chuckles.

I want to batter him with the nearest blunt object. A sharp object would do too. I'd settle for a toothbrush if that's all I can find.

While I straighten my skirt and blouse, I glower at him. "Thank you for turning back into a *bod ceann*. Makes it so much easier to never have a poke with you again."

"Until the next time you get horny."

I slip my feet into my shoes. Then I catch sight of myself in the mirror attached to the dresser. My hair is a mess. Bloody hell, I have sex hair. Logan cannot see me like this. He'll know I've been shagging Luke for sure, and a scientific experiment will turn into a battle the likes of which no one has seen since Bannockburn. The Scots won that fight, and Logan will pummel Luke into the ground as surely as Robert the Bruce trounced the Brits.

Not sure if I'd mind him doing that.

Yes, of course I'd mind. I might despise Luke, but I don't want him to be murdered. My brother would go to jail then, and I definitely don't want that to happen. Despise him? I wish I felt that way, but if I did, I wouldn't have begged him to hold me.

I glance at the bed, with its rumpled bottom sheet and lumped-up pillow, not to mention the covers that are hanging off the foot of the bed. "We need to clean this up before Logan gets here."

"Sure, I'll help."

"You want to help? Without any griping or sarcasm?"

"That's right. Maybe I'm not as much of a *bod ceann* as you think. What does that phrase mean, anyway?"

"Dickhead."

We work together to make the bed, though I'm not sure it looks any less like we had a poke there once we're done. Does this room smell like sex? I should go downstairs to get a bottle of air freshener spray. I am hungry too, so I could get a piece at the same time. Luke follows me downstairs, though I didn't ask him to do that, and I didn't tell him what I mean to do there either. I find air freshener in the pantry.

"What's that for?" he asks while smirking. "Afraid your brother will smell what we did in the tower bedroom?"

How did he know I was worried about that? He's not telepathic, I hope. But I suppose it's not too difficult to figure out why I wanted air freshener.

I do not answer his question, however.

"Relax, kitten," Luke says. "Only somebody with a superpowered nose would sniff out our naughty little secret."

No, I will not respond to that statement. He wants to get me flustered, and I won't let him do it.

Ignoring him, I head for the kitchen and grab a muffin from the basket on the counter. Mrs. Brody always leaves snacks out for whoever might want them. Cranberry nut muffins will satisfy my craving—for food. Heaven help me, I still crave Luke, despite all my denials. He's gorgeous and brilliant at sex, so of course I want to have a poke with him again. But I won't do it. Only in my own thoughts will I ever admit I still want him even though he's a *bod ceann*.

Mhac na galla. What sort of dunderhead have I become?

I grab another muffin and toss it to Luke.

He catches it in one hand, sinks his teeth into the muffin, and chews languorously. "Thanks, kitten. But I'm hungry for more than a muffin."

"No more sex." I glance at the clock on the wall. "Logan will be here soon, anyway. Twenty minutes at most."

"Then we've got time for a quickie."

"What part of 'no' are you confused about? I will never let you shag me again."

He takes another bite of muffin, chews it slowly, and drags his tongue across his lips to clean off the crumbs. "Okay. *You* can shag *me* this time."

"Absolutely not."

"Hmm." He sets his muffin down on the island and strides up to me. "Guess I'll have to kiss you so hard you come for me."

"Donnae be ridiculous. No one can do that."

"Give me a chance to prove the scientific validity of my hypothesis."

For reasons I don't understand, whenever he speaks in science jargon, it makes me randy—especially when he speaks in a husky tone.

Luke backs me up to the island, penning me with his hands at either side of my body. "Let's test my hypothesis."

I should move. Shove him away. Tell him to go to hell. But my muscles refuse to obey my commands, instead softening while I exhale the breath I hadn't realized I was holding. My lips open, though I didn't want them to do that. A tingling heat starts between my thighs, spreading outward little by little while he leans in until our mouths are millimeters apart. My lips are tingling now, and I can't pull in a full breath.

"Bet you're still wet for me," he rumbles.

Aye, of course I am. Donnae want to be, but my body has overruled my brain. I sag against the island, and he lashes an arm around me to keep me from falling to the floor at his feet.

He flicks his tongue out to tease the seam of my lips.

And heaven help me, I moan.

Groaning, he sneaks his tongue between my lips, then withdraws it. He does that three more times while every swipe makes me wetter and more tingly. I grasp his shirt, hauling him closer until our chests collide, and I thrust my tongue into his mouth.

He groans so deeply it vibrates in his chest.

A door slams shut elsewhere in the house.

"Kirsty!" Logan shouts. "Where are you?"

While his footfalls pound in the hallway, I push Luke away. "My brother is here."

Luke sighs. "It was just getting good."

I'm silently thanking the universe for my brother's arrival, because I'd been about to let Luke do whatever he wanted to me, even shag me on the kitchen island. Worse, I still want him to do that.

I rush into the hall and bump into Logan. "Oh! Didnae see you."

"What's the rush?" He squints at me, then glowers at Luke, who has just exited the kitchen. "*An Diabhal fhéin.* What has he done to you?"

My brother just snarled "the devil himself" in Gaelic, but I don't think he's asking me what Satan has done to me. He was simply swearing. Luke might be an erse, but he is not the devil.

"More Scottish nonsense words, eh?" Luke says while smirking. "Nice to see you too, Logan."

My brother skirts around me to stop inches away from Luke. "What's this I hear about an experiment? If you're using my sister in some idiotic scheme to further your career—"

"Calm down. Kirsty agreed to participate."

"*Ith do chac, ye bod ceann.*" Logan straightens, now towering over Luke. On purpose, I'm sure. "That means eat your own shit, ye dickhead."

"Logan!" I snap as I shove myself between the two men. "You promised to behave like a mature adult, not assault Luke with Gaelic insults."

"When I mean to assault him, he'll know it."

I smack my brother's arm. "Stop acting this way, or I will throw you out the door myself."

Logan lifts one brow at me, his lips ticking up on one side. "My sister thinks she can throw me out the door?"

"Kirsty's tougher than she looks," Luke announces. "Bet she could kick your ass from here to Glasgow."

My brother narrows his eyes to slits as he looks at my ex-boyfriend. "Still might kick yours—if I decide you're abusing my sister's trusting nature."

"That's very sweet, Logan," I say. "But can you two stop the testosterone festival and behave like adults?"

"Sure," Luke says.

"Aye," Logan agrees.

I take a step away from them. "Good. Let's go upstairs to continue Luke's experiment."

Only as we're walking into the tower bedroom do I realize I left the bottle of air freshener in the kitchen.

Mhac na galla.

Chapter Fourteen

Luke

Logan isn't exactly glaring at me, not anymore, but he watches me like I'm a terrorist and he's infiltrating my sleeper cell. I didn't do any sleeping in this bedroom. I screwed his sister, and I'm starting to think he might've figured that out. No, if he knew, I'd be a bloody stain on the floor. Since I still have all my limbs and my neck isn't broken, I assume Logan hasn't realized what happened in this room earlier.

Well, we did make the bed. It's not like we left it messy to ensure everyone would understand that I drove Kirsty out of her mind on those sheets.

Damn, I'd loved doing that.

Logan squints at me, his lips tightening.

I hope he can't read my mind. Since his sister claims to have supernatural abilities, maybe he thinks he does too. No, I don't really believe that. Logan was a soldier and a spy, so I kind of doubt he buys into the malarkey his sisters believe.

"How does this work?" Logan asks. "Your barmy experiment."

"I sit here"—I point to the end of the table where I'd left my papers and the deck of test cards—"and the subject sits at the other end. I blindfolded Kirsty earlier, just to make sure I wasn't giving her any inadvertent visual cues."

"Donnae trust her, do ye?"

"Of course I do."

Kirsty's gaze flies to me, and her eyes widen a touch.

Yeah, I'm kind of surprised that I said I trust her too.

"I'll be your subject this time," Logan says. He stalks over to the chair Kirsty had sat in earlier and settles onto it. His gaze veers to her. "Who's minding your store? Or have you closed it just to make this *cacan* happy?"

"No, Logan, I haven't closed it. Isla is filling in for me."

Logan seems satisfied with that answer, but I'm confused. "Doesn't your sister have a job of her own?"

"Aye. But Isla runs a business over the internet, so she can work from anywhere."

"What kind of business does she have?"

"Graphic design."

Logan makes an annoyed growling noise. "Can we get on with this barmy experiment?"

"My brother's favorite word is 'barmy,' " Kirsty tells me. "You'll get used to it. My cousin Rory's favorite word is 'ridiculous.' "

"What's your word of choice?" I ask.

She shrugs. "Donnae have one."

"Of course you do," Logan says. "It's *da-shealladh*."

He gives his sister the kind of teasing smile only a family member would offer. Logan clearly loves his sister, and I can tell from the things she's said about him that Kirsty adores her brother. She adores her cousin Magnus too and has good relationships with all her extended family. That much I could tell just by listening to her talk about them. I don't think she realizes it, but hearing about the amazing MacTaggarts makes me feel kind of...depressed. Being an ass, I show my feelings by acting sarcastic and dismissive. I hadn't thought about it much until yesterday, when I barged in on a huge family get-together, but now I realize the truth.

Seeing Kirsty with her family, I realized that I have no one.

That knowledge hurts like a hot steel spike driven straight through my chest, but I will never tell her. Well, unless she coaxes it out of me. I can't believe I told her I was an orphan, so I can't swear I won't spill the beans about my idiotic, pathetic feelings.

"Should we get started with your barmy experiment?" Logan asks, his gaze trained on me. Though he wears a neutral expression, he has his arms barred over his chest.

I opt to ignore the fact he called my scientific endeavor "barmy."

"Yes," I say. "We can start now. But I think Kirsty should leave the room to avoid giving you any subconscious cues."

"Aye, he's right," Kirsty tells her brother. "I'll wait in the sitting room. Ring me on my mobile when you're done."

She leaves the room, shutting the door behind her.

I pick up the necktie. "Mind if I blindfold you? It's strictly to prevent me from accidentally giving you any cues about which card I'm looking at."

"Go on, then." He narrows his gaze. "But I can see you even when I'm blindfolded. It's secret agent magic."

"Yeah, sure, whatever." I assume he's joking, but it's hard to tell with Logan. I sit down. "We'll do one round without the blindfold, then another with it. Okay?"

"Aye."

I still can't get a read on this guy to figure out whether he genuinely hates me or he's having fun tormenting me with his "I'm a super-tough, murder-ready ex-spy" stuff. Yesterday, he told me I was seconds away from being "dead on the grass." Now, he wants to help me with my study of so-called supernatural abilities. If Logan is this opaque and strange, I wonder what Magnus is like. Kirsty told me no one in the family understands him, except for her, apparently.

"Let's get started," I say as I shuffle the deck of cards. "Each card has a symbol on it—circle, triangle, square, or wavy lines. When I lay down a card, you make a guess. Don't think about it, just do it. I'm looking for your initial subconscious response, which means—"

"I understand the concept. Don't need an American laddie to explain it to me like I'm a daft bairn." He speaks in a calm voice, though he keeps his sharp gaze leveled on me.

No, I am not intimidated by his act. He wants to unnerve me, but I won't let him.

"Glad you get the concept," I say. "First card."

I lay down a card with wavy lines on it.

"Circle," Logan says.

"Next one."

"Square."

"And the next one."

"Triangle."

We go on like that until I've had him guess one hundred times, just like I did with Kirsty. Logan guesses correctly some of the time, on par with the average for random responses. If I'd hoped testing Logan would give me any idea about how Kirsty got half the answers right… Well, I was dead wrong. When I blindfold Logan, he gives a similar percentage of correct answers, all within the norm for wild guesses.

How the hell did Kirsty guess right fifty percent of the time? She must've cheated somehow, but I still can't make myself believe she would do that.

"Satisfied?" Logan asks.

"With what?"

"Your results."

"I need more data." Gathering up the cards, I shuffle them. "I'd like to try a slightly different experiment, one that involves putting electrodes on your fingers to measure the skin conductance response and neural activity. That means—"

"You want to see how my brain reacts to your tests by measuring what sort of emotional response your experiment triggers. It's like a lie detector test."

"That's right. Though 'lie detector' isn't an accurate description."

"No, but you mean to measure my anxiety level or some such bollocks."

"Yes. How do you know about the skin conductance response?"

He grunts. "I'm not an eejit, for one. And for another, I've interrogated suspected terrorists and watched while an expert measured the 'skin conductance response.' He explained to me how it works."

"Interesting. I didn't realize MI6 used scientific methods."

"You think every spy uses his fists to get information. Aye?"

"Um…" Yeah, that's exactly what I'd assumed. Guess I watched too many spy movies. "Sorry. I didn't mean to insult you."

"You haven't." He leans forward a few inches. "If and when you do insult me, ye willnae have the chance to apologize. Your jaw will be wired shut."

He's implying he'll break my jaw, but I'm starting to think he just enjoys harassing me.

I rise and retrieve my equipment for measuring the skin conductance response and lay all of it on the table behind the barrier I'd set up at Logan's end. "Mind if I attach the electrodes?"

"Go on."

The electrodes are attached to nylon strips that have Velcro to hold them in place, and it only takes a moment to attach the two sensors to Logan's fingertips. The wires connected to the electrode leads are themselves connected to the digitizer, a small box that will both convert the signals from Logan's skin response into digital data and transmit that data wirelessly to my computer. I explain all of that to Logan to make sure he understands how the experiment will work.

He glances down at his hands, one brow lifting briefly, but then he just sits there with his arms crossed and a neutral expression on his face.

"All done," I say. Though I feel a bizarre impulse to pat his shoulder, I ignore it. "The test is simple. I'll do the cards, and then we'll try a different way of attempting to measure psychic faculties."

"Get on with it, laddie."

I turn on the digitizer, then hustle back to my chair at the opposite end of the table. "First card."

"Triangle."

We do fifty cards this time, and Logan's answers are well within the normal range for guessing. The skin conductance readings appear on my computer screen, and they seem normal too. He didn't even get the tiniest bit anxious. But then, I hadn't expected him to get nervous. He was a spy, for pity's sake. The man must have cool composure down to an art form.

"For the second part of the experiment," I say, "you're going to attempt to alter the pattern I'll be running on my computer. I want to measure your skin conductance response while you do this. The test involves a series of random numbers, and your job will be to push that sequence out of randomness."

"How am I meant to do that?"

"By thinking about it. I didn't make this up on my own. It's based on studies conducted by other scientists."

"What did they determine from their tests?"

"I can't tell you that. It might bias the results of what I'm trying to do here. Are you okay with this test?"

Logan sighs and shrugs. "Might as well give it a go."

"Okay." I start the random sequence running on my computer, then turn off the screen so I can't see the numbers. "Start now."

He stares at me.

"No, don't look at me," I say. "Focus on the numbers."

"Cannae see them."

"Imagine them. Then try to affect their randomness."

Logan growls out a sigh. But he closes his eyes as if he's trying to do what I asked.

Seconds tick by. I'm starting to feel oddly claustrophobic in this room, with the window covered up and both doors closed. I've never suffered from anxiety about enclosed spaces, so I have no idea why it's bothering me now. It can't have anything to do with Kirsty's brother—or Kirsty. I don't give a crap that Logan dislikes me or that Kirsty and I had sex again. It didn't mean anything.

My gaze darts to the bed.

And my thoughts rewind to earlier, when Kirsty lay naked on that bed, writhing and moaning and begging me to make her come. She had looked more beautiful than ever while I coaxed her to orgasm twice.

Then she asked me to hold her.

Why do I keep thinking about that?

"You shagged my sister in here, didn't you?"

Logan's sharp tone yanks me out of my memories, and I swerve my focus to him. "What? Why would you think that?"

"Because you keep looking at the bed." He nods toward the floor at the foot of the bed. "And you left your underwear down there."

I bend over, holding on to my chair's arm, and peer under the bed. Oh shit. He's right. My briefs are under there. I hadn't noticed them earlier because I'd been sitting at the wrong angle. Naturally, since I have crap luck, Logan happened to be seated at the perfect angle to see my underwear.

"Must've fallen out of my suitcase," I say. I'm lying, of course. What else can I do? Kirsty will freak out if Logan mentions my underwear to her.

"What suitcase? You only have your equipment for this barmy experiment."

He's right, of course. And I'm a complete moron.

And of course, Logan is now speaking in a tone so measured and soft that it projects menace like he's got psychic powers and can affect my emotions. Not that I'm intimidated. Or embarrassed. No way.

Logan is also staring at me with an expression I can only describe as the eerie calm before a tornado hits. Is the sky turning green out there? If Logan destroys his cousin's castle, it won't be my fault. No, I haven't given him any reason to smack me down—like, say, screwing his sister twice, including once in this very room.

"Better check the results of the test," I say. Then I turn my computer screen back on and survey the data it's showing me. "No deviation from randomness."

"Disappointed? Maybe you're wanting to prove the paranormal exists so Kirsty will love you again."

"That's the dumbest thing I've ever heard." Yes, I'm exaggerating. But I have this annoying knee-jerk response whenever Logan speaks to me. It's worse when Kirsty speaks to me. I spout snarky garbage to both of them, but even more so to Kirsty.

Yeah, I've become a total dick.

Even with electrodes stuck to his fingers, Logan projects menacing calmness.

"I need to run this test on Kirsty," I say. "To compare the results."

Logan's results don't help me at all because he seems never to get nervous or truly upset about anything. In fact, he might be the coolest cucumber I've ever tested.

"Why donnae ye run your experiment on every MacTaggart?" Logan asks. "We've got enough cousins, aunts, and uncles to keep you busy for the rest of your life."

"Just Kirsty is fine."

Logan tips his head sideways toward the bed and rolls his eyes in that direction too. "Best pick up your underwear first."

Chapter Fifteen

Kirsty

I'm sitting at the table in the tower bedroom again while Luke sets up his next experiment. Logan insisted on staying in the room with us. I don't know what happened while those two were alone in here, but Luke seems anxious and Logan keeps his deadly calm stare aimed at my ex-boyfriend, watching every little move he makes. I know Logan can be overprotective, but this is bordering on obsession.

Luke might be an erse, but he wouldn't hurt me—physically.

Once he has attached the electrodes to my fingers, he returns to his end of the table and types on his computer. The sound of the keys ticking away echoes in the room. "Okay, the test is ready to go."

"Should I start concentrating on your numbers now?"

"Hold on." He hits one last key. "Start now."

I close my eyes and think of numbers. Any numbers. The only ones that come to mind are the digits of my mobile number, so I focus on those. Can I affect a randomly generated sequence? Not sure, but I'm giving it a go to help Luke. Why do I want to help him? I prefer not to think about that.

Luke told me a few minutes ago that he would turn off his computer screen during this test. When I'd asked if that meant he was afraid he might telepathically influence his own computer, he gave me an annoyed look and told me to "just focus on the damn numbers." He gets testy whenever I question him about his methods, but he seems particularly sensitive when it comes to any suggestion that he might have witchy powers of his own. I was joking, but I think I touched a nerve without meaning to do it.

With my eyes shut, I imagine numbers floating in space. The digits for dialing my mobile phone. They hover and bob around while I try to communicate those numbers to Luke's computer. Honestly, I'm a Wiccan, not a New Age sorcerer. But I'm doing my best because I promised to take part in this experiment.

I lose track of the task I'm meant to be focusing on because my mind insists on rewinding to earlier, when Luke had been making love to me on the bed that sits a few yards away from us. The look on his face, it had been more than lust. He'd gazed at me like I mean more to him than just a lass he wants to shag one more time, or a casual sex partner. I will not use that stupid phrase he'd said earlier. I'm not his fuck buddy. So aye, that is the last time I will ever think or speak that phrase.

"The test is over," Luke says, and he doesn't sound irritated anymore. "You can open your eyes."

I look at him, but he's fixated on his computer. I hear the keys clicking away again.

His brows squish together. His lips tighten. "This isn't—It has to be a mistake."

"What's wrong?" I ask. "Did I change your random numbers?"

Luke flashes me a scowl, then glares at his computer. "We need to run the test again."

"All right. I'm ready whenever you are."

"Your brother needs to leave the room."

"Like hell I will," Logan says. "If you don't like the results of your experiment, donnae blame Kirsty. And I willnae leave her alone with you."

"Even if I am having sex with your sister, it's none of your goddamn business."

I leap out of my chair. "You told Logan? I'll strangle you myself, ye *bod ceann*."

Luke's face blanches. He struggles to get out of his chair, which results in it tumbling over backward and him tripping over its legs. Catching himself by grabbing the table's corner, he shuffles over to me. "I didn't tell him, I swear. He figured it out on his own."

My brother chuckles darkly. "Aye, because I saw his black briefs that he left under the bed."

Luke left his what where? I don't understand any of this. But apparently, my ex-boyfriend who shagged me earlier forgot to put his underwear back on. How did it end up under the bed?

"I'm really sorry," Luke says. "I swear I didn't do it on purpose so your brother would find out what we did."

"The experiment is over," I announce. "And I need to get away from both of you."

Pushing past Luke, I race out the door and down the stairs into the long gallery. Then I burst into a sprint as I cross the space and run for the spiral staircase. I've reached the vestibule when I hear footfalls pounding down the stairs behind me.

Luke trips on the last step but grabs the railing for support. He's breathing so hard he's almost wheezing. "Wait, please, Kirsty."

"How could you let Logan find out what we did? It's humiliating enough that I let you seduce me again, but now my brother knows about it."

"I didn't do it on purpose." He shuffles up to me and reaches out as if he means to clasp my hands, but he pulls them away before he's touched me. "After everything I've done, I don't expect you to forgive me, not even for accidentally letting your brother find out we had sex. You definitely shouldn't forgive me for anything else. But I…" He scrubs a hand over his mouth. "I don't like knowing I've hurt you."

"As if that's a novel event." I'd wanted to sound annoyed when I said that, but instead, my voice quavered. The start of tears stings in my eyes too. "It might be hard to believe, but having Logan find out I slept with you isn't the worst of it. You think I'm insane. You've called me that more than once. Every time you say it, I remember the first time you told me I'm crazy, on the day you broke up with me twelve years ago."

"I should never have said that. I wish I hadn't. I'm sorry."

He wishes he hadn't? And he apologizes? I don't know what to make of those statements. Just yesterday, he called me insane.

"You're confused," he says. "I know it's my fault. Even if I don't believe in the things you do, I have no right to label you as mentally ill. I'm an intolerant bastard, and I can't for the life of me figure out why you wanted to have sex with me yesterday or today."

"I don't know why either." Is that true? Or am I deluding myself?

He grips the back of his neck, his expression pinched. "I need time to collate and analyze the results of the experiments we did today. Hopefully, I can still get a room at the Loch Fairbairn Arms."

"You'll stay here," Logan declares, his voice reverberating in the stairwell.

Luke and I both glance up at the first-floor landing, where Logan stands with one hand on the banister.

"Why would you want me to stay in your cousin's castle?" Luke asks, sounding genuinely confused. "I'm an asshole."

"Aye." Logan slowly walks down the steps. "But we can keep an eye on you here."

"We? Guess you're planning to bring in the army to keep me away from Kirsty."

"My sister is a clever woman. She can take care of herself." Logan reaches the vestibule, stopping beside us. "The clan will watch you."

I shake my head at my brother. "Are you making Luke your prisoner? This is silly. You say I can take care of myself, but you plan to 'keep an eye on' my ex-boyfriend while he's staying at Dùndubhan."

"Not worried about what you might do." Logan aims his hardest stare at Luke. "I'm making sure this one isn't up to anything he shouldn't be. Things not related to shagging my sister."

Luke's face goes blank.

Does he think Logan knows something about him that he doesn't want me or anyone to know? That can't be the problem. Then again, I hadn't seen Luke in more than a decade until yesterday. He's clearly changed during the intervening years, and I don't know him the way I used to, not anymore. The sweet boy I'd loved at university has become someone else.

But I swear I've seen glimpses of the old Luke. Like when he made love to me earlier. Or when he raced down the staircase after me to apologize.

"I've rung Jack," Logan says. "He will be here soon to take the first shift."

"First shift of what?" I ask. "Luke's imprisonment?"

Logan folds his arms over his chest and raises his brows at me.

Oh no. How could I not have foreseen this? So much for my witchy powers. My brother is bringing in Jack, our psychologist cousin, to shrink Luke's head. Well, Luke does sometimes act like he has an enormous ego, so his head could probably use some shrinking. But I don't believe he's as arrogantly certain of everything as he wants everyone else to believe.

"What's going on?" Luke asks, his gaze aimed at me. "Who's Jack?"

"My cousin. He's a—"

"Let's make it a surprise," Logan says while smirking. "Give the laddie something to look forward to."

I doubt Luke will be looking forward to meeting my cousin, considering the way Logan seems extremely pleased with himself for planning an intervention. Jack is brilliant at his job and a very kind person, so Luke will be in good hands. If Jack can convince him to submit to therapy.

Aye, the sun might turn purple before that happens.

Logan grasps my shoulders and turns me toward the door that leads out of the vestibule, into the outdoors. "Go home, Kirsty. Let the rest of us handle Luke Turner. We'll ring you when the time is right for you to come back here."

He pulls the door open and gives me a wee shove.

"I can't leave you alone with Luke," I say. "Besides, the experiments—"

Logan leans in to whisper in my ear, "Trust me. I know what I'm doing."

Of course I trust Logan. I'm being an eejit about this. Neither Logan nor any of my cousins will hurt Luke. Maybe they can help him, especially Jack.

I glance back at Luke. "Are you sure this is all right with you?"

"Yeah, sure. I'm an adult, not a dumb kid. I can handle your family."

What else can I do? I walk outside and head for my car, while I hear Logan shut the vestibule door.

On the drive back to Loch Fairbairn, I try to figure out what Logan means to do with Luke, other than having Jack talk to him. My brother used to be a spy, so he knows how to make someone talk. He won't hurt Luke, but he might give him that deadly calm stare until Luke cracks. Logan knows every way to be intimidating without laying a finger on the other person.

When I get to the village, I drive to my shop and tell Isla she can go home now. Fortunately, she doesn't ask what happened at Dùndubhan. My older sister knows when to ask questions and when not to ask them. I probably seem a wee bit anxious, and I'm sure Isla will ring Logan to find out what he's doing out at the castle with my ex-boyfriend. But she'll be tactful about it. Isla is good at that.

I feel more relaxed once I get back into my environment—the shop. The day is almost over now, so I help two customers, then decide to close up twenty minutes early. I've just walked out from behind the counter when I spot a receipt on the floor and bend to pick it up.

The door chime rings as someone enters the store.

"There you are, *gràidh*. Need a hand?"

My heart leaps at the familiar voice calling out from the doorway. I race over to hug the big ox and kiss his cheek. "Magnus! When did you get home?"

"Just now. I came to see my wee cousin first."

I had to stand on my tiptoes to kiss his cheek, and now I settle back onto the floor. Aye, Magnus is a large man, even by MacTaggart standards. But it isn't his height or his bulging muscles that make people wary of him. He has tattoos and wild hair that almost touches his shoulders, but even that isn't the whole picture of why everyone feels uncomfortable around him, even family members. Magnus always dresses like a hoodlum, or so other people say. Today, he's wearing worn jeans and a black T-shirt with a skull-and-crossbones on it. His scuffed black boots have tarnished silver buckles, and his goatee looks like it needs a trim.

The most intimidating aspect of him is, without a doubt, his job. Magnus MacTaggart is a bounty hunter, known for bringing in fugitives no one else could catch. He's often away from home, which only adds to the mystique that encourages everyone else to relegate him to black-sheep status.

I adore Magnus, though no one else understands why. Magnus is a sweet man at heart, under the gruffness and the bad-boy exterior. Aye, people think I'm barmy when I say that out loud. The only other human being who appreciates Magnus is my brother, Logan.

"How long are you staying this time?" I ask.

"Not sure. A few days, at least."

"I'd ask if you got your man, but I know you always do."

He scratches his chin. "Not the blokes who give me trouble."

Though I'd love to hear whatever story goes along with that statement, right now I need to finish closing up the shop for the day. Magnus helps me put everything back where it belongs. Tourists are notorious for picking up an item, carrying it around, and then changing their mind and dropping it wherever. It's not just my store where they do that. I've talked to other shopkeepers, and they all say the same thing. It's part of running a tourist-oriented business. A metaphysical shop might not seem like a place sightseers would visit, but it makes sense once you understand Scotland. We have the sort of landscape visitors won't find anywhere else, and we have ancient sites like cairns and standing stones. Tourists love those places. And after visiting a mystical stone circle, they want to buy mystical kitsch.

And I love telling them about the metaphysical side of my homeland.

"Why did you come to see me first?" I ask Magnus. "Your parents must want to see you too. Shouldn't you have gone there before seeing anyone else?"

"The last time I saw my father, he told me never to come back."

"What? Oh Magnus, I'm so sorry. But I'm sure Uncle Baltair didn't mean it."

Magnus gets a look on his face that reminds me of Logan—deadly calm. But with Magnus, there's a darker undercurrent to the expression. What has he needed to do to get his job done? Not even I know that. I don't think anyone does, though the MacTaggart grapevine is full of gossip about him.

"I spoke to Logan while I was on the plane," Magnus says. "Rang him to see if we could have lunch sometime while I'm here—you, me, Logan, and his wife. I haven't met her yet. At any rate, he told me about your ex-boyfriend."

His voice took on a darker edge when he mentioned Luke.

"You don't need to batter him," I say. "Logan has brought in Jack to shrink Luke's head."

"Aye, Logan told me about his plans for Luke Turner." Magnus leans in close. "I need to meet the *tolla-thon*. But first, you're going to tell me everything that's happened between you and him since he turned up at Jack's wedding."

I decide not to comment on the fact he just called Luke an ersehole in Gaelic. I can imagine what Logan told him about my ex.

Why shouldn't I tell Magnus everything? Logan already knows I've had sex with Luke. Besides, I trust Magnus completely, just like I trust my brother. I sort of like having a cousin who would do anything to protect me, but I can't help wondering.

What will Magnus do with Luke?

Chapter Sixteen

Luke

Who the hell is Jack MacTaggart, and why does Logan want him to "talk" to me? Anything the ex-spy decides is a good idea for me probably involves lots of glaring and threats. I can handle that. What bothers me, and makes me nauseous and itchy all over, is the idea of what I'll have to do to Kirsty, eventually.

I can delay for a while. But only a while.

Then it will be decision time.

Logan doesn't give me much time to think about my moral dilemma, or to think about anything. Not long after Kirsty left, Logan herded me into the sitting room and ordered me to park my ass on one of the chairs that sit alongside the tall windows that overlook the compound. Yeah, I'm in a compound. I suppose technically it's a fortress, but nobody wages war from this castle these days.

At least I hope they don't. Most of the Scots I've met so far seem weird enough and so outrageously macho that they just might start a war for the hell of it. I wouldn't be surprised if I looked out the window and saw Kirsty standing on top of a siege engine, about to hurl huge, flaming projectiles at me.

She should hate me. But I don't think she does.

Why not?

I have trouble focusing on my own thoughts while Logan paces the width of the room, back and forth, over and over. He keeps his posture straight and his head up, while he clasps his hands behind his back. Every time he walks past my chair, his gaze flicks to me, though he has no discernible expression. I guess that's what they call inscrutable.

He's trying to intimidate me, I'm sure. *Fat chance, jerk-off.*

I get bored with alternately staring out the windows and watching Logan pace like a panther waiting for his chance to pounce. So I ask, "Isn't Jack the cousin who got married yesterday?"

"Aye."

"You're ruining his honeymoon just to screw with me. Nice. Will you tell him Santa isn't real too?"

Logan grunts. "Your sense of humor needs work, laddie."

"I save my best jokes for emergencies." I shift a little in my seat because this spiffy chair doesn't seem to have much padding. "It's kind of rude to drag a newlywed away from his bride."

Logan grunts again. "It's their second wedding. Besides, when I told Jack why I needed his help, he was glad for the chance to meet you and dig out all your secrets by whatever means necessary. Medical attention will be required."

He's implying I'll suffer some kind of injury. Yeah, right. Logan loves to intimidate me—or rather, try to intimidate me—but I don't fall for that shit. A foster kid learns how to take care of himself pretty damn quick.

Logan's phone chimes with a new text message. He checks it, then turns his gaze toward me and smirks. "Jack is just coming up the drive."

I jump out of my chair. "Good. Can't wait to meet him."

Maybe I'm trying a little too hard to sound happy about the idea that I'm going to meet yet another MacTaggart. I could do without the parade of family members who come to glare at me. They don't make me uncomfortable, but I'd rather spend my time with Kirsty. Having sex, not...doing other things. So what if I've fantasized about holding her? Every man is allowed the occasional dumb thought.

"Stay here," Logan says. Then he walks out the door.

I hear a click, almost like a lock being engaged. No, he wouldn't lock me in here. Would he? His "I want to murder you" shtick is just an act, not a sincere promise of a gruesome death to come. Still, I find myself shuffling over to the door and grasping the knob. It turns. Not locked in after all.

No, I wasn't worried.

I sit back down, on the sofa this time, and wait. Seconds tick by. *Ticktock, ticktock.* I prop my feet on the coffee table and cross my ankles, then lean back so I can link my hands behind my head. *Ticktock, ticktock.*

Three minutes later, according to the grandfather clock on the other side of the room, the door swings inward.

Logan holds the door open while another man enters the room. "He's all yours, Jack. You may feel a powerful urge to skelp him, and I willnae tell anyone if you give in to that impulse."

The former spy steps back and shuts the door.

Now I'm alone with a stranger.

I've seen this man before. He was sitting at the same table with Kirsty at the wedding reception. His blue eyes aren't as pale as Kirsty's, but he has the requisite MacTaggart muscles, though he's not as ripped as Logan. Who is Jack? Maybe he's the family enforcer, though I don't get that vibe from him. He seems relaxed, and his lips form the faintest smile.

And he's wearing a kilt.

The men in attendance at the wedding reception had worn kilts too, even the Brit who invited me to come here. The fabric is blue and green plaid with orange lines running through it. The MacTaggart clan tartan, I'd guess, since all the men at the reception wore the same plaid.

I sit forward but stay on the sofa. "You're the guy Logan thinks can uncover all my secrets."

"Aye." Jack glances at the chairs by the windows. "Let's sit over there. It's a better position for what we need to do."

"Uh-huh." I follow Jack over to the chairs, and we each take a seat. "Logan said I'd need medical attention when you got here."

"That's true."

"If you plan to punch me, you should know I can handle it. Nothing you do will make me run away."

"That's not what I do." He offers his hand to me. "Dr. Jack MacTaggart. It's a pleasure to meet you, Luke."

"Doctor?" I eye him with suspicion while we shake hands. "What kind of doctor are you?"

"A psychologist."

Oh, that sneaky bastard. Logan made out like he was bringing in a mafia hit man. His vague statements gave me that impression, and I have no doubt that was Logan's plan. Get me on edge so I'd be relieved when I found out Jack is a psychologist who just wants to mess with my head for a while.

I think I'd prefer the hit man.

Jack sets one ankle on the opposite knee and folds his hands over his belly. "Now, tell me what the problem is."

"Logan. He's the problem."

"Is he? Or are you making him the villain so you can avoid dredging up deeper issues?"

Oh yeah, I'm going to hire my own hit man to take Logan out. Tricking me into therapy? That's a capital offense for sure.

Jack smiles. "Donnae worry. I put everything back where I found it after I rummage around in her head."

"Gee, thanks. But I didn't ask for therapy, and I don't want it."

"Well, I don't think Logan will let you leave the castle until I let him know you finished a wee session with me."

I study him for a moment, trying hard not to glare at him. "Don't suppose I could convince you to pretend you shrank my head, then tell Logan it's all good so I can leave."

"Where will you go? I understand you've been living in England."

"I meant leave the castle, not leave the country." I slouch in my chair, resting my hands on its arms. "Can't leave, anyway. Not yet."

"Can't you? Despite what Logan wants you to think, you're free to go anytime."

Free to go? Technically, yeah. But I can't leave until I've done what I have to do. Christ, I wish I had never mentioned Kirsty to Melvin Prickett.

Jack waves a hand in a vague gesture. "Go on. Leave. That's what you want, isn't it?"

"Told you, I can't go yet."

"But you haven't explained why that is."

Why am I not walking out the door? I can stay in Scotland but leave this castle. If I have any luck left, there will be a room available at the Loch Fairbairn Arms. Or I could go to one of the neighboring villages. Must be a room available somewhere.

But I'm not getting up. I keep sitting here while Jack gazes at me with a slightly amused expression.

"Why are you wearing a kilt?" I ask. Yeah, that's Deflection 101. To avoid answering questions, ask a dumb one of your own.

"I enjoy wearing a kilt," Jack says. "It's comfortable. Besides, my wife wanted me to wear one today while we played sex games, and I didn't want to waste time changing clothes when you desperately needed my help."

"Desperately? That's bullshit." And no, I will not comment on his statement about sex games with his wife. That's TMI of the worst sort. I didn't need that much information about the guy who wants to, as he put it, rummage around in my head. "The only thing I need right now is for you to sign off on this bogus therapy session so Logan will leave me alone."

"Are you afraid of him?"

"No."

"Then why do you care if Logan is satisfied? You can walk out the door right now, but you seem to need his approval." Jack rests an elbow on his chair's arm and braces his chin on his raised hand. "Why do you think that is?"

"I don't care what Logan thinks of me."

"Ah, then it's Kirsty whose opinion matters."

"No. Well, maybe." I throw my head back and groan. "Why am I talking to you? Sharing my feelings with counselors never did me any good."

"Counselors? More than one, eh?"

This guy is good. And I hate it. "No comment."

"Hmm." Jack taps one finger on his chin. "We'll be in this room together until you open up and let me help you. I can stay awake all night if that's what it takes."

"Why do you care if I 'open up and share'? Logan must be paying you shitloads of money to break me."

"I don't want to break you, Luke. I want to help you."

"Sure you do. Because we're such good buddies."

He leans forward, resting his elbows on his thighs. "Sometimes talking to a stranger allows a person to say things they wouldn't tell a loved one or a friend. I won't judge you. My only goal is to help you in whatever way I can. But therapy only works if you're willing to give it a go."

Do I want to try this? Tell a stranger all my secrets? It will be confidential. That's how therapy works, right? But I've been through this garbage before, and it didn't work out well for me. Still, Jack isn't just some jerk with a PhD. He's Kirsty's cousin. She must trust him. I can't believe she would've agreed to Logan's plan otherwise.

"Well?" Jack says. "Are we moving ahead, or do you want to leave?"

"I'm staying."

"Glad to hear it." Jack leans back in his chair. "So, how is the sex this time around?"

"Not discussing that with you."

"All right. We'll work up to that topic." He watches me for a moment. "Let's start with your experiments."

"What about them?"

"Kirsty agreed to be your test subject. But I'm wondering why you asked her to do that."

"Because she claims to have supernatural abilities, like her second-sight thing."

"Do you believe her?"

I wriggle in my chair, though I know this discomfort has nothing to do with the upholstery. "It's not about belief. It's about what I can prove with scientific methods."

"Scientific? It's not very objective to use your girlfriend as a test subject."

"Kirsty is not my girlfriend. Not anymore."

"But you're shagging her."

As much as I don't want to hear about Jack and his wife playing sex games, I'd rather listen to those details than talk about my relationship with Kirsty. We don't have a relationship anymore. Why did I think of it in those terms? Habit, that's all. I was involved with her for more than a year. Long ago. In another lifetime. But since I kind of agreed to this therapy crap, I guess I'd better roll with it.

"Yes," I tell Jack, "I've had sex with Kirsty twice since we got forcibly reunited yesterday."

"And how was the sex?"

Damn that Logan. He set me up for Humiliation 101. I'd rather go back to Deflection 101, but that won't make Jack stop interrogating me.

"Can we talk about something else?" I ask. "Don't know how to answer that question, anyway."

"Why not? If you enjoyed the sex, then it shouldn't be hard to say so."

"It's complicated."

"All right. We'll set that topic aside for the moment." Jack studies me with what I take for measured curiosity or maybe the psychologist sizing me up. "Let's go back to a previous topic. You're using your ex-girlfriend as a test subject. How does that make you feel?"

"Oh great. I knew you'd get to the 'how does that make you feel' bullshit eventually."

"If you want this session to end before midnight, best start opening up. Everything we discuss will be completely confidential."

Maybe I do need to talk to someone, and Jack seems like a nice enough guy, but I can't tell him the real reason I convinced Kirsty to participate in my experiments. I can't tell anyone that. Not even Kirsty. How did I let things spiral so far out of control? I'd intended to do the experiments and go home. The consequences of what I'd done wouldn't have been my problem because I'd be far, far away when the aftermath hit.

Yeah, I'm a goddamn coward.

My plans have gone sideways, and now I'm trapped in the middle of a family effort to help me and probably to force a reconciliation between me and Kirsty. I don't know if I want that. Yesterday, I was positive I didn't want to get back together with her. But now that we've done the deed twice, I have no fucking idea what I want. The first time had been a quickie I could easily dismiss as meaningless. But today when we got naked, it had felt like something else. Something more? No, I can't accept that.

I flunked out of Deflection 101. But scoring an A-plus in Denial 101 doesn't sound like a win, not anymore.

Jack is good at his job. I can tell that already. But I can't let him coax my secrets out of me, no matter how much I might need to expunge all that garbage. It's too dangerous.

For which one of us? Me or Kirsty? I don't know anymore.

"Listen, Dr. MacTaggart—"

"Call me Jack."

"Okay, whatever. Jack, you seem like a nice guy. And I appreciate that you're trying to help me. But this just isn't going to work for me." I stand up. "Sorry you wasted your time coming out here."

I head for the door, but stop with my hand on the knob when Jack speaks.

"Helping someone who needs it is never a waste of time. I'll be here whenever you're ready."

Can't help it. I glance at him over my shoulder. "Do you mean here in this castle?"

"Aye. You'll find me in the guest bedroom at the end of the hall, at the opposite end from the dining room doorway. But I also have a house in Loch Fairbairn."

"Okay. Thanks."

I leave the room and don't look back again.

No, I can never let anyone root out my secrets.

Chapter Seventeen

Kirsty

When I arrive at Dùndubhan the next morning, a shocking sight awaits me. I can't believe what I'm seeing, but aye, it's reality and not a hallucination. Has the world started spinning in the opposite direction? I can't think of any other explanation for this.

My brother and my ex-boyfriend are sitting at the dining room table eating a hearty Scottish breakfast while chatting to each other and laughing—loudly. No, they're not pretending to have a good time. They genuinely are enjoying each other's company.

Jack is there too, but that doesn't surprise me. My psychologist cousin spends a lot of time helping people get along with each other, since he specializes in couples therapy, so he knows how to handle difficult situations. Logan and Luke aren't a couple in the romantic sense, but they do need to work out their interpersonal issues. It would help if my brother didn't keep threatening to murder Luke. But despite their current attitudes, I have no illusions the death threats are in the past. Logan enjoys tormenting Luke. It may have started out as genuine dislike, but now my brother is using suggestions of bodily harm as a way of bonding with my ex-boyfriend.

Men are all bampots.

When they see me, Luke and Logan both grin and say, "Good morning."

"Aye, good morning," I say. "Jack, did you hypnotize these two and program them to get along?"

My cousin smiles. "No, but that would've been brilliant. I should try that with some of my clients. Maybe if I make them bark like dogs, they'll stop being so bloody-minded and figure out how to get along with their significant others."

Not sure how barking like a dog would do that. But it doesn't matter. Jack is joking, I think.

I look at Luke. "Therapy worked, aye?"

He averts his gaze, staring down at the food on his plate.

Jack chuckles. "Luke refused my offer of therapy. But I suggested to Logan that maybe he should stop thinking of Luke as the barbarian storming the gates to abduct his sister and start seeing him as a human being."

"A bloody annoying one," Logan says with a smirk. "But I don't think I'll disembowel him today."

"Thanks," Luke says. "I'm touched by your kindness."

I square my shoulders and clear my throat. "I have news that will be of interest to you, Jack and Logan. Family news."

All three men focus on me.

"Magnus is back," I say. "He's staying for a while."

Logan sighs with mock wistfulness. "Another pair of hands that can throttle Luke Turner. Aye, that is good news."

"Magnus?" Luke says. "That's your favorite cousin, right?"

Jack clutches his chest as if he's having a heart attack or experiencing severe heartburn. "I'm wounded, Kirsty. Thought I was your favorite."

"I can have more than one favorite, Jack." I pull out the chair beside Luke's and sit down. "I told Isla about Magnus last night, so I'm sure the entire clan knows by now."

"And the blethering will have begun," Logan says. "MacTaggarts love to gossip, especially about Magnus. Donnae see what's frightening about him. The rest of the family needs to stop watching mafia films."

"Magnus isn't in the mafia," I tell my brother. "He's a bounty hunter."

"To the family, that's the same thing."

"Aye," Jack agrees. "But it's partly his fault. If he didn't dress like the captain of a devil-worshiping biker gang, maybe the rest of the clan wouldn't feel uncomfortable around him. Not that I'm judging. I believe everyone should find their own personal style and be true to themselves."

Luke shoves a chunk of Lorne sausage into his mouth and chews it while eying me with curiosity. "When do I get to meet this Magnus guy? He sounds like someone I need to study."

My brother chuckles. "Like to see ye try to put electrodes on Magnus. You'll be a lump of blood and pulverized bones on the floor."

"Haud yer wheesht, Logan," I snap. "Magnus is a sweet man, and you're making him sound like Attila the Hun."

"No, I'm making him sound like Jack the Ripper."

My cousin Jack clucks his tongue. "Mind your history, Logan. Jack the Ripper only killed women."

I sag against my chair. "Ugh. You lot are driving me insane."

Luke smirks at me. "I was right after all, then."

"Very funny." I push up straighter and look at Jack. "Since Luke doesn't want to do therapy with you, I was thinking maybe I could help him deal with his issues."

"Aye, that could work. I suspect you are one of the major issues he needs to deal with. Might as well let you have a go at rummaging around in his head."

"Good. I have a plan for—"

"Hey!" Luke shouts. "I'm sitting right here, you know. Don't I get a say in who shrinks my head and how that gets done? I don't need therapy, anyway."

I pat his shoulder. "Of course you do. No one as pent-up as you should go without counseling. Since you won't let Jack do that, I've decided to take over the task."

"Perfect. My ex-girlfriend wants to poke around in my brain."

"Aye. And maybe I'll attach electrodes to you so I can measure your skin conductance response."

He stares at me, sliding his tongue over his bottom lip while his eyes darken.

I know that look. His pupils have dilated, making his eyes seem darker. What about my statement gets him randy? I stand by my assessment that men are bampots.

"Have at it," Jack says. "Use whatever means necessary to crack the laddie's shell."

"What shell?" Luke asks. "I don't have one."

"Of course ye do." Jack leans across the table to thump his fist lightly on Luke's chest. "See? I can hear the echo inside there."

I stand up. "All right, you lot have had your fun. Now I need to speak to Luke alone."

Logan lifts one brow. "Speak to or shag?"

"*Pòg mo thòin*, Logan." Aye, I just told my brother to kiss my erse. He deserved it.

I grab Luke's arm and tug. "Come on. I need to talk to you. Just talk. In case anyone else here has a filthy mind and thinks everything is about sex."

Luke follows me out of the dining room, down the hallway to the kitchen.

"What now?" he asks.

"You know what." I plant my hands on my hips. "You refused to let Jack help you, which means you've left me no choice."

"I don't need help from anybody."

"That's rubbish, and you know it." I lean against the island, searching his face for some clue to his state of mind, but I can't tell anything from his bland expression. "What happened to you, Luke? Why are you so angry?"

"What makes you think I'm angry?"

"Are you honestly going to stand there and pretend the truth isn't true?"

He grumbles out a sigh, shaking his head. "We're not a couple anymore. That means I'm not required to share all my secrets with you."

Aye, but I think he needs to confess. Keeping things to himself has made him tense and rude and not very pleasant to be around. This isn't the Luke I knew. I've seen glimpses of the way he used to be, but he seems determined to quash it.

"You aren't going to tell me anything," I say. "Are you?"

"That's right."

"Fine. I have another idea, then."

He rubs his forehead, wincing. "Do I want to hear this? It probably involves your brother glaring at me while your cousin Jack asks me 'how does that make you feel.' Maybe I'm not hating on them anymore, but I don't want to go through another round of male-bonding baloney."

"This would involve only two people. Me and you."

Luke jerks his gaze up to mine while he keeps his hand on his forehead. "What exactly did you have in mind?"

"You want to debunk my witchy powers, aye?"

"I want to measure your potential psychic abilities to determine the veracity of your claims."

"That's debunking, Luke." Before he can complain, I raise a hand. "Listen to my idea before you call me insane again or tell me my plan is nonsense."

"Yeah, okay. Tell me."

"Donnae say that like I'm about to drag you away to the worst prison on earth. This will be fun."

His brows squish together. "Fun? You Scots have strange ideas about what constitutes entertainment."

"Don't you trust me?"

"I do, but—"

"Hush." I push away from the island but keep my hand on its granite surface. "You can't study my abilities when you know nothing about Wicca or the metaphysical side of life. Let me enlighten you. This won't be a lecture. I want to show you my world through my eyes by taking you to the places that have informed and inspired my beliefs."

"What exactly are you suggesting?"

"A road trip."

He groans. "How long will this road trip last?"

"We can see most of the places I want to show you today. If after that you don't want to continue, I will stop havering about it and leave you be."

"And my experiments?"

"I'll continue with them."

He regards me for a moment, without expression, giving me no clue what he might be thinking or feeling right now. I've offered to show him my world. When I'd told him I was a witch all those years ago, he'd left without even explaining why. He thought I was insane, yes. But that didn't shed any light on the reasons he ran back to America, abandoning his studies in the middle of the semester. Now that I know he was an orphan, I'm certain the answers to all my questions revolve around that fact.

"Okay," he says at last. "I'll go on your little road trip. But I will not be chanting spells or dancing naked under the full moon."

"No, of course not." I pat his cheek. "It's the new moon tonight."

He rolls his eyes. "What a relief."

"You might enjoy this, you know. Tourists love this sort of thing and pay for the privilege. I'm giving it to you for free."

"Hmm." He moves closer, lowering his head to gaze straight into my eyes. "If you want to commune with the universe in the nude, I'm all for getting it on with you outdoors. Guarantee you'll be screaming 'oh God' multiple times."

"You have to earn the right to have sex with me again."

"Do I?" He wraps an arm around my waist, pulling me snugly against him. "Bet you're already wet for me, kitten."

"Being aroused doesn't mean I'll let you have a poke with me."

"We'll see." He takes two steps backward. "When do we start this meta-physical journey?"

"Right away. I already packed snacks and water bottles, and I put every-thing in the car. Are you ready to go?"

"Yeah, sure."

"Good." I wave toward the doorway. "Let's go."

I lead Luke back down the hall and through the dining room, where Logan and Jack are still talking and eating. They glance at us with raised brows, but I tell them only that Luke and I are going for a drive and will be gone all day. That statement encourages them to smirk. Let them think whatever they like. I don't care.

Once we exit the vestibule, I march straight to the car parked nearest to the house. The other vehicles belong to Logan and Jack.

Luke freezes, his unblinking gaze trained on the car we will be us-ing. "That's a Jaguar F-Type. Isn't it?"

"Aye. My cousin Rory lent it to me when I told him I wanted to take you on a tour of the mystical sites in the Highlands."

"That's very generous of him."

"You seem to think all my relatives are erses."

He approaches the car, gliding his fingertips along the edge of the hood. "I've only met a few of them. Maybe I have kind of assumed all MacTaggarts would hate me, but I don't think that anymore. Even Logan isn't so bad once you get used to his weird sense of humor."

"I'm glad you feel that way, because I love my brother."

"And he clearly loves you. Everybody does, as far as I can tell." Luke drags his fingers up the frame of the windscreen until he touches the roof. "This is a convertible. Maybe we could put the top down."

"That would be nice." I didn't miss the fact that he paid me a compliment. Everyone loves me? He hasn't met everyone I know, so he can't say unequivocally that no one dislikes me. Still, I feel an odd sensation, like butterflies in my tummy have migrated into my chest.

Luke smiles at me. "You can drive, kitten. Take me anywhere you want."

Chapter Eighteen

Luke

I never could have imagined my trip to Scotland would turn into a drive in a Jaguar with the top down and a beautiful, sexy girl behind the wheel. Am I lucky or what? My experiments can wait because I want to see whatever mystical hooey she plans to show me. If anyone else had suggested I go on a road trip like this, I would've said hell no and told them to go jump in a lake. But Kirsty asked, and I said yes.

Maybe I do want to get it on with her again. But I also honestly want to explore her world. Not that anything I see will change my mind about Wicca. It's bullshit.

Still, I can't deny the scenery is stunning. Craggy green mountains. Lochs so deep and dark they seem almost black. Quaint villages that echo the past in their architecture and their history. We pass through Loch Fairbairn, then Fort William, and continue to the northwest toward the Isle of Skye. Kirsty tells me we won't be heading to that island, not today, though she promises to take me there if I stay long enough. Is she trying to convince me to stick around? That would suggest she wants me in her life. Since I've acted like a jerk since the day I turned up at the wedding reception, I can't understand why she seems to hope I'll hang around for a while.

Maybe I'd like to do that. But I can't. Melvin will eviscerate me if I don't complete the mission he forced me to undertake. The longer I'm with Kirsty, the less I care about Melvin and his garbage. Even my freedom doesn't mean as much anymore.

"How long will this tour of the mystical Highlands take?" I ask.

"All day. Is that okay with you? My favorite places are spread out through this part of the Highlands."

"Sure. All day is fine by me, especially since we get to ride in style. I've never been in a luxury sports car before."

"My cousin Rory bought the Jaguar for his wife, Emery, not long after they got married. It was a wedding gift."

"A Jag as a wedding present. Can I marry Rory too?"

She laughs. "I'm afraid bigamy is illegal in this country."

"Dang. I was excited to get myself a rich Scottish sugar daddy."

"You'll have to make do with me."

"I can handle that. You are sweet as sugar and sexy as hell."

Her lips curl up into an almost shy smile. "You're full of compliments, aren't you? What did Logan and Jack feed you this morning?"

"Well, they tried to feed me black pudding, but I said no thanks."

"Americans are so squeamish about eating pig's blood."

"Oh, so now you're insulting Americans." I lock my arms over my chest, pretending to be offended. "When was the last time you ate black pudding?"

"When I was fifteen. It was the first and last time I ate it. Logan dared me to try it."

"Am I right in assuming you didn't love it?"

She feigns gagging. "Does that answer your question?"

I can't help laughing. "I get the picture. Some authentic Scots lass you are."

As we drive through the village of Spean Bridge, I finally ask Kirsty where she's taking me.

She aims a sweet smile at me. "It's a surprise, Luke. That means I can't tell you until we get there."

"I'm a scientist. That means I need facts, not surprises."

"What you need is to stop being so uptight and learn to go with the flow."

"Back in college, you were too shy to tell me when you wanted to have sex. Now you boss me around and refuse to say where you're taking me on this kidnapping expedition."

She sighs with a bit of sarcasm and shakes her head. "It's not kidnapping if you volunteer to come along."

"But it's not voluntary if I have to come along so I can get you to have sex with me again."

"Who said anything about sex? You're obsessed with shagging, aren't you?"

"Only since I saw you again."

Why did I say that? It was a dumb thing to blurt out, even though it's true. I've slept with other women since I broke up with Kirsty, but I've never needed to screw anyone as much as I need to screw Kirsty

MacTaggart. There's no deeper meaning hidden beneath the surface of that fact. We have awesome sex, that's all. Even if I wanted this thing between us to be more than friends having a good time, I can't let that happen. Eventually, she will find out the real reason I came here, and she'll hate me again.

Is work the real reason I flew to Scotland? The longer I'm with Kirsty, the less sure I am of the answer to that question she keeps asking me. *Why are you really here?*

For the rest of today, I'll forget about all the crap. This is my day off, I've decided, and I want to enjoy the mystery tour Kirsty has arranged for me.

We drive alongside Loch Duich, heading northwest until we turn off onto a one-track road where I see only a smattering of houses. After I park the car, we get out to walk the rest of the way.

"It's about a mile's walk," Kirsty tells me. "Can you handle that?"

"Are you trying to annoy me? It won't work. My manly pride isn't that fragile." I lean in close enough I could kiss her if I wanted to do that, which I absolutely do. But this isn't the time or place. "If you can survive the hike, so can I."

Our hike takes us up a long path that rises the whole way, and to a high spot that overlooks the other side of the water. Is that still Loch Duich? Not sure. We stop in front of a spiffy sign that tells us this is Caisteal Grugaig. Okay, yeah, I have no idea how to pronounce that until Kirsty demonstrates it for me. The sign also announces this is "a desirable Iron Age residence."

Is that Scottish humor? I don't think anyone would call a prehistoric dwelling "desirable."

"This hill is called Faire an Duine," Kirsty says, "which means 'watch place of the tower.' That castle you could see as we approached the site is Eilean Donan castle."

"Right, I noticed a building on an island. That was the castle, huh?"

"Aye." She takes hold of my hand, guiding me toward the ruins of a stone structure. "This is a broch. No one knows for sure what the ancient people who lived here thought brochs were for, but today, archaeologists believe they were homes or perhaps fortified dwellings."

"Interesting." And I mean that. I am interested in what this place might've been and who might've lived here. But I'm most interested in why she decided to hold my hand while we explore this broch whatsit. Not that I mind. It feels nice to have her hand wrapped around mine.

"The broch would've been a tower originally," she says as we approach the structure. "Now all that's left is the first floor."

"Somebody needs to weed-whack this place. It's all overgrown."

"I like that it's wild and natural."

"That wasn't a complaint. It was a statement of fact."

She eyes me sideways. "And facts matter more to you than anything else."

"What else is there?"

"How you feel." She stops me at the opening of the tower, a doorway fashioned from gray stones with one large, triangular rock as its lintel. "Do you never let go of the cold, hard facts and let your intuition guide you?"

"No, never. I like data. It makes sense to me, and people rarely do."

She turns toward me, still holding my hand. "I'm sorry, Luke. It must've been awful to grow up in foster homes, but you can't let your past taint your future."

"How did anything I've said imply I'm sad about the past?"

"You told me people rarely make sense to you. I inferred the rest." She smiles and winks. "I have witchy intuition, you know."

"Uh-huh. If you say so."

"By the end of our journey today, I predict you will have softened your stance on the metaphysical aspects of life."

"Don't hold your breath."

While we wander around the broch and appreciate the view across Loch Alsh—Kirsty told me the name of that lake—I can't help wondering if she has a point. Maybe I was talking about my childhood when I said people don't make sense to me. I wasn't consciously referencing my past, but everything that happened to me when I was a kid has affected me as an adult. I can't deny that. It's a cold, hard fact. But all that emotional garbage confuses the hell out of me. I don't understand my own feelings, so I have zero chance of understanding other people. Even Kirsty is a mystery to me, though I'm getting more clues the longer I'm with her. Maybe that was her plan. Trick me into a getting-to-know-each-other session in the guise of a tourist outing. No, she's not tricking me. I think she might be...

Helping me.

Not sure it'll work, though. I might be a lost cause.

I insist on driving when we leave that broch with the hard-to-pronounce name. Kirsty seems skeptical, since I've never visited Scotland before and therefore have no knowledge of the roads. But I convince her that, with her instructions, I can get us to our next destination. I love to drive, anyway. Kirsty tries half-heartedly to talk me out of taking the wheel, but I can tell she doesn't really mind. We stop off at a shop in a village that's on the way to wherever we're going, so Kirsty can introduce me to one of her friends, a fellow Wiccan called Morwen. Turns out she's Cornish by birth but now lives here in the Highlands. And she runs a metaphysical shop, just like Kirsty.

No, I'm not so dense that I don't get what she's doing. Kirsty wants me to meet other Wiccans so maybe I'll realize they're normal people, not kooks who perform sex rituals in the woods. Morwen is a very nice lady and smart too, but that hardly changes my opinion of metaphysical stuff. It's pure hokum.

After our chat with Morwen, we get back on the road and sing along with the radio. Since we have the top down, Kirsty's hair whips in the wind, making her seem every bit the wild Scottish witch. She's beautiful, and when she smiles, she is the most stunning woman on earth.

We take a lunch break to enjoy a picnic at the Glencoe Visitor Centre near Ballachulish, eating our meal while gazing at the impressive mountains that stretch across the horizon. I can see why Kirsty loves living in the region and why she came back after…that thing I did when she told me she was a witch. Yeah, now I don't even like thinking the words. I called her insane, that's what I don't want to think about. Then I abandoned her. Today, when I remember what I did, I get a weird pain in my chest and feel a little nauseous.

After lunch, Kirsty reclaims the wheel and navigates toward a destination she says is about an hour away, though she still won't tell me what it is. The sexy witch claims she wants it to be a surprise. I swear, if there are naked people dancing and chanting… I'll do what? I promised I'd go wherever she wants to take me, and oddly, I'm looking forward to seeing the next site she's chosen. During our drive, I decide to bite the bullet and ask Kirsty some questions. I know this means I'll have to answer some of hers, but I'm not as anti-sharing today as I had been, well, yesterday. My attitude shift might've happened quickly, and that makes no sense, but I've stopped caring about the facts and logic, at least for this afternoon. Tomorrow, I'll probably revert to being an asshole.

I don't want to be like that anymore, though.

So, I ask my question. "Why aren't you mad at me anymore? I called you insane, and I haven't been very nice to you."

"Aye, you have—today. I don't believe in holding grudges."

"Two days ago, you called me evil. And I deserved it."

She shrugs. "You're different today. More like the boy I knew twelve years ago."

"What does that mean? I'm an immature, ignorant kid again?"

"No," she says in a tone that implies I'm exactly that. "It means you've let that crusty shell crack a wee bit. You're much happier and more relaxed today."

"Great sex will do that to a man."

She shakes her head. "You can't chase me away with that rubbish. Even if you turn surly again, I'll know it's an act."

"You'd be better off accepting the truth. I'm an evil jackass."

Kirsty laughs, the sound so sweet and affectionate that I get that pain again. Then she starts singing—not to the radio, though. She's singing a song I've heard before, so I know it's called "Westering Home." It's a pretty song that embodies both longing for home and certainty that home will always be waiting for you. But no, I don't have a real home to go back to or anyone waiting for me there. I'm a loner.

But not today.

I gaze at Kirsty while she sings, her expression soft and happy at the same time, without a trace of sadness. She's always had a big extended family to go home to, no matter where she wanders. And suddenly, I want that too.

Yeah, I have zero chance of ever finding a place I can honestly call home.

"My turn," she says once she's finished her song. "I want to ask you a question."

"Go on." Do I sound pathetically resigned to answering her question? Yep, I do. It's embarrassing.

"Why did you come to Scotland? Donnae give me that bollocks about Alex telling you I needed help. I want the real reason."

Time to spill my guts. I knew when I asked her a question that I'd need to reciprocate.

I slouch in my seat and stare straight ahead. "I wanted to see you again."

"Why? If you honestly think I'm insane."

"No, I don't think that. I never did, not really." I slouch a little more, like I think I can disappear into the upholstery. "The valid reason I came here... Well, I didn't know what it was until today. I convinced myself I was here to... I don't know. Put the ghosts of the past to rest. But that's, as you and your brother would say, a load of bollocks."

"So why *did* you come here?"

Am I about to confess? Thinking about it makes me itchy from head to toe, deep under my skin. Part of me wants to speak the words, but the rest of me is stuck in jackass mode and won't let me do it. I tell her the only sliver of the truth I can make myself say. "I needed to know how I'd feel if I saw you again."

"How do you feel?"

"Not sure yet."

She pats my thigh. "You can tell me when you're ready. I'm a patient person."

Kirsty sets both hands on the wheel again, focused on the road ahead.

And yes, I lied to her when I said I don't know how I feel. I do know, but I can't say it. Can't believe it. The truth is impossible and makes no sense and I have no data to help me figure out what might happen if I speak the words. But I can't stop myself from thinking them while I gaze at her profile.

I'm still in love with you, Kirsty.

Chapter Nineteen

Kirsty

This is it?" Luke says. "Rocks in a field? Considering the way you hyped this when we started getting closer to the site, I kind of expected something more…impressive. I'm taller than these chunks of stone. You led me on, kitten."

"No, I didn't. And I know you're teasing me. I'm not fooled for one second."

"I'm only half kidding. This isn't exactly Stonehenge."

"Maybe not, in terms of scale, but it is a Scottish monument built by mysterious ancient people."

We needed permission from the landowners to come out here and view the stones, but it was worth the extra effort. Despite what Luke says, I can tell he's fascinated by the Kinnell Stone Circle. The oddly shaped slabs of rock form a rough circle in the middle of a pasture used for livestock and growing crops. But right now, there are no animals out here. Not even people, except for me and Luke.

He comes up behind me, slipping his arms around my waist. "This is cool, but I was hoping for some mystical naked sex rituals."

"Thought you were horrified by the prospect of pagans chanting and dancing in the nude."

"I'm talking about a private ritual, just you and me."

"No sex, Luke. Not yet."

He nuzzles my neck. "Not yet? There is hope, then."

"There's always hope, though it depends on what you're hoping for." I wriggle out of his arms, turning to face him. "I have one more place to show you, but it's personal, not for public viewing."

"Personal? Do you own a wee henge of your own? It should be called Kittenhenge if you do."

"Very funny. You'll find out what our last stop is when we get there."

I drive the final leg of our journey, which takes us back toward Glencoe and through Ballachulish. We wind up at a site that I know Luke would never have expected me to take him to, and that's partly why I chose it. He thinks he understands everything about me, but the man has a lot to learn. This site isn't about me, though. It's about a different sort of history from what I've shown him so far.

"A cemetery?" he says as we climb out of the car.

"That's right." I lead him toward the wooden gate that opens into the graveyard. "This is the MacTaggart family burial ground. Or it used to be. The plot has been filled up for decades, and we had to start burying our loved ones in a different place, on the other side of the village. My Uncle Baltair takes care of this cemetery. That's Magnus's father."

"How many people are buried here?"

"I haven't counted. Only three times have I come to this place, and always to bury one of my older relatives. That was back before the cemetery was filled up. But that's not what I want to show you." I guide him toward the back of the cemetery where the oldest gravestones lie. "This is the medieval section, where a few of my ancestors are buried."

"Medieval ancestors. Your family's been here for a long time, huh?"

"Aye, we have." I stop in front of a grave marked only with a slab of stone that has the deceased's name scratched into the surface. "Remember the prehistoric monuments we saw earlier? I told you no one knows for sure who built those structures, which is true. But there's plenty of evidence that the tribes who lived in Scotland thousands of years ago were pagans, or at least spiritual people. They buried their dead in ceremonial ways, with great care that suggests they probably believed in an afterlife."

"Yeah, I've read stuff about that. Not Scottish pagans, but the ones who lived around Stonehenge."

"They might have been pagans, but they were also scientists. Monuments like Stonehenge featured astronomical alignments, and there's evidence similar structures in Scotland have the same alignments. That's science, not mysticism."

He shoves his hands into his trouser pockets. "What's your point? That I'm a hypocrite because I don't believe you have 'witchy' powers?"

"No. I'm not as closed-minded as you are. That's the point." I gesture at the grave in front of us. "This is the final resting place of Kieran MacTaggart, who was executed in fifteen ninety-eight."

"Executed? What did he do?"

I kneel at the foot of the grave, staring at the name of my ancestor carved into the stone. "According to family legend, he was a practicing witch who never did anyone any harm. But a jealous rival, who wanted to seize control of the clan when Kieran's father died, conspired with a few loyal associates to accuse Kieran of witchcraft. All witch trials were rigged. If you were accused, you were deemed guilty whether you passed their tests or not. The trial was for show, to keep the people scared, even the ones who weren't witches."

"You said Kieran was one."

"Not the sort who did black magic. According to stories passed down through the centuries, he was a white witch, a devout pagan, not a devil determined to cause harm." I run my fingers through the grass, focused on the movements while I explain to Luke. "According to our family stories, a man called Simidh Gunn started the rumors that claimed Kieran was in league with the devil and all that nonsense. Gunn was responsible for Kieran being arrested, tried, and executed. But I don't know how much of that is true since those events happened so long ago that it's essentially a myth."

"Hasn't anyone checked the local records? I thought churches always kept track of things like that. Not just witch trial records, but births and deaths and marriages too."

"I have no idea how to find that information."

"Lucky for you, I'm a research aficionado." He hunches his shoulders. "Though I should tell you, in the name of full transparency, that historical research isn't my forte."

"Are you offering to help me research the true story of what happened to Kieran?"

"Yeah, I guess I am. If you want me to help."

"I've always wondered what the real story is, but it never occurred to me to research my family history. My older relatives told stories, and I assumed that was all the information that's available."

Luke kneels beside me, bumping his shoulder into mine. "See, I'm not just an annoying jerk after all."

"Won't the research take too much time away from your experiments?"

"No. This is more important." He lays a hand on my thigh. "You should know the truth about your ancestor."

"Why do you care so much about this?"

He hunches his shoulders again and looks away. "I've never known anything about my family. My parents died when I was four years old, so I never knew them and never heard any family stories. I thought about researching my ancestry, but I just couldn't make myself do it."

"I don't understand. Why couldn't you?"

He picks at the grass, his gaze focused on the task. "Guess I was afraid of what I might find out. Maybe I'm the orphan child of two lunatics who ran a cult."

"Tosh." I hook my arm around his. "Let's research your family too. Maybe it will be easier to do when you're not alone, when I'm with you the whole time to see you through the process and support you no matter what we learn about your family."

He jerks his head up, eyes wide. "You would do that for me?"

"Aye, of course."

"Even after the way I've treated you?"

"I'm a forgiving person, though my forgiveness does have its limits."

He kisses my cheek. "You are a wonderful woman, Kirsty. Can't promise I'll never hurt you again, but I hope you know that if I do, I won't have meant to do it."

What is he trying to tell me with that statement? I'm not sure, and I don't want to ask for clarification. We've had fun today, together, and I don't want anything to spoil that.

Luke takes a picture of the headstone with his mobile and also photographs the other medieval graves. He thinks it might be helpful to have pictures when we're researching the oldest known branch of the MacTaggart clan. I'm sure there were MacTaggarts before the Middle Ages, but no one knows where they were buried. I still can't quite believe Luke wants to investigate my ancestor's life. He hasn't made any derisive comments about Kieran being a witch either. I don't expect Luke will ever become a pagan, but I'm glad he seems to have opened his mind a wee bit more to the possibilities, enough that he might not call me or anyone else insane simply because we have beliefs he doesn't understand.

We stop at the cafe in Loch Fairbairn and take our food with us, sharing a meal on the shores of the loch that gave the town its name. Sunset lights the sky on fire with shades of orange and red laced with purple. Once we've finished eating, I decide it's time to explain something to Luke.

"Have you ever wondered why my sisters and I became Wiccans?" I ask.

"Of course I have. But it's none of my business."

"You're wrong. I think you need to know, so you'll understand me better. Don't you want that?"

"Sure, but you don't have to—"

"I know I don't have to tell you anything." I wriggle closer to him, though I focus on the dark waters of the loch instead of looking at him. "When Elspeth was nine years old, she contracted bacterial meningitis. None of us realized how sick she was until it had gotten quite serious. My baby sister tried to hide the fact she was ill because she didn't want to upset the rest of us. Even at such a young age, she cared more about the welfare of others than about her own health, and she kept hoping the illness would go away. Instead, it got worse. She was hospitalized. The doctors couldn't tell us when or if she would recover."

Luke clasps my hands. "You must've been terrified."

"Aye. Especially when the doctors had to put a tube down her throat because she couldn't breathe on her own. We would all take turns sitting at her bedside, holding her hand, talking to her, praying she would wake up and be fine. One day, I overheard Logan talking to Elspeth, begging her to come back to us. Even then, my brother wasn't the sort to say things like that, so hearing him plead for her recovery made me even more terrified that we might lose Elspeth."

Tears sting in my eyes, making me suck in a breath.

Luke slides an arm around me and tucks me into the crook of his shoulder. "You don't have to tell me anything more. It's clearly still an awful memory for you."

"It's all right." I grab a napkin and dab at my eyes, though I'm not actually crying. "I still get a bit choked up when I talk about it, but I'm not as upset as it probably seems like I am."

"Good." He gives me a light squeeze. "Obviously, Elspeth recovered."

"Aye. She's partially deaf in one ear, but otherwise fine." I rest my cheek on his shoulder. "Elspeth is eight years younger than I am, and twelve years younger than Isla. Logan is ten years older than Elspeth. She's the baby of the family in every sense, and what happened to her affected us all deeply. Logan joined the army, and though he's never admitted to any of us why he did that, I'm sure it has something to do with Elspeth. While our brother chose to fight to save the world, my sisters and I chose a different path. We became Wiccans."

"It's not unusual for an experience like that to make people look to spirituality for answers, but I don't get why you guys chose Wicca."

"Would you be more tolerant of our beliefs if we were Methodists?"

"That's not what I meant. You have to admit becoming a pagan isn't the most obvious reaction to what your family went through."

"It makes sense if you understand the underlying ideas of Wicca. The concept of the sacred feminine is important to our beliefs, the idea that divinity is not exclusively a male domain and that even men have a bit of the feminine inside them." When I glance up at Luke, he has a look on his face that I know well. It means he's about to balk at what I just said. So I hold up a hand to silence him. "Let me finish. I'm not saying men are feminine in the traditional sense. The sacred feminine is about accepting that God or whatever deity you worship is neither male nor female, but it's also both. The concept is that we all should share in the traditionally feminine ideas about what motherly love and understanding mean, and that we should appreciate and accept sexuality as a natural condition."

"Hmm. I think I get it. Wicca is about girl power."

"If you want to make it sound like we're all teenagers braiding each other's hair while we blether about boys."

"No, I just meant that women like Wicca because it empowers them more than some other belief systems do."

"That's a fair assessment." I lift my head, gazing into his eyes from inches away. "Thank you for not making snide comments about my beliefs."

"I shouldn't have ever done that. I'm sorry." He pulls me tighter against him and presses a kiss on my forehead. "Thank you for telling me all of that. I finally understand why Wicca is important to you, and I respect that."

"You do?" I raise my brows. "What happened to 'you are insane, Kirsty'?"

He groans and shuts his eyes briefly. "I've been a complete ass. I know that. But there is a reason why I've been so antagonistic toward your beliefs."

"Are you going to tell me what it is?"

"Yeah, I guess it's time I explained myself."

Chapter Twenty

Luke

I just promised to tell Kirsty the real reason for my dickish behavior. Why did I do that? I'm not sure she can ever understand, not completely, and I will end up sounding like a jerk again. I don't want to be that way anymore. This is my third day with Kirsty, and already I know I'm still in love with her and I never want to walk away from her again. Being an idiot, though, I haven't told her any of that. Even if she wants me the way I want her, I doubt she'll be able to forgive me for what I will do to her, unwillingly.

No, I'm not being forced to betray her. I signed up for this.

Why? Because I'm a raging idiot.

"You know I was an orphan," I begin, "and I got knocked around from one foster home to another. Sometimes I literally got knocked around. So I learned to take care of myself and not let anyone get too close because they would probably get rid of me sooner or later. I wasn't a jerk back then like I am now."

"I'm sorry I called you evil. You are not a jerk, not once you stop trying to keep a wall around yourself."

Yeah, that's exactly what I've done, and she knew that without me telling her. Maybe she does have supernatural powers. No, she's just very intuitive—and very kind.

"The last social worker I met helped me get into college," I say. "He was good friends with some people at a big charity that helps orphans get a good

education. With the scholarship they gave me, I was able to get into the
university I'd most wanted to go to, the University of Edinburgh."

"Why a Scottish university? You're American."

"Born in Milwaukee, raised in foster care. But yeah, American." I rub my
hand up and down her arm, letting the comfort of her body ease the tension
inside me a little bit. "I wanted to escape from my old life. Get far away and
start over. Edinburgh has a good physics program, so I went there."

"And we met in our second year at Edinburgh."

I wrap both my arms around her, gazing down into her pale blue eyes. "It was
the best thing that ever happened to me. I was completely in love with you."

"Until I confessed that I'm a Wiccan."

"Yeah, that threw me for a loop. And I should explain why."

"Only if you want to."

I touch my lips to hers. "Yes, I want to tell you."

She lays a hand on my cheek, brushing her thumb across my mouth. "I'm
listening."

"When I was in foster care," I say, "the only thing that kept me from going nuts was science. I started reading books about it when I was eight, and
I never stopped being interested in the subject. Science is about facts and
data, what we can quantify and explain unlike people, who are confusing
and sometimes mean. I couldn't understand why one foster family after another kicked me to the curb, but I eventually figured out most of them only
wanted the extra money the state paid them. When I became too much of
a bother, they got rid of me."

"But you were such a sweet laddie when I met you. How could anyone
think you were a bother?"

"I was shy and quiet, so they figured I had mental deficiencies."

"What sort of eejits were these people? You're very clever."

Can't help smiling a little. She's defending me, the way no one else in my
life ever has. But my smile fades quickly as I go on with my explanation. "I
guess you could say I developed my own belief system that revolved around
cold, hard data. Science saved my life. I wasn't depressed or anxious when
I was reading about Einstein's theories or Newton's laws. It made sense in
a way nothing else in my life did. Then I went to college and met you, the
most beautiful, sweetest, smartest girl I'd ever known. I fell for you at first
sight, and I was sure one day we would be married and have kids. Then you
told me your secret."

"And you didn't want a life with me anymore."

"That's the thing. I did want it. I wanted you in my life forever, but I
couldn't reconcile what you believed in with what I'd convinced myself
was the only rational way to view the world." I pull away from her, though

I'm not sure why. Getting some space feels vital right now as I confess the rest. "The only person in the world, in all my life, who made me feel like I belonged somewhere turned out to be a pagan. I'd built my safe little world inside myself out of bricks made of scientific laws and principles. But here you were telling me you believed in metaphysical mumbo-jumbo, and I felt like my whole world had exploded. That's why I ran away."

She can't understand that. How could she? It's dumb, but I need to tell her the truth about this since I'm keeping another secret from her. Any second, she'll say I'm an idiot and order me to go away. What kind of moron abandons his girlfriend because she doesn't share his beliefs? And yeah, maybe science has become my religion. I've turned into a closed-minded bigot who can't accept that facts aren't the ultimate answer to everything.

"I didn't expect you to become a Wiccan," Kirsty says. "All I wanted was for you to accept me as I am and love me anyway."

"But I did love you, despite everything. I wanted to be with you, but I freaked out and did what I do best. I ran away from the problem instead of trying to work it out with you." I bend my knees, resting my elbows on them, and let my head fall into my raised palms. "I gave you up because I'm a coward and a jackass."

"You were afraid. After everything you'd been through, it was natural to be scared. But I wish you had been honest with me and told me about your past at the time."

She is the most amazing person on earth. So kind, loving, intelligent, open-minded. All the things I've never been good at. Pushing people away, that's what I excel at doing. I don't want to lose her again, but what I want doesn't matter. I made a deal with the devil.

You can get out of this mess if you tell her everything.

And risk losing her again? No, I can't do it. But she'll find out eventually and then I will lose her.

"Why did you become a psychophysicist?" she asks. "Psychology isn't all about facts and data."

"I know, but I needed to understand people better."

"Because you can't understand me."

Though I raise my head, I stare at the dark water of the loch to avoid her gaze. "Yeah, I guess so."

"Where did you go after you left Edinburgh?"

"Back to America. My old social worker pulled some strings to get me into USC. That's the University of Southern California. They have amazing science programs."

"And now you study how what people think and feel affects them in ways that you can measure."

"With physics as the foundation, yes."

Kirsty combs her fingers through my hair. "I'm glad you opened up to me."

"Oddly, I'm glad too."

"Let's go back to Dùndubhan and have sex."

"What?" I jerk my head up to gape at her. "You said no sex."

"Not yet, that's what I said. Now it's time."

"You seriously want to sleep with me again."

She laughs softly. "Not sleep, Luke. We can do that after. I want you to make love to me."

Am I going to say no to that? Even I'm not that stupid.

I leap up and offer her my hands, helping her stand. "Let's put the pedal to the metal and see how fast that Jag can get us back to Dùndubhan."

"We obey the speed laws, Luke. I'm a good girl, remember?"

"Not sure you're one hundred percent good anymore. I think you've got a naughty streak too. You did have sex with me in the garden, after all. While your entire family was on the green."

"Aye. We can be naughty later. Right now, I want to lie on a soft bed while you show me how good you can be."

"Oh, I'm very, very good. But you already know that, kitten."

We climb back into the Jag and obey the speed laws. I'd been mostly joking when I suggested we should drive like speed demons, but I would love to do naughty things with her. Next time.

It's dark by the time we turn onto the driveway that takes us through the woods and to the castle. Maybe I should feel wiped out after the long day we've had, and the intense confessions we shared, but I feel more awake than ever before. I should tell Kirsty about that thing I've tried not to think about ever since I came here. I know I should tell her. But that little devil on my shoulder keeps reminding me I'll lose her if I confess my last secret.

Just a little more time with her. That's all I need. Then I'll tell her everything and accept the consequences.

A hard pang throbs in my chest. Even if it means I can never make love to her again, I should rip that Band-Aid off and let the blood flow.

"Luke? Are you all right?"

Kirsty has just parked the Jag in the courtyard and shut off the engine. She's watching me with a concerned expression, waiting for my response.

"I'm fine," I say, not lying because that pain is gone now. Just looking at her makes me feel good. "Let's go to our room and get naked."

We walk to the vestibule door hand in hand. Kirsty is the only woman, the only person, I've ever let hold my hand. Just as we reach the door, it swings open.

A massive man stands there. His longish hair hangs wild around his face, and his somewhat scruffy goatee only enhances his wild-man aura. The guy is dressed like a biker, complete with tattoos on his arms—and his chest, I think, since I can see hints of designs poking out above the neck of his T-shirt. He has more muscles than even Logan, and he glares at me with a lot more menace than Kirsty's brother had.

"Magnus," Kirsty says, her voice tinged with surprise. "What are you doing here?"

"Checking on my wee cousin. After our talk yesterday, I knew I needed to make sure you're all right."

The guy speaks in a deep, rough voice. Christ, he even sounds like a wild man. At last, I've met the infamous Magnus, Kirsty's favorite cousin and the black sheep of the clan.

I hold out my hand to him. "Luke Turner. I'm Kirsty's…ah, friend."

Magnus looks at my hand, his lip curling slightly. "You would be the *cacan* who's harassing Kirsty and forcing her to do your experiments."

Everybody else is probably terrified of this guy, but I met my fair share of creeps in foster care. If I could handle them, I can handle one surly Scot. Kirsty adores Magnus, so he must have a softer side too. Not that I expect to experience that side of him. I'm the American ass who's misusing sweet little Kirsty. That's undoubtedly what Magnus thinks.

"Kirsty agreed to participate in my experiments," I say. "She's free to back out anytime."

Magnus eyes me up and down, his gaze narrowing. "I heard about your 'experiment' in the tower bedroom."

His tone makes it clear he knows I screwed Kirsty in that room. Oh great. Every MacTaggart in creation must know by now. I never would've pegged Logan or Jack as the gossiping type, but nobody else knows what happened here yesterday. Kirsty wouldn't tell anyone.

The badass Scot eyes me up and down again. "I've been to the tower bedroom. The evidence is clear. But ye willnae be taking advantage of her again, not under my watch."

"Magnus," Kirsty snaps. "I do not need anyone to protect me. If I want to shag Luke, I'll do it. Donnae need permission from you or anyone."

"I'm not leaving," Magnus says. "Not as long as this *cacan* is here."

Kirsty smacks his arm. "Stop it. You're the *cacan*, not Luke. Anything he's done to me was something I volunteered for. Donnae treat me like a bairn unless you want me to call your parents and tell them you're back."

"I'm dead sure they already know."

Kirsty turns to me. "Let's get your equipment and our suitcases and go back to my house. We can finish your experiments there." She aims a sharp look at her cousin. "Alone."

Magnus is still blocking the doorway, so I don't see how we'll get inside to collect our stuff.

The giant Scot sighs and steps aside. "No need to leave. I won't interfere as long as you're all right. But I did promise Logan I'd stay on the premises to keep an eye on that one."

He spears me with a hard look.

Give it up, Big Mac. I'm not that easy to intimidate.

Kirsty and I head through the vestibule and upstairs to collect my equipment. Magnus remains at the bottom of the stairwell, leaning back against the last post, arms crossed over his chest. His gaze stays glued to me as I follow Kirsty up to the second floor. He's still watching when we enter the hallway. I can see him down there, his head tipped back so he can keep an eye on me.

But he can't see me now. We're walking through the long gallery, headed for the stairs that access the tower bedroom. Once we're inside the room, I stop.

"Why are you sticking up for me?" I ask.

Kirsty swivels her head toward me, her lips curved in a sweet, if small, smile. "Why do you think? I want you to stay with me."

"But why?"

She walks up to me, settles her palms on my chest, and feathers her lips over mine. "You answer my question first."

"Which question?"

"You know what I'm talking about."

She wants to know the rest of my valid reason for coming to Scotland. And I realize it's time to admit to the whole truth.

"I'm here for the experiments, like I said," I tell her. "But I wouldn't have come here without a better reason than that."

"What is the reason?"

"I'm still in love with you, Kirsty."

Chapter Twenty-One

Kirsty

He loves me? That can't be true. Luke wouldn't have behaved like such an erse when he first turned up in Scotland if he still loved me. Would he? Men often do things that make no sense, particularly when their pride is involved. He seems to have let go of the anger, or maybe that was fear making him act that way.

Should I trust his change of heart? I want to, so much, but I can't help worrying it's temporary. Regardless of whether I have psychic abilities, I've always been intuitive. The MacTaggarts all know it's true and tease me about it, in an affectionate way. Right now, my intuition warns me that Luke is still keeping a secret from me. Maybe I shouldn't tell him how I feel until I know what he's hiding, but I've never liked holding back—or lying.

"I'm still in love with you too," I say. "But I don't know if we can ever be a couple again, no matter how much I wish we could. I hope you can understand why I feel that way."

He bows his head. "Yeah, I get it. After the way I ended things twelve years ago, I don't expect you to leap into my arms and beg me to stay."

"You live in England now. Aye? That means we have a geographic barrier between us, besides the issue of whatever you're hiding from me."

Should I not have mentioned that? Probably. But I can't take secrets. They make me feel sick.

Luke lifts his head to study me. "I wish I could tell you everything, but there's more going on here than just my experiments or what we want from each other."

"I don't understand."

"Yeah, I know. Just give me some time to sort out the mess I've gotten myself into. Please. All I'm asking for is a little time."

Mess? What has Luke gotten involved in? Though I want to ask him that, I realize I need to wait until he's ready to explain. Then, I'll decide if I can be with him, if we belong together. Our lives are so different, more so than back at university. It's more than the fact I'm a Wiccan and he's a scientist. We've both changed, and we need time to figure out whether our lives can mesh.

"Work out your problems," I say. "But I hope you'll still have time to help me research Kieran."

"Absolutely. You have my word that I will see it through to the end, however Kieran's story goes."

I think he might be talking about more than my ancestor's life story when he says that. He might be talking about us too.

Luke grasps my upper arms, tugging me closer. "I love you, Kirsty. Whatever happens, remember that."

"Are you sure you're all right? You seem...almost sad."

"No, not sad." He pulls me into his arms, and I rest my cheek on his chest. While he combs his fingers through my hair, he whispers, "I don't know how this will end, but I promise you, I'll do whatever I have to do to protect you."

"Protect me? From what?"

"Later. I'll explain everything after I've set things right."

I still have no idea what he's talking about, except that it's something he thinks he needs to protect me from, something that fashes him.

A throat-clearing makes us both glance toward the doorway.

Magnus stands there, his expression unreadable. "You don't need to leave the castle. I will not interfere in whatever you two are doing. Logan told me about the experiments, and if you need another participant, you can have me."

"You want to help me?" Luke says, sounding genuinely baffled.

"Aye. Logan said your tests are barmy but entertaining." Magnus strides into the room, halting halfway to us. "I've been told I'm intense and scary, and maybe I like perpetuating that image. But Kirsty is like a sister to me. I owe it to her to give you a chance to prove you're not a *bod ceann*."

"Oh, I am a dickhead," Luke says. "Won't deny it."

"But you clearly care for my cousin." Magnus glances at the table with its partition and equipment. "I spoke to Jack, and he assured me you're not insane, just a bloody-minded man with some issues to confront."

"I thought therapy was private."

"Aye. Jack didn't tell me anything that wasn't, according to him, dead obvious to everyone who meets you."

"Guess that's true." Luke pulls away from me. "Well, if we're still doing the experiments here, might as well get started first thing in the morning."

"I'll be ready."

Magnus saunters out of the room and down the stairs, his footfalls receding with every step.

"Guess your cousin isn't going to murder me after all," Luke says. "That's good to know."

"I told you Magnus is a good man. He needs to have a rough image so fugitives will respect his authority, but he's not a demon."

"No, but he is even weirder than Logan."

"Donnae be insulting my brother or my favorite cousin." I smile when I say that, so he knows I'm teasing.

"Insults are the secret code men use to express their feelings." He pulls me into his arms again, my body snugly molded to his. "Should we sleep in our separate rooms downstairs, or share a bed?"

"Donnae want to sleep in here, with the window covered up. But we could share my room in the guest wing. It has a bigger bed than yours."

"You got a bigger bed? But I'm a man, which means I'm much larger than you."

"Aye, but my brother decided which rooms we should have."

"Right, of course. Logan wanted me to feel like a big lug sleeping in Little Red Riding Hood's bed."

"No, he wanted you to be uncomfortable."

"Yeah, I get it. Your bedroom it is."

We make our way downstairs and into the guest wing, but by the time we reach my room, we're both too jeeked for sex. I don't even need to tell Luke that. He snatches my nightie from the dresser and tosses it to me, ordering me to get ready for bed. Then he strips down to his boxers and climbs under the covers. I join him a moment later. He lifts an arm, silently inviting me to cuddle up to him, which I do. He curls his arm around me while I drape my arm across his bare chest.

And we sleep. Only sleep.

I can't remember the last time I slept with a man, only slept, with no sex involved. I don't think I ever did this with Luke either. It feels intimate in a different way, as if the words we spoke to each other earlier in the tower bedroom have become embodied in our desire to share a bed tonight. Aye, I love him. Always have, always will. But I still have no idea how this will end. Will we work out our differences and make a life together? Or will his secrets and our clashing beliefs force us to go our separate ways?

When I wake in the morning, I'm lying on my side facing Luke, who lies on his back. His mouth is open, and saliva trickles from the corner of his mouth. That might not be the most romantic way to wake up, but it is what a real couple would do. Isn't it? I never saw Luke drooling in his sleep before, but oddly, I find it endearing—because it's normal.

I tickle his lips.

He stirs but doesn't wake up.

So I tickle his nose.

He jerks his head, then sneezes. His lids flutter open, and he gazes at me with bleary eyes, mumbling something I can't understand.

"Good morning, Luke," I say. "Time to get up and start your experiments again."

"Breakfast first," he mumbles, though more coherently than he'd mumbled a moment ago. He yawns and stretches, careful not to whack me in the face with his elbow. Sounding more awake, he says, "Or maybe we should do something else first."

He rolls onto his side, palming my breast through my nightie.

"Aye, that sounds like a reasonable plan," I say. "Wake ourselves up with sex before we have breakfast."

"Exactly." He flicks his thumb over my nipple, making me gasp and arch my back. "A nice long shag to start the day."

"Shag? Since when do you say that?"

"I'm trying to matriculate with all you barmy Scots by adopting some of the lingo. Besides, I've been living in England for a while now, so I already know what 'shag' means."

"Let me teach you a few words I guarantee you've never heard in England or America." I slip my hand between our bodies, pushing it inside his boxers, and wrap my hand around his stiffening cock. "First word, *bigealais*. That's what I'm holding right now."

"Yes, you are. Think I like that word better than *slat*." He shifts his hand down to my thigh and glides it up under my nightie. His fingers tease my mound, then he slides them between my folds. "What's the Gaelic word for this?"

"There are several terms for it, but I like *ròmag*."

"I like that one too. Think I'll start using it all the time." He nuzzles my throat, then drags his tongue up to my ear. "I want to eat you up, kitten, in whatever language you like."

"Mm, I'd love to take your *crann* in my mouth and suck until you *caith*." I slide my hand up and down his length. "That means I want to take your erection in my mouth and make you come."

"Let me tell you what I want to do to your—"

Someone knocks on the door. "Time to rise and shine, children."

I moan, but it comes out slightly petulant. "Go away, Magnus. We're still sleeping."

"So that's what lasses your age call it." He hesitates, then adds, "I've made breakfast, the full Scottish sort. Ye wouldnae want it to get cold while you…sleep."

Luke flops onto his back and groans, muttering, "Guess we better rise and shine before he storms in here to drag me off you."

"We're coming, Magnus," I call out.

"The food's in the dining room."

His footsteps assure me he is going away.

"We best save sex for later," I tell Luke. "Sorry. But he did make us a proper Scottish breakfast, which must mean he likes you or at least doesn't want to batter you anymore."

"I'm touched by his kindness."

We get dressed and wander into the dining room, where Magnus has set up a formal dining experience complete with the good silverware and place settings. Each dish lies inside a silver platter or a bowl. We even have cloth napkins, neatly folded.

"This is lovely, Magnus," I say as Luke pulls out my chair for me and I sit down. "You've cooked up a feast for us."

My cousin takes the seat at the head of the table while Luke settles onto the chair beside mine.

As Magnus pulls his chair up to the table, he says, "Thought I'd show your laddie a wee bit of the MacTaggart hospitality. Can't have Logan seeming like the civilized one in the family."

"Oh, I'm sure everyone will be impressed when I tell them how you served us a feast worthy of a medieval laird. Though Mrs. Brody might not appreciate you raiding her pantry. But I'm sure you'll glare at her until she runs away in terror."

"Cheeky lass. Eat your food."

"This looks delicious," Luke says. "Thanks for whipping up a big breakfast for us."

"Kirsty seems to like you," Magnus tells him. "And I want my cousin to be happy. Of course, if you hurt her, I will hunt you down to the ends of the earth and rip your *bagais* off right before I snap your neck."

"I might be more terrified by that statement if I knew what that word meant."

Leaning in, I whisper in Luke's ear, "*Bagais* means testicles."

"Oh. Still not terrified."

Magnus spears a chunk of sausage, raising it near his mouth. "Ye will be, laddie. Just wait."

Chapter Twenty-Two

Luke

After breakfast, Magnus offers to clean up the dishes. Seriously. The man who told me in a menacing, growly tone that I would be afraid of him offered to wash up. That guy confuses the shit out of me. I'm not terrified of him, and I never will be, but he seems determined to make me believe he'll murder me sometime if I do anything to tick him off.

What is with MacTaggart men and death threats?

I want to get started on the research into Kieran MacTaggart, but Kirsty insists on helping me with my experiments first. We tromp upstairs and lock ourselves in the tower bedroom. Not literally. The door isn't locked, but we have sequestered ourselves here, in the same room where we got it on the other day.

"Don't you want to know the results of that last test?" I ask as I sit down at my end of the table.

Kirsty is watching me from her end. "Only if you want to tell me."

"You're not curious at all."

"Of course I am. But this is your study, not mine. You make the rules and decide when to tell me what."

Why is she suddenly so cooperative? Well, I guess she always has been during the experiments. And in light of our sharing session yesterday, when I'd confessed to being a lonely loser, I guess I shouldn't be surprised that Kirsty is giving me space.

I don't want space. I need to…hold her.

Damn. What is wrong with me?

"Whether you want to hear it or not," I say, "I'm going to tell you the results of the random numbers test."

"If that will make you happy."

Huffing, I lean back in my chair. "Come on. You can't honestly tell me you aren't the least bit curious."

"I don't need to understand every last thing in the universe. The unknown is perfectly acceptable to me."

"But not to me. I care only about facts, right? That's what you mean. I'm an uptight asshole scientist."

She lifts her brows. "That must be what you believe, deep down, because it's not my opinion."

How can she stay so calm and reasonable while saying things like that? Yeah, okay, I'm being unreasonable. Like I told Kirsty yesterday, my world has revolved around science for most of my life. Facts made me feel safe, and this "witchy" mumbo-jumbo makes me uncomfortable.

"Go on," she says. "Make yourself feel better by telling me your results."

"But it's not comforting if you have to order me to do it."

She leans forward, her lips curled in a slight smile, but she says nothing.

Though I'd like to cling to my self-righteous indignation, I can't do that anymore. "Fine, I'll tell you. The number sequence came out slightly less than random. The difference was tiny, but detectable."

"Are you saying I influenced your computer?"

"Not exactly. It might've been a glitch. Sometimes things that seem statistically significant turn out to be nothing more than a sampling error."

She straightens and nods once. "Let's do it again to be sure. And if it will make you feel better, I'm sure Magnus would be fine with doing the same test."

Yeah, I want to experiment on the guy who looks like a demonic biker and talks like a Scottish psycho. Good plan. I don't say any of that to Kirsty, though. She worships Magnus. I am not afraid of him, but I do get a little tired of the graphic threats of bodily harm.

"Maybe we could call somebody else in," I say. "Like Logan or Jack."

"Why don't you run the test again on me before we call for reinforcements."

"Sure. That, uh, makes sense." I don't get flustered around women, or anyone. But yeah, I'm feeling that way right now.

It's the bed's fault. Why does that thing have to squat there taunting me with its puffy pillows and padded quilt? I bet nobody has washed the sheets, which means it must still smell like sex and Kirsty.

Dammit. I drop my head into my raised hands and groan miserably. After all the times I've called her crazy, now I'm the one acting that way.

"Are you all right, Luke?"

"Just dandy." I scrape my fingernails over my scalp, but nothing in the world will snap me out of this weird mood. This can't be me starting to…believe her. "Gimme a minute. I'll be ready for the test in just a minute."

"Repeating words doesn't sound like the behavior of a man who's all right."

I groan again. This was not how I imagined things going when we came up here to this bedroom. Maybe that's the problem. I keep thinking of this as a bedroom instead of a makeshift laboratory. *Come on, idiot, get your head on straight. Lab, not sex room.* Uh, bed. That's what I meant.

This is my lab, not a bedroom.

Soft, warm fingers pry mine away from my face.

I keep my eyes closed so I won't have to see the look on her face. "Go ahead. I give you permission to call me nuts."

"I don't want to do that, Luke. You're struggling, and I'd like to help you."

"Seeing my ex again shouldn't throw me for a loop, not like this."

What on earth am I babbling about? I slump against my chair. This must be a bizarre panic attack.

Kirsty settles onto my lap. "You think your test might show that I do have witchy powers. Aye? That's why you're in such a state."

"No, that's not it. The test was indicative of some type of minute alteration in the randomness of the pattern, but that doesn't prove anything."

"But it raises questions, and you don't like mysteries." She brushes her fingers through my hair in a gentle, lulling rhythm. "I remember when we went to the cinema and saw a science fiction film. When it turned out the aliens had telepathic powers, you swore you would never go to another movie again."

"That was a totally ridiculous plot twist."

"Life is one long ridiculous plot twist. Whether you choose to dismiss witchy powers as rubbish, you still need to accept that not everything in life will make logical sense."

She's right, I guess. Facts and science can only take me so far. But I'm not ready yet to dive into a swimming pool in the pitch black. The longer I'm with her, though, the more I think I might like falling headfirst into the unknown.

And that scares me more than anything else.

I open my eyes to look at her. "You do realize you're sitting on my lap."

"Am I? Hadn't noticed."

"But you are, and I'm starting to get ideas. The kind that might lead to nudity."

"Wouldn't mind that." She picks up the box I keep the electrodes in and brings one out. "You could wire me up again—but all over my body this time. Then you can take measurements of my skin conductance while you're inside me."

"That sounds like lots of fun, but your surly cousin is probably hovering outside the door."

"So what?" She slithers off my lap and under the table, placing her head between my thighs. "Maybe I should put those electrodes on you instead."

"What are you doing under there? I can't kiss you this way."

"But I can kiss you." She takes hold of the button on my pants and unhooks it. "This will be a deep kiss."

She licks her lips while gazing up at me with half-closed eyes.

And suddenly, I'm having trouble catching my breath. She can't intend to give me head. Here. In the tower bedroom. With Magnus who-knows-where, ready to pounce and tear my throat out. But this won't be my fault, will it? Kirsty initiated this, so she's to blame.

She pulls the zipper down inch by inch.

"Let's wait until we're at your house," I say, though my voice comes out strained. Probably thanks to my dick stiffening faster every second. "More privacy there. Unless your cousin and your brother plan on camping out on your lawn."

"Quit worrying. I thought you were adventurous, considering that you had a poke with me in the garden during the wedding reception."

She's right. Why am I complaining? The woman I love wants to get my dick in her mouth, so I should be fist-pumping, not whining.

I relax in my chair, exhaling a long breath. "Go for it, kitten."

With a sexy smirk, she pulls my cock free of my pants and wraps her hand around it. I groan, loving the feel of her skin on mine. She pumps slowly while gliding her tongue across her lower lip, then she traces her tongue along the bottom edges of her top teeth. Damn, that's hot. I want to fuck her right now, but the need to let her do what she wants overrides my lust for her body. Sweet little Kirsty never touched my cock, much less took it in her mouth, during the thirteen months when we'd been together. She's all grown up now and ready to take control of the situation. Of me.

"Mm," she moans. "Cannae wait to taste you."

"Better hurry it up. If you keep looking at me that way and talking that way, I'll go off before you even get started."

That sexy smirk returns, and she slides her hand down to the base of my erection. With deliberate slowness, she lowers her head while keeping her gaze glued to mine. I can't help it, though. My attention swerves to her mouth as it dips down, down, down until her lips hover millimeters from the crown of my cock.

She puckers her lips and blows.

Cool air shivers across my flesh, making me suck in a ragged breath. Twice more, she blows a stream of air over my crown. I grip the chair's arms and grit my teeth too, but it's the best kind of torture triggering those reactions. When a drop of moisture beads on my crown, Kirsty licks it away, then moans as if I taste so damn good that she almost can't stand it. I won't be able to withstand this onslaught for much longer, not when she has that sexy, hungry look on her face and she's doing incredible things to me.

Who knew Kirsty MacTaggart could be such a naughty kitten?

She opens her mouth and swallows my cock.

I gasp and almost lift off my seat. The feel of her hot, slick mouth enveloping me just might drive me insane for real. And when she begins to move her mouth up and down while lapping and sucking, I think my eyes actually roll back in my head, if only for a second, and everything inside me tightens and gets ready for what's to come, thanks to the woman crouched between my legs. She pumps with her hand while she works me with her mouth, her tongue coiling around me in leisurely sweeps while I start to breathe even harder. I can't look away from her, though my focus shifts back and forth between her eyes and her mouth wrapped around me. Though I try not to move, my body has other ideas. My heart pounds, my hips jerk forward, and I can't stop my fist from thumping on the chair's arm even while my other hand clamps onto the chair so tightly my knuckles ache.

"Kirsty—ah—I can't—"

No idea what the hell I'd been trying to say. I gasp and thrust into her mouth, doing my damnedest not to hurt her, but I've lost all control over my own body. Can't stop the inevitable. The spasms in my cock hit so hard and fast that my back arches and I let out a strangled shout, coming inside her mouth until I have nothing left to give.

Kirsty lifts her head, licks her lips, and smiles. "I love the way you taste."

I still haven't regained the power of speech. My sweet little Kirsty just sucked me off like nobody's business, and I'll need time to recover—from the shock of her doing that, and from the intensity of my climax.

"That was amazing," I say when I finally manage to speak. "You're a genuine sex kitten, aren't you?"

"No one has ever called me that before, but I've never had a complaint."

"Are you saying you've done that to other guys?"

"That's right. Did you think I'd been a nun since you left me?"

"No, I just… I never thought about you being with other guys, that's all."

She laughs softly, wriggling out from between my legs, and stands up so she can lean over to kiss me. "You are adorable after sex. So sweet and confused, not at all a grumpy grouch."

"You don't need to say grumpy and grouch. They mean the same thing."

Kirsty pecks a kiss on the tip of my nose. "You need the extra emphasis of both words."

She starts to move away.

I grab her wrist. "Don't I get to reciprocate?"

"Later. It's time for more tests, so you can debunk me."

"Not sure I want to do that."

She stares at me, her eyes wider than usual. "I thought that was the whole point of these experiments. You wanted to study me, so you could prove I don't have witchy powers."

"I'm seeking the truth, not debunking you." So what if that's exactly what I'm supposed to be doing? Debunking doesn't sound as appealing as it used to, and besides, this cockamamie scheme wasn't my idea. I should never have said yes when Melvin brought up the subject.

Maybe I can still get out of it before things go too far.

Kirsty touches her lips to mine again and ambles over to her end of the table. She sits down, aiming a sweet, gentle smile at me.

My chest hurts just looking at her. We're still in love with each other. We both said those words. But if I don't finagle a way out of this snare I voluntarily walked into, I will lose Kirsty forever. How could she ever forgive me? Melvin used my one stupid mistake to trap me into hurting the only woman I have ever loved, the only one I ever will love. I never knew my parents, but losing them still ruined me in ways I don't fully understand even now. To lose Kirsty…

I should confess. Tell her everything.

But I can't make the words come out of my mouth.

<h1 style="text-align:center; font-style:italic; font-weight:normal;">Chapter Twenty-Three</h1>

Kirsty

Though we continue with the experiments, Luke keeps getting distracted and asking me the same questions repeatedly. He also keeps dropping things, which involves cursing under his breath and glaring at nothing in particular. Oral sex makes most men relaxed and happy, but instead, Luke seems tense and anxious. Once we've gone through the same tests as before, and done each twice, he slumps in his chair and blusters out a sigh.

"What's wrong?" I ask. "Did you not get the results you wanted?"

He flashes me a scowl. "I'm a scientist. I don't 'want' certain results. I go where the data leads me."

"I didn't mean to imply you rig the results or some such thing. I only meant that you seem unhappy with how the tests went this time, so I wondered if you had trouble with your machines."

"No. Everything worked perfectly."

"Glad to hear it. Why are you morose, then?" I give him a teasing, sexy smile. "Maybe I should help you get your end away again. That seemed to relax you very well."

"I don't need you to do that. I just need… Never mind." He shoves his chair backward, scraping it across the floor, and heaves himself out of it. "Think I should find a hotel somewhere."

"Why? You can stay with me, at my house. I have a guest room if you suddenly don't want to share a bed with me."

"I need a quiet place to go over the data I've collected and figure things out."

Though I have no idea what happened to make him sullen again, I realize he won't tell me anytime soon. Maybe never. Men are all so pigheaded. Since I grew up with a brother and an assortment of male cousins, I'm used to the way they behave. Still, I am getting weary of trying to drag answers out of Luke. We had a wonderful time yesterday, and this morning started out good too—until I went down on him. Then everything changed, and I can't understand why.

He told me earlier that the random numbers test resulted in the sequence being "slightly less than random." Then he tried to dismiss it as a "sampling error." I have no bloody clue if that's what it was, but I'm dead sure he wants the results to be an error. Luke needs to believe science can explain anything, solve any mystery, ensure the world makes perfect sense.

But that's not life. Science might have hard data and logic, but humans are inherently illogical.

Still, he must decide what to believe. I won't bully him into accepting that not everything in life makes sense. If he decides to place all his faith in data, I will accept that and still love him. But will he lose interest in me if I don't give up my beliefs?

"You can find quiet places here," I say. "Where you can think. The castle is big enough that you can hide anywhere you like."

"I don't know. Hard to think clearly when I'm in your cousin Rory's castle with your cousin Magnus hanging around."

"He won't bother you. I know Magnus likes everyone to think he's a beast, but he's actually a sweet man."

"Guess I have to take your word for that since I have no empirical data to support the hypothesis."

"You must be feeling better if you're talking in science jargon again." I walk over to his chair and rest my bottom on the table's edge. "We need to trust each other. Do you want to have a relationship with me again? As a couple?"

"Do *you* want that?"

"That willnae work this time, Luke. You answer my question first."

He sighs and rubs his forehead, then looks up at me. "Yes, I want that."

"So do I."

"But honestly, I don't know if we could ever work out as a couple."

I move onto his lap, draping my arms around his neck. "Nobody ever knows what the future will be, not even those of us who are gifted with *da-shealladh*."

"Then what's the point of having witchy powers if you can't foresee the outcome of anything?"

"Second sight isn't a computer program. It provides insight, not a roadmap."

He grunts. "Sounds useless to me."

"Maybe you just need a break from all your experiments. We could start researching my ancestor Kieran instead."

"Yeah, we could do that." He sets his hands on my hips, and his body slackens. "Don't know why you're putting up with me, but I'm glad you are. Somehow, you know exactly what to say and do to pull me out of whatever funk I might sink into."

"That's what you do for the people you love."

He watches me for a moment, almost as if he's weighing the pros and cons of telling me something. Or maybe he's just knackered. Sometimes it's hard to tell with him.

"Think we can borrow the Jag again?" he asks.

"Aye. Rory said we can use it anytime."

"Let's go find out more about your ancestor."

I kiss him. "Thank you, Luke. I never would have tried to learn more about Kieran if you hadn't encouraged me to do it and offered your research skills to help me."

"Well, I figure there might be more sex in store if I do something nice for you."

"Donnae need to do anything. I'll have a poke with you anytime."

"And I love that about you." He tugs me closer. "I love everything about you, even your witchy powers. Not that I subscribe to that idea."

"I love everything about you too, even your stubborn skepticism."

He kisses me as if he's in no hurry to leave this room, taking his time and drawing out every movement of his tongue and lips. When he finally separates his mouth from mine, he gazes into my eyes. "How about another road trip right now?"

"Aye. That sounds perfect."

I help Luke put away his equipment, then we leave the tower bedroom. Despite what Luke jokingly said, Magnus is not waiting at the bottom of the stairs for us. I don't see him in the long gallery or on the stairs. We don't bump into him in the ground-floor hallway either. In fact, we see no evidence he's still in the house until we go into the kitchen to grab some snacks for our trip.

Magnus is standing in front of the refrigerator, with the door open, eying the food options. When Luke and I enter the room, Magnus peers at us over his shoulder. "Finished with your tests already?"

"Not completely," Luke says. "We're taking a break from that for the rest of the day to do some personal research."

"We're investigating Kieran MacTaggart," I say. "Luke thinks we can learn more about him by combing local archives."

Magnus shuts the refrigerator and leans back against the door. "Does he now. Someone who doesn't even live in Scotland thinks he knows more about our history than we do."

"No, Magnus," I say, "Luke doesn't think that. But he's good at research, so I'm going to work with him to see what we can find out. Nobody in the family ever bothered to look into what the truth about Kieran is, so it's about time we did that."

"I'll go with you."

"That's not necessary. Why don't you visit with your parents instead?"

His features crimp, but only a wee bit. I doubt anyone else would notice the change. But I've spent more time with Magnus than anyone but Logan, so I recognize all his expressions, even the minute ones. Magnus is worried about seeing his parents again.

My cousin pushes away from the refrigerator and hooks a thumb inside his waistband. "Maybe I'll spend time with Logan like I planned. Haven't met his wife yet. I missed Jack's wedding too, so I should take him and Autumn out for a nice meal."

"I'm sure they understand why you couldn't be at the wedding. Your job is grueling."

This time, his expression is obvious to anyone. He grimaces. "Aye, but I should've been there."

I walk over to him and kiss his cheek. "You're here now. That's what matters."

Magnus shuffles out of the kitchen.

Luke and I gather our snacks and climb into the Jaguar. Soon, we're away on our research road trip, following the itinerary Luke crafted by searching online for places that might have historical information about my ancestor. We stop in Loch Fairbairn so I can open the store and take care of customers until Isla can take over for me. I'd called her as we were leaving Dùndubhan, so she should arrive any minute.

While I talk to customers, Luke watches me from halfway across the shop. He's browsing the medicinal herbs, allegedly, but he keeps looking at me so often that I doubt he sees anything on the shelves.

Isla arrives a wee while later, and Luke and I get back on the road.

Our first stop isn't far away. The Loch Fairbairn Historical Society is on the other side of town from where my shop lies, but it takes only a few minutes to get there. The village isn't large. I'm amazed that we have a historical society in such a small village, but fortunately, we do. Will Luke and I find any information about Kieran here? We're about to learn the answer.

I feel a strange combination of excitement and dread as we enter the building. Am I worried I'll find out Kieran was a devil-worshiper after all? No, I can't believe that. But I might learn things that will change how

I view the history of my entire family. Not sure what exactly I worry I'll find, but I can't help feeling conflicted about the search.

An elderly man sits at a desk just inside the doorway. When he sees us, he stands and gives us a pleasant, if impersonal, smile. "Welcome to the Loch Fairbairn Historical Society. We offer self-guided tours of the exhibits, and admission is five pounds each for adults. Children are free."

"Really?" Luke says with a mischievous twinkle in his eyes. "I thought kids were expensive, what with diapers and food and college tuition."

The gent behind the desk crinkles his brows. "I meant admission is free for children."

"Yeah, I know. Sorry. That was a dumb joke." Luke smiles and offers his hand to the man. "I'm Luke Turner, and this is my friend Kirsty MacTaggart. We'd like to see the archives to research one of Kirsty's ancestors."

I don't know the gent who works here. But then, I don't know everyone in the village, and I never had a reason to visit the historical society before.

"Diarmid Fraser," the man says as he shakes Luke's hand. "But most people call me Dee. You can too. Let me show you to the archives."

He leads us past the exhibits and to a doorway hidden behind a screen. As he unlocks the door, he tells us, "Hardly anyone wants to search the archives anymore. If it's not on the internet web, folk aren't interested. Ye see, we donnae even have a card catalog, much less a Goggle account."

I think he means Google. Aye, some older people haven't kept up with the times. But since Isla calls it "that Giggle engine," I know it's not only age to blame. Of course, she's being silly on purpose.

"You should talk to Calli MacTaggart," I tell Dee. "She's a librarian and very skilled at organizing books and papers and whatnot. Emery MacTaggart is a computer programmer, so she could help too."

Dee's expression brightens. "Maybe I should speak to them. Thank you for the advice, lass."

He pushes the door inward and leads us down a wooden staircase into a basement that's been converted into a storage room with concrete walls and floors. Rows of shelves hold boxes—some with lids, some that sit open. Every row has a range of years posted at the end, in the form of handwritten paper signs housed inside plastic sleeves and taped to the shelving.

This is going to take forever to search.

Dee scurries away into the maze of shelves and returns a moment later, pushing a wheeled wooden ladder. "This will help you reach the upper shelves."

He gives us some general advice about searching the shelves, then politely excuses himself, leaving us alone amid the stacks.

And we start searching.

Chapter Twenty-Four

Luke

I've done my fair share of research over the years, beginning in college and continuing into my professional career. I've never enjoyed doing this kind of research, though. It's time-consuming and duller than dull. None of the archives I've ever visited looked like this one, though. It reminds me of a horror movie where mummies or zombies or whatever burst out of the floor to wreak their vengeance on the world.

Okay, maybe I've watched too many movies.

And maybe that was vampires, not mummies or zombies. Vamps rise from their graves, right? I stifle a groan. Like it matters which kind of horror movie monsters are most likely to burst up out of the earth.

Kirsty and I develop a routine for searching the rows of boxes. I stand on the ladder to reach the top shelves while she searches the lower ones. By grasping the shelves, I can slide the wheeled ladder down the aisle, always careful to keep track of where Kirsty is so I don't crash into her. Though there are numbers on the ends of the rows, it seems like nobody ever paid much attention to re-shelving the boxes in the proper place. I find files from the year thirteen ninety-two stashed right next to the ones for nineteen thirty-four.

We agreed before we started our search that if we found any records from the time of Kieran's birth until his death, we would set those aside and peruse them later. First, we need to make sure we've got all the boxes we need so we can come up with a proper chronology.

After an hour of combing through the stacks, we take a break to go outside and stretch our legs. The historical society building lies on the edge of the village, where there aren't many houses. Rolling hills carpeted in green grass and wildflowers surround the area, and the sun has peeked out from behind the clouds too, giving us a touch of natural warmth.

Kirsty lies down in the grass and closes her eyes, her lips curling into a smile of blissful satisfaction. I settle in beside her and thread my fingers with hers.

"Sorry the search is taking so long," she says. "I had no idea the archives would be such a mess."

"Not your fault. We've made a good start."

"Aye. And I never would have thought to research Kieran if it wasn't for you. So thank you, Luke." She turns her face toward me, still smiling, her blue eyes gleaming in the sunshine. "I'm glad you're here."

"Me too."

She rolls onto her side, half onto me, and lowers her mouth toward mine.

My phone rings. Damn.

When I glance at the caller ID, I freeze. It's Melvin, of course. Why he feels the need to keep harassing me, I have no idea. But I'm getting sick of it.

I gently push Kirsty off me. "Sorry. I need to take this call."

She sits up, brushing grass off her blouse. "I don't mind. You aren't my slave, after all."

"No, but I'd love to be." I kiss her cheek while my phone rings for a third time. "In bed, anyway."

I jump up and walk a little ways from Kirsty so I can tell my boss to go suck a lemon without my girlfriend hearing it. I swipe to accept the call. "What is it now, Melvin?"

"Have you completed your task yet?"

"No. I needed to talk to you about that." I take a deep breath, exhale it, and dive in. "I can't do what you wanted. It's wrong. I won't risk ruining someone's life just so you can get the funding you're lusting after."

A pause follows. When he speaks again, his voice is almost a snarl. "You are my employee, Mr. Turner. You do my bidding—if you want to keep your job. The directive was clear. I expect you to comply within forty-eight hours, or I will terminate your employment and all your research will become the property of the institute. Of me. We both know why you agreed to this plan. I own you, Luke, so do what I say."

I have a PhD, but he always calls me mister instead of doctor. Just to piss me off, I'm sure. Sometimes he even uses my first name.

But Melvin is right, of course. The bastard does own me, all because

I made one bad call. Now I'm compounding it with another, much more devastating mistake. Why? To keep my job? I'm not sure it's worth it anymore. But like Melvin said, I have no choice if I want to save my career—and my future.

My gaze veers to Kirsty. She's still sitting there with that serene smile on her face, her attention on me. God, she's beautiful. And sweet. And kind. Smart, passionate, and loyal too. The only one of those things I can claim to be anymore is passionate. I crave Kirsty every minute of every day, and as much as I long to make love to her again, I shouldn't do it. I shouldn't be with her at all, not even to research her ancestor.

Within the next forty-eight hours, she will learn the truth about me— and I'll lose her forever.

For the rest of the afternoon, we sit on the concrete floor of the archives, searching box after box, file after file, for some clue to the life and death of Kieran MacTaggart. We find other MacTaggarts, including his three aunts, but nothing about the man himself. All we get about the others is the historical equivalent of basic driver's license info along with genealogy stuff. But Kieran's genealogy is murky. We learn the names of his parents and his aunts but can't find out if Kieran married or had children, or if his aunts had any children. Did he have brothers or sisters? If so, we haven't found that information yet. This could take weeks or months, even years.

I have two days at most.

Dee comes down to tell us the building will be closing in ten minutes.

Kirsty and I put back the boxes we've already searched, then drive back to the castle. There, we decide to grab our stuff and take it all back to her house instead of staying another night at Dùndubhan. The castle is amazing, but I'd rather sleep in a cozy home than a giant medieval fortress, and Kirsty agrees. She calls her cousin Rory to make sure he's cool with us keeping the Jag for another day or two. He is, naturally. Anything for his cousin. We order takeout from the cafe, and while we eat, I mull over my choices.

Tell Kirsty the truth and lose her. Keep the secret until she finds out anyway—and lose her. Somehow stop Melvin from outing me or forcing me to betray Kirsty.

Of the three options I can think of, the third seems the least likely to happen. How can I convince Melvin not to do this? He's one determined son of a bitch, and I have no leverage against him. I should never have come here, should have guessed that Melvin would exploit the situation. But how could I have known? I only mentioned Kirsty to him in passing, then made the mistake of answering honestly when he asked me why I'd broken up with her.

What a damn idiot I am.

After dinner, Kirsty takes my hand to lead me down a short hallway. I see two doors, one on either side, and both look like bedrooms.

"Where would you like to sleep?" she asks.

I want to sleep with her, but I shouldn't. Somehow, I need to create distance between us so it might not hurt either of us quite as much when the shit slams into the proverbial fan. But I can't make myself tell her I should sleep in the guest room. Different words come out of my mouth.

"With you," I say. "If that's okay."

"Of course." She smiles in that same sweetly serene way she had done earlier. "I'd love to share my bed with you."

A pang stabs into my chest so hard that I wonder if I'm having a heart attack. But no, I'm not. It's just the knife-sharp pain of guilt. *Tell her now. You know you should.*

My throat constricts. I struggle to breathe evenly.

Kirsty clasps my hands. "What's wrong, *mo leannan?*"

"Nothing. I'm tired, that's all."

She hooks her arm around mine. "Let's crawl into bed and fall asleep together. You'll feel better in the morning, after a good night's rest."

Not sure I'll ever have a good night's rest again, but that's my problem, not hers.

Do I sleep well that night? Of course not. But I don't toss and turn because that might disturb Kirsty, and I don't want to wake her. I like watching her sleep. Eventually, I do slide into slumber, though nightmares haunt my dreams and I don't wake up rested.

I also wake up alone in Kirsty's bed.

Since I hear noises coming from elsewhere in the house, I figure she's in the kitchen making breakfast. I get dressed and amble out there, finding her doing exactly what I thought—cooking. She's just taking a batch of muffins out of the oven when I walk into the kitchen.

"Morning, kitten," I say while admiring her ass. The way she's bent over gives me a great view of her beautiful backside, but only until she straightens. Then I sigh with sarcastic disappointment. "You ruined the view, baby."

"You can stare at my erse later, when I'm naked." She kicks the oven door shut and sets the muffin pan on the counter. "I hope you like oatmeal walnut."

"I'm not picky. Anything you cook, I'll eat." I walk up to her and slide my arms around her waist, tucking my chin on her shoulder. "But I do know how to make my own food. Maybe I can cook lunch for you."

"Aye, I'd like that." She peeks at me over her shoulder. "Donnae remember you cooking when we were together."

"No, I was still a dumb college kid. Only later did I figure out making food for a woman is the most potent aphrodisiac." I pause like I'm thinking hard. "Taking out the garbage works too. But cleaning the bathroom... Now that's a surefire way to get laid."

She laughs. "Donnae need to clean my bathroom. Mrs. Brody comes in every Tuesday to do the whole house for me. She usually brings a batch of her famous blueberry tray cake too."

"I might fall in love with that woman when I meet her."

"Do I need to fight her for you?"

"No, kitten, I'm yours." I tear a piece off one of the muffins and shove it into my mouth. "Mm, delicious. These will definitely fuel me up for another day of combing through the historical society archives." I slide my hand down to her thigh. "Though I might need a little exercise to keep me motivated."

She gives me a teasing smile. "You're wanting exercise? Well, there is a gym here in Loch Fairbairn. You can use the treadmill and do some weight training—"

"I'd rather exert myself in bed."

"Let's eat first. I did slave away making breakfast for you."

I nibble on her earlobe. "Already love what I'm tasting."

Our breakfast turns out to include not only muffins, but also omelets and bacon. We take our meal out into the backyard where Kirsty has a pergola that's covered with ivy, which provides a bit of shelter and looks nice too. We sit at a small table and talk while we eat, telling each other jokes and discussing her enormous and rather strange family. Kirsty shares stories about the crazy things her relatives have done, and I don't need to pretend to enjoy listening to the details. MacTaggarts are weird, but they're good people too. Yes, even Logan and Magnus are included in that statement.

Whenever Kirsty tells me about her family, I try very hard not to get morose about it. I never had a family, so I can't help feeling uncomfortable and even a little sad whenever other people talk about their relatives.

Kirsty has just finished relating a funny story about Logan and his friend Alex when she stops mid-sentence to reach across the table and touch my hand. "I'm sorry. Shouldnae be havering about my family when you don't have one of your own."

"I like hearing about your crazy clan. But yeah, maybe I sometimes feel a little bit jealous in a depressed way. I must've looked really bummed if you could see it on my face."

"No, you didn't look 'bummed.' But I can sense your pain, Luke."

"With your witchy powers."

She shakes her head. "Because I know you."

Kirsty knows me. We'd been apart for twelve years, which means she shouldn't know me that well, not anymore. I think she does know me, though, better than she should. I still don't believe in second sight, but I do believe this woman sees things in me that nobody else ever has. For sure, she makes me feel things nobody else ever has.

Doesn't matter. I'm going to wreck us both, whether I want to or not.

Just as we finish cleaning up after breakfast, the doorbell rings. Kirsty rushes off to see who it is, and I follow her. Not because I'm a sad little puppy who's desperate for attention. I just want to be with her as much as I can until the day she kicks my ass out the door. I stand beside her as she swings the door open.

A man I recognize from the wedding reception smiles at us. "Good morning, Kirsty. And it's Luke, isn't it?"

Kirsty smiles right back at the British guy. "Alex, what are you doing here? It's wonderful to see you, but I thought you were busy getting ready for the baby."

"We are, but Cat lets me off my leash from time to time."

"Come inside." Kirsty shepherds me out of the way while our guest walks into the house. Then she waves toward the sofa and chairs in the living room. "Have a seat, Alex, and tell us what's on your mind."

The British guy holds out his hand to me. "I don't believe we were ever formally introduced. I'm Alex Thorne, also known as the British Bastard, the Limey Louse, and the Soulless Sassenach."

I shake his hand, though I'm feeling a little confused. "You're the guy who called me and said Kirsty needed my help. But I thought the MacTaggarts liked you. Kirsty's been telling me stories about everybody, and she never mentioned insulting nicknames."

Alex winks. "Only my wife calls me those names. Kirsty is too polite to share the sordid details of how Catriona and I eventually ended up together. She cursed my name for more than a decade. That means you and I have something in common, Luke." He nods toward Kirsty. "Your girl thought she hated you too. Of course, you broke her heart, whereas Cat broke mine, sort of. But that's a long story, and I did come here for a reason."

"What is it?" Kirsty asks.

"I'm going to save your lives."

Chapter Twenty-Five

Kirsty

ave our lives?" I say, and I'm fair positive I'm gaping at him. Alex loves to say outrageous things, then announce it was a joke or maybe possibly might be true. We've all gotten used to his strange ways. Even compared to the MacTaggarts, he is the strangest man in the Highlands. "Luke and I aren't in danger. If Logan sent you to check up on us—"

"No, no, it's nothing of the sort. When I said I want to save your lives, I was speaking in a more metaphorical sense." He drops onto an armchair and sighs. "I plan to save your lives by sparing you the agony of searching through the Loch Fairbairn Historical Society's archives. I've been there, and honestly, it's not a user-friendly environment."

Luke and I sit down on the sofa, side by side. He seems even more confused than he had been when Alex first turned up on the doorstep, so I offer a brief explanation. "Alex is married to my cousin Catriona, who's one of Rory's sisters. Logan and Alex are best mates, though neither one will admit to that. And Alex is also an archaeologist, so he knows about archives and all that rubbish."

"Uh-huh," Luke says, though he still seems a wee bit baffled.

Alex has that effect on everyone.

"How are you going to spare us from the historical society?" I ask.

"You and Luke are clearly a clever pair, but you don't have my intimate knowledge of how to conduct historical research. And you seem surprisingly unaware of the treasure trove of information available to you."

"What are you talking about?"

He smiles in the way Cat always describes as Alex in "roguish devil mode." He looks that way whenever he's dead sure he's about to give someone information they would never have found on their own.

"The answer has been right in front of you the entire time," Alex says. "Metaphorically. The actual destination you need to visit is a bit further away but well worth the trip."

"And where might it be?" I ask. Aye, I'm getting a wee bit irritated with Alex's need to always draw things out for dramatic effect.

"You two need to visit the Highland Archive Centre at Inverness."

"The what? I've never heard anyone mention it before. Not even Iain, and he's an archaeologist too."

"Did you ever ask him for advice on how to conduct your search?"

"Well…no. It didn't occur to me."

Luke clears his throat. "Guess I should've done more internet searching when I was looking for archives to go to. But I thought local ones would be best. I did try some of those genealogy sites, without any success. I screwed up. Sorry, Kirsty."

"Not your fault," I say. "Your specialty is psychophysics, not historical research."

"There's no need to blame yourselves," Alex says. "You're very fortunate to have family members who know about these things. In fact, I would wager you've got family who are experts in practically any subject you care to know about, what with MacTaggarts infesting the entire Highlands."

Only Alex could get away with calling my family an infestation. I know he's joking. People think my brother is strange, but Logan has nothing on Alex. He's even stranger than Magnus, though no one is afraid of Alex.

They shouldn't be afraid of Magnus either. He's a good man.

"And if the Highland Archive Centre can't help," Alex tells us, "there's always your Uncle Tam. Calli cataloged and classified every last document in that hoarder's collection. Not sure how much of it is useful, but you might give it a go if Inverness doesn't work out."

"Thank you, Alex," I say. "We're grateful for your help. And I know we may not be able to find anything about Kieran, so I won't be devastated if we fail."

"Glad to hear it." Alex leans back in his seat, hands resting on the chair's arms. "Now, about you two. I understand Luke ruthlessly broke your heart, Kirsty, and accused you of being insane."

"I've apologized for that," Luke says. "We're cool now."

"Are you? That happened quickly. I'm sure Jack would say no wound heals in five minutes, and you should expect bumps in the road ahead before you genuinely reconcile."

Luke gets an odd look on his face when Alex tells us that. He almost seems grey, like he might vomit. Why should what Alex said affect him that way? Later, when we're alone, I can ask him about that and assure him Alex didn't mean that we won't work out. Luke explained why he left me, and I've forgiven him. Aye, of course there will be bumps in the road, but nothing we can't handle together.

We chat to Alex for a bit longer, mostly about the family and how "utterly barmy" they are, though Alex speaks those words, not me. He might say things like that, but I know he loves my family as much as I do. Logan, Rory, and Lachlan rushed to rescue Cat and Alex when his birth parents kidnapped them, and the entire clan gathered for a celebration afterward to show that we accepted Alex.

Catriona cursed him for more than a decade before she finally married him, and yet my entire family embraced him as one of our own the moment she brought him home to us. It helped that Logan had already become friends with Alex before he reconciled with Cat. Still, the fact everyone accepted Alex without reservation gives me hope that Luke can become a part of this family too.

As our conversation winds down, I finally ask Alex the question I've wondered about ever since the wedding reception. "Why did you connive to get Luke here?"

"To help you both. I've embraced the meddling ways of the MacTaggarts."

"No, Alex, I'm asking for the real reason. Why did you do it?"

He taps his chin with one finger as if he's considering how to respond. After a moment, he sighs. "The love story of you and Luke bears a striking resemblance to the path Cat and I took to our happy ending. Luke has never been a con artist, as far as I know, but he did shatter your heart. And you did swear you could never love him again. It's clear neither of you got over the other, and you've carried that torch with you ever since, along with the pain it brings."

Of all the people I know, Alex might be the one most likely to understand what Luke and I have been through, what we've done to each other. Jack would understand too, I think, since Autumn walked away from him until Alex meddled to get them back together. But their love story only took two years to reach its fairy-tale ending. Alex and Cat, like me and Luke, needed a long time to realize we never got over each other.

"I wanted to help two kindred spirits," Alex tells us. "And maybe I wanted to be a part of saving your love story and rewriting the ending."

"Thank you, Alex," I say. "That was a very sweet thing to do, even if it was bloody annoying of you to meddle."

"Ah, the typical MacTaggart response. 'Thank you, but you're an arse.' I've gotten used to you lot and your strange ways."

I can't help smiling. "Aye, and we've gotten used to you."

Luke smirks. "Do we all need to hug it out now?"

"Good lord, no," Alex says with mock disgust. "That wouldn't be manly, would it?"

I roll my eyes and walk over to Alex's chair, leaning over so I can give him half a hug. Then I kiss his cheek. "You're a good man, Alex."

"Don't spread that rumor. The British Bastard has a reputation to uphold."

"Too late. Everyone knows the truth."

As Luke and I escort Alex to the front door, our guest pauses with his hand on the knob. "By the way, the American Wives Club is in full swing. Don't be alarmed if you come home from your little trip to find they've arranged some sort of outrageous event designed to help you two rekindle your relationship."

"We don't need their help," Luke says. "The rekindling is already a bonfire. And what kind of club is that, anyway?"

Alex chuckles. "I'll let Kirsty explain."

He ambles out the door, shutting it behind him.

Luke raises his brows at me. "American Wives Club?"

"So many MacTaggarts have married Americans that they started an informal club. It was Emery's idea."

"Emery, right. She's married to Rory, who lent us his castle."

"Aye. Emery is the unofficial president of the American Wives Club, since she came up with the name for the group. Back then, it was just her, Erica, and Calli. Now, it includes even more wives—and husbands too, like Gavin Douglas, who married my cousin Jamie. Alex is an honorary member since he has dual citizenship in the UK and the US. He's technically American."

"Uh-huh. So Logan's wife is a member too? Can't picture him taking part in meddling."

"Serena is a member, yes." I smile as I recall the events of last year. "But you'd be surprised what Logan will do these days. He brought Alex from America to Dùndubhan so he could reunite with Catriona. That is a form of meddling."

"A form of meddling? No, it's the full-on version."

"You haven't seen full-on meddling from the American Wives Club."

He feigns terror—eyes bulging, mouth agape—and speaks in a shaky voice that's equally false. "Oh no, someone save me. A bunch of women are going to attack me and gnaw the flesh from my body."

"They aren't monsters, ye cheeky erse." I lean closer and speak in an overly dramatic whisper. "It's Logan and Magnus you should fear. An ex-spy and a bounty hunter? They'll make the American Wives Club seem like blue-haired ladies in a nursing home."

"Your brother and your cousin don't scare me."

"Not yet."

He pulls me close. "Should we get on the road to Inverness?"

"Aye."

We gather snacks to take with us and climb into the Jaguar. I've learned that a luxury sports car can be surprisingly comfortable. We don't go as fast as the Jaguar can go, because that would mean violating the speed laws, and we prefer to take it easy. Luke wants to drive, so I decide to let him.

As we approach Loch Ness, Luke pulls over at a secluded spot alongside the road. He parks under a stand of trees that shade us and shield us from the traffic, though someone could see us if they stopped to look. This doesn't look like an official place for tourists to stop and enjoy the scenery, though it is a lovely spot.

Luke gets out of the car and strides around to my side to open the door for me. He holds out his hand. "May I assist you in exiting the vehicle, my lady?"

"Please do." I lay my palm in his, letting him help me out though I don't need help. But I appreciate the gesture.

He leads me to the front of the car and stops.

"What are you doing?" I ask.

"Something I've dreamed about ever since the first time we took a ride in this car." Luke grasps my waist and lifts me onto the hood of the car. "I want you, kitten. Right here, right now."

"You want to have a poke on the car bonnet?"

"I guess you mean the hood. Yeah, that's what I want to do."

"What if someone sees us?"

"Let them." He moves closer, pushing my legs apart. "It'll be worth it, baby. I know you've got a wild heart, but you don't need to hide it, not with me. I love your passion."

"You weren't like this before."

"I've grown up." He unhooks the button on my jeans and slides the zipper down. "You make me crazy with lust. Tell me to stop, or say you want me to take you right here on the car...bonnet? That's what you called it."

"Aye, that's what we call it in the UK." I plant my palms on the car and lift, elevating my erse. "And aye, please fuck me, Luke."

He drags my jeans and knickers down to my ankles, but he doesn't bother trying to remove my shoes. Instead, he lets my clothes stay lumped around my ankles. From his pocket, he pulls out a condom packet. I watch him undo his trousers and pull out his cock, which is already stiff, fascinated by the efficiency of his movements while he rolls the condom onto his length. And I find myself doing something I never imagined I would do.

I tell him, "You have the most beautiful *bigealais* I've ever seen, long and sleek and thick. That's why I couldn't stop myself from swallowing you whole and tasting every inch of that *crann*."

To make sure he understands how much I mean what I said, I wrap my fingers around his length, though the condom keeps me from feeling his skin.

He closes his hand around my wrist, peeling my palm away from him. "I loved what you did to me yesterday, but you'd better keep your hands off my dick until we're done. I won't last long enough to make you come if you keep touching me that way."

"I'm so wet for you, Luke, I know I won't last long once you're inside me."

"A roadside quickie it is, then. Lie back, Kirsty my sensual kitten."

Despite the fact I've always thought "kitten" was a silly pet name, I love it every time he calls me that. Even when he called me his sensual kitten, I loved it because he spoke those words in the sexiest voice I've ever heard.

I lie back on the bonnet. It still feels warm from the engine, though not too hot, just enough that the heat of it against my backside has the odd effect of making me even more aroused. Luke tugs my hips, making me slide down the bonnet, and sets his hands at either side of my body.

Then he spreads my thighs and thrusts into me.

I gasp and grip his biceps while he keeps pushing inside me and pulling out, pushing in and pulling out, the pace measured as if he wants this to go on forever despite calling it a roadside quickie. I want to lock my legs around him, but my jeans lumped around my feet stop me from doing that. So I hold on to him with my inner muscles, clenching them around his cock every time he thrusts deep inside me.

He splutters. "Don't do that, or I'll go off too soon."

"Donnae care. I need to feel you come inside me."

"Back to a roadside quickie, then." He punches into me, starting a rough and almost frantic rhythm that makes me slide up and down the hood while the sounds of our bodies colliding echo around us and mingle with the cries we both unleash. My climax builds inside me like a volcano about to erupt, the pressure increasing exponentially with every lunge of his cock. He grunts and shouts while I dig my nails into his arms and cry out multiple times, screaming his name at the instant I come. My body clenches him in powerful waves while I go rigid and the orgasm robs me of breath.

He pulls his hips back and pounds into me twice more, letting out a hoarse shout as he comes too.

I'm breathing too hard to speak. All I can do is gaze into his eyes and marvel at how quickly everything has changed between us. A few days ago, I thought I hated him. Today, I'm reveling in the bliss of feeling his *crann* softening as we both try to recover from bloody amazing sex on the bonnet of a Jaguar.

"That was some roadside quickie," Luke says.

I lash my arms around him and hold him close.

Chapter Twenty-Six

Luke

We get back in the car, and Kirsty offers to drive the rest of the way. She knows the roads better than I do, so I don't argue about it. Besides, she's even cuter when she's driving, the way she squints and bites her bottom lip whenever she knows she needs to turn soon, like she has to concentrate hard not to miss the corner. The rest of the time, she either sings along with the radio or tells me more crazy things her relatives have done. I've only met a handful of MacTaggarts, but already I feel like a member of the family.

Not for long, though. If I don't tell her the truth, Melvin will. And then she'll hate me again.

Maybe I'd seduced her today because I know I'm going to lose her soon. I've never had sex on a car, or in a car, not until today. But the impulse hit me, and I had to do it. I needed to feel her body wrapped around me one last time, so I'll have a final memory to cling to after the catastrophe strikes.

When we reach our destination, as we're getting out of the car, Kirsty tells me, "Here we are. *Tasglann na Gàidhealtachd.*"

"What does that mean?"

"It's the Gaelic name for the Highland Archive Centre."

"Oh. Are you trying to force-feed me Gaelic?"

She laughs. "No, *mo chridhe.* I'm teaching you about my culture."

"What did you just call me? Yesterday, you said something else that sounded similar but different."

"I called you *mo leannan* yesterday, and today I said *mo chridhe*. The words mean 'my sweetheart' and 'my heart.' They're Gaelic endearments."

She called me her heart. Tomorrow, she won't be calling me anything nice in any language ever again.

Kirsty leads the way as we enter the building and head for the Family History Room, which Kirsty calls by its Gaelic name—*Ionad Eachdraidh Teaghlaich*. When I fumble the pronunciation, she patiently repeats it several times while enunciating each syllable with care, until I sort of understand. She kisses me when I get it mostly right, and she calls me *mo chridhe* again.

I call her kitten, but that's not quite as sweet as her Gaelic endearments. I also called her baby a couple of times. That doesn't count as romantic either. Does it? No point in worrying about that. Judgment Day arrives tomorrow, and I doubt any angels will swoop down to take me to heaven. No, I'll be going somewhere a lot less pleasant.

A nice lady who works in the Family History Room helps us research Kirsty's family via online databases, including one called ScotlandsPeople that has tons of census records. Those don't go far enough back, though. Church registers of births, marriages, and deaths date back further but don't give us any info about Kieran. Either he wasn't born in Scotland, or nobody bothered to register his birth. I can tell Kirsty is disappointed, though she hides it well, giving me sweet smiles to cover up the fact she feels like our search is a waste of time. She never says that. I can tell by her expression and the tone of her voice.

I won't give up yet. There must be a way to get more information.

"Can you call your uncle?" I ask. "The one who has a bunch of old books and files and stuff. Ask if he knows anything about Kieran."

"Doubt he knows. Uncle Tam is a hoarder, which is why he has so many books and other documents, but he never kept track of them. Calli, my cousin Aidan's wife, offered to catalog and classify everything he has in his library. She would've done it for free, but he insisted on paying her." Kirsty pauses, flattening her lips the way she often does when she's thinking. "Maybe I should ring her. Tam asked Calli to keep the database she created when she cataloged his collection. She would know everything that's in it."

"Now that's a plan. Give her a call."

"Right now?"

"Yeah. No point in bothering your uncle if he doesn't have anything that's useful to us."

Kirsty and I are sitting on a bench along the River Ness, having left the Highland Archive Centre. Before we vamoosed, we thanked the nice lady who helped us search the archives and assured her it wasn't her fault we didn't find what we'd hoped we might. She seemed to feel bad she couldn't do more to aid our search. When Kirsty calls her American cousin-in-law, Calli, she puts the call on speaker so we can both hear what she says and talk to her.

Is there such a thing as a cousin-in-law? There must be. After we talk to Calli, I'll do an internet search to find out the answer for sure.

Yeah, that's what I should worry about right now. Not Melvin and his demands.

After the usual pleasantries, Kirsty explains what we've been doing. "So you see, we need help. You cataloged and classified all of Uncle Tam's library, and I was hoping you could search your database for any references to Kieran."

"Not sure that will work," Calli says. "I didn't index every document. It took for-freaking-ever just to catalog everything, so I gave up on scanning and indexing. But I could search for anything that dates back to the right time period."

"Please try."

"Give me a minute."

We hear the clacking of a keyboard as Calli executes her search. Then silence. I assume she's scrolling through the search results.

"There is one item that might be helpful," Calli finally says. "No idea if Kieran is mentioned in it, but the item is a diary written by Efrica Mac-Taggart. It's not in Tam's library, though. It's in the private collection of another man who paid me to catalog his historical library. He gave me permission to let interested parties search the database of his collection, but so far he hasn't let anyone actually view it."

"Who is this man?" Kirsty asks.

"Not sure it'll do you any good to know. He's even more of a hermit than Tam, and he does not like visitors."

"Please tell us anyway. It means a lot to me."

"His name is Mungo Gunn."

Kirsty and I swerve our gazes toward each other at the same instant. My eyes must be as wide as hers. Gunn? That was the name of the creep who got Kieran executed, according to the MacTaggart family legend. Of course, Simidh Gunn lived hundreds of years ago, and I doubt his descendant still carries whatever grudge his ancestor had against Kieran. But our search has led us to a descendant of the man who ruined Kieran's life. This feels almost like…fate.

I don't believe in that crap.

Still, our search has brought us to an unexpected crossroads and turned this into an epic quest. Will we find out Kieran was an evil witch or what-ever they called men who claimed to have supernatural powers? Or will it confirm he was a good man? Will we discover the whole truth behind the family legend? Kirsty wants to know, and I intend to make sure she gets those answers.

"You guys still there?" Calli asks.

"Aye, we are," Kirsty says. "It's a shock, though. Simidh Gunn was responsible for Kieran being executed, and it seems like a bizarre coincidence that another Gunn might have the answers we're looking for. Can you put us in touch with Mungo? I know you said he doesn't like visitors, but I need to try."

"Of course. But I think you'll have a better chance if Iain makes the initial contact. He and Mungo have become… well, not exactly friends, but something like that."

"Ring me when you know if we can go there."

"Just hang on. I'll get on the landline to call Iain. I'm going to mute you while I do that."

Why did this Mungo guy let Calli catalog his collection and tell people what's in it if he doesn't want anyone to see it? Sounds like a kook of the first order to me. He should fit right in with the MacTaggarts. I'm joking, naturally. Kirsty's family might be strange, but the members I've met so far do have brains in their heads, not balls of plaid.

Mungo might be the plaid-headed type.

Scots have some strange names, that's for sure. Mungo, Magnus, Isla, Catriona… I probably don't want to meet every MacTaggart or I'll go nuts from trying to remember all their unusual names.

"Okay," Calli says. "It's all set. Iain will meet you at Mungo's place this evening at seven o'clock. He wants to be the buffer between you guys and the recluse. Is that cool with you?"

"Aye, of course," Kirsty says. "Thank you for arranging this, Calli."

"No problem. I hope you find what you're looking for."

Kirsty and I drive home to Inverness, but we have some time before we leave for the Haunt of the Hermit. I don't think that's the official name of Mungo Gunn's home, but it seems appropriate to me. Not that I plan on saying those words out loud. I might be a bastard, but I'm not that rude. Since we have time, we invite Magnus to join us for an early dinner. It was my idea. Yeah, I suggested we invite the tattooed, leather-clad, demon-biker MacTaggart over for a meal. He doesn't seem to like me, and I half expect he'll string me up in the tree behind Kirsty's house and let the vultures devour my carcass.

I don't know if they have vultures in Scotland, but I assume there's some type of similar animal. I might be getting a bit morbid, what with Melvin's deadline looming. Maybe I won't die, not physically, but I know it will hurt like hell when that ax drops. Losing Kirsty might feel like a kind of death.

When Magnus arrives, he doesn't glare molten steel nails at me. He doesn't smile either, but he does say hello and shake my hand. Guess a hug is out of the question. That's another joke. I don't hug anybody except Kirsty. I suppose that's part of my foster-kid mentality. Keep my distance because other people tend to disappoint me in the worst ways.

Kirsty never did. She loved me and trusted me, and I panicked. That's the sole reason I lost her the first time. With this go-round, I've wrecked things so badly that I can't see a way out of the hole I've dug for myself.

I try not to think about any of that during dinner. Magnus and Kirsty tell stories about the wacky MacTaggarts and the sporting events they undertake strictly to show off. That's not me being sarcastic. Magnus said it—when I asked him how he feels about Scottish sports.

"The Highland games are an excuse for my cousins to impress their women with how powerful they are," the demon biker says. "But I don't need to prove anything to anyone. Men cower when they see me coming."

"Even your family?" I ask.

"Why do you think they call me the black sheep? They whisper when I'm around and look at me like I'm a serial killer." He picks at his food while staring down at his plate. "It's better that way."

"You want everyone to think you're a badass demon biker?"

Magnus lifts his gaze, one side of his mouth quirking upward. "Demon biker? Donnae own a motorcycle, laddie. Donnae want one. Cars are more fun for doing things ye shouldnae be doing."

I decide not to ask what that means. He might tell me a story about getting naked with handcuffed women in his hatchback. That would totally ruin my image of him as the demon biker.

Once again, Magnus does the dishes. Yeah, that skews my image of him too. How can he maintain a bad-boy persona when he politely washes up after meals?

We leave right after Magnus and pull up in front of Mungo Gunn's house at five to seven. A Land Rover sits parked in the driveway, and Kirsty tells me that's Iain's car.

As we climb out, I ask, "Have I met Iain yet?"

"No, of course not," she says with a laugh. "You'd remember if you had. Or are you developing early onset senility?"

"Ha-ha. I only asked because it's hard to keep track of all you MacTaggarts."

"You can't keep track of me?"

I sling an arm around her waist. "Oh no, I never need help figuring out how to find you. Not since Alex Thorne made his SOS call."

Her cousin emerges from the house and waves to us. "Come on, ye bairns. Mungo doesn't like waiting, and he might not let you inside if ye dawdle."

We trot to the door and follow the man inside.

So this is Iain, the archaeologist. I don't know how old he is, but I see a few gray hairs and a few slight wrinkles. When Kirsty leans close to whisper to me that Iain is in his fifties but he married a woman fifteen years his junior, I can't help being surprised. The guy doesn't look middle-aged. Kirsty also whispers that later she'll tell me the story of how Iain and his true love, Rae, were reunited after thirteen years apart.

The MacTaggarts have a lot of stories like that—love lost, then rekindled. Maybe they've found their happy endings, but Kirsty and I won't have one of those. Unless I can somehow rewrite our story.

Hmm... Can I do that?

Iain leads us down a rather long entryway into a living room that has only one tall, narrow window. A man sits in a high-backed leather chair, eyes closed, dressed in the kind of threads I've seen in old movies. The shirt and pants of a suit, but with a smoking jacket or whatever they call it instead of a suit jacket. He reminds me of Sherlock Holmes, especially since he's holding a pipe. No smoke wafts out of it, though.

The most surprising thing about Mungo is his age. He looks not much older than I am.

He doesn't look at us when we enter the room.

"Mungo," Iain says in a patient tone, "your guests are here. Kirsty and Luke have come a long way to see you."

Technically, I guess we did since we drove from Inverness back to Loch Fairbairn, then traveled down winding roads on the outskirts of the village. But it's not far compared to where I came from to get to Scotland. The institute in England is much farther away than Inverness is from Mungo's place.

Iain approaches our host's chair and gently shakes his shoulder. "Wakey-wakey, Mungo."

The man in the chair sighs and wriggles in his seat, then he clamps his teeth over the end of his pipe. "What do they want?"

"The diary of Efrica MacTaggart. I told you that earlier."

"Oh, aye." Mungo straightens and sets his pipe down on the table beside his chair. "Why do they want it?"

He sounds confused rather than annoyed. Earlier, Kirsty had jokingly asked if I had early onset senility, but I'm wondering if Mungo does have that. Or maybe he's got other kinds of mental issues. He might've suffered a brain injury, I suppose.

Only now do I notice the small plastic bag on the table next to Mungo's chair. The bag contains greenish leafy stuff that seems to have been chopped up.

Iain notices me looking at the bag and pats our host's shoulder. "Best not to discuss Mungo's, ah, recreational habits. The law doesn't look kindly on these things, and we wouldn't want you two to become embroiled in any of his shenanigans."

Sounds like Iain is politely informing me that Mungo uses marijuana. I've never done any kind of drugs, but I had a roommate in college who liked to smoke it on occasion. I recognize the stuff in Mungo's baggie. Does he smoke it in his pipe? Well, that would explain his kind of loopy behavior. Whatever this guy does in his own home is none of my business, and all we need from him is that journal.

"The diary," Iain says. "Where is it, Mungo?"

Our host jerks his head to look at Iain, as if he's only just noticed there are other people in the room. He glances at me and Kirsty before returning his attention to Iain. "It's in the library. Let me show you."

Mungo groans and grunts as he gets up out of his chair. Iain tries to help, but Mungo flashes him a scowl and shakes his hand off. Our host stretches and groans again, more deeply, then straightens and strides toward a closed door to our left. He brings out a set of keys, fumbling with them until he finds the right one and jams it into the slot. "Do not touch anything unless I expressly state that you may."

Iain chuckles. "Donnae worry, mate. They won't break anything. Luke is a scientist, which means he knows how to handle delicate things."

My field is psychophysics, so I'm not sure I deserve the endorsement Iain has given me. I have no clue how to handle very old documents. My best option is not to touch anything unless Mungo or Iain tells me it's okay.

Our host unlocks the door and shepherds us into the library.

Chapter Twenty-Seven

Kirsty

We are inside Mungo's library, the place he doesn't like anyone else to see. I have no idea how Iain convinced the recluse to let us look at the diary, but I get more excited as we walk further into the room. It has shelves that fill every wall from floor to ceiling, as well as rows of shorter shelves that reach my waist height. I also see glass cases that apparently house the most delicate documents in his collection. A single overhead light illuminates the space, which has no windows.

I feel like I've stepped into an ancient Egyptian tomb.

Mungo halts once we've all stepped inside the room. He waves to Iain, who shuts the door. Then Mungo points to a cardboard box that sits on the floor beside the door. "Masks and gloves are required. I have many documents that are quite fragile and might be damaged by your exhalations."

Iain digs around in the box, bringing out three masks and three sets of gloves. While Luke, Iain, and I put on the required gear, our host pulls a mask and gloves out of his trouser pocket.

"Follow me," Mungo says. "But do not touch anything."

He guides us through the maze of shelves and display cases toward a far corner of the library. The overhead light barely illuminates the space, but I can see an ornate metal box stuffed into the corner. It sits on a waist-high table.

Mungo pulls his keys out again. "Try not to breathe."

I glance at Iain, who shrugs and rolls his eyes.

Donnae care what Mungo says. I'm going to breathe.

Our host unlocks the box and carefully picks up the item housed inside it. The small book features a leather cover, worn and cracked, but I see no words printed on it. He turns toward us while cradling the book in his hands. "You will not touch this. I'll turn the pages so you can have a peek."

A tingle of anticipation sweeps over my skin as Mungo gently opens the book to the first page. The name "Efrica MacTaggart" is written there, in a sprawling, elegant hand. Is that Efrica's handwriting? Before I can examine it more closely, Mungo turns the page.

And there it is. The first lines of my ancestor's diary.

"May I take pictures of the pages?" I ask. "That way we can study the diary more closely later."

"Certainly not," Mungo snaps. "No MacTaggart may touch or photograph this diary."

"But it belongs to my ancestor. I only want to—"

"I said no." He lays the book back in the box, the pages still open. "This was a mistake. You lot have cursed my family for centuries. I should never have let you see the diary, and you will never possess it. If the ruddy thing weren't infected with poisonous magic, I would burn it."

"You will not destroy a piece of my family's heritage. I'll steal the bloody thing if necessary to stop you from erasing Efrica MacTaggart from history."

Mungo's lip curls as he growls, "She was a black witch who hexed my lineage. We've had no luck since then, and we all suffer from maladies that strike us when we reach the age of twenty-eight." He jabs a finger at me. "You lot did this to us. The MacTaggarts are a pox on the Highlands."

I open my mouth to argue with the wanker, but Luke intervenes.

"Let's all calm down, hey?" he says. "This is just an old book. Maybe we should come back later when everybody's more relaxed."

"Aye," Iain agrees. "We'll come back another time, Mungo."

"Willnae let ye in," our host says. "Should never have been friendly with any MacTaggart. And none of you will ever get a glimpse of that diary again." He swings an arm up, stabbing a finger in the direction of the door. "Get out of my house."

The three of us stare at Mungo. Is he honestly never going to let me see the diary? I didn't mean to upset him, but when he accused my family of hexing his...I admit I lost my temper a wee bit.

"Get out!" Mungo roars, his face turning crimson.

Iain ushers us out of the library and the house. We stop in the driveway.

"Sorry," Iain says. "Mungo has never been like that before. I think he genuinely believes that book is cursed. If I'd known that, I would never have suggested you come here, Kirsty. Now you've lost any chance to study Efrica's diary."

I hug my cousin. "It's all right, Iain. You did your best. And it's my fault for getting upset."

"No one would blame you for that." Iain steps back. "You two go home. Let me think on this. There might be another way to convince Mungo."

"Calli says you're the only one he might listen to."

"Try not to be upset anymore. I'll find a way, you have my word."

Luke snorts. "Looks like the only way Kirsty will ever see that diary is if Mungo's stoned out of his head and we steal the thing right out from under his nose."

"I doubt that will be necessary," Iain says. "Though if it comes to that, my da can help you with your plan."

My cousin gets into his car and drives away.

Once Luke and I are in the Jaguar, heading back to my house, he asks, "What did Iain mean when he said his father could help us with my plan?"

"Uncle Angus used to be a petty burglar. He did it only to feed his family, and he only ever stole from wealthy scunners who most likely stole the things in the first place. Angus went to prison several times, but now he's retired."

"I see. Your family gets weirder and weirder."

"Not as weird as Mungo, though."

Luke chuckles. "Oh yeah, that guy wins the prize for the kookiest kook on earth."

"It sounds like he has mental issues. I'd say Jack should talk to him, but Mungo thinks MacTaggarts are evil witches."

"Maybe Jack can find somebody else to help that guy."

By the time we get home, meaning my house, we're both so jeeked all we want to do is go to sleep. We remove all our clothes, but only so we can lie in bed together with nothing between us, only my skin on his. It feels lovely. Warm, comfortable, sensual but in a softer way, not like we want to have a poke. Luke lies on his back while I drape one leg over his and lay an arm across his chest, where I rest my cheek. He combs his fingers through my hair with one hand while he strokes my back with the other.

"I love you so much, Kirsty," he says. "You're my soul mate, and I would never do anything to hurt you, not if I could help it. You're everything to me. No matter what happens, remember that."

That almost sounds like he's expecting something bad to happen. But that can't be what meant.

Snuggling closer, I murmur, "I love you too, Luke. More than anyone in the world."

He wraps his arms around me, holding me tight, but he says nothing else. Though I want to ask him about what he said, I can't stop myself from falling asleep. An embrace from Luke Turner is better than any tranquilizer.

When I wake in the morning, Luke isn't in bed with me.

I get dressed and walk into the bathroom, but I don't find Luke there. He's not in the living room either, or the kitchen. I go outside to check the backyard and the front lawn, even the garage. He's nowhere. Has Luke left me again? No, he wouldn't do that. I believe that because I believe in us, in what we've forged over the past few days. Maybe he went to the cafe to get us breakfast.

With that thought, that hope, in my mind, I sit on the sofa and wait.

An hour goes by. No Luke.

I grab my mobile and ring his number. No answer. I leave a message on his voice mail.

Where is Luke? I eat a quick breakfast and then ring Logan to see if he knows what's become of Luke. He doesn't have "a sodding clue," as my brother colorfully says. So I ring Magnus.

"I know where he is," my cousin says, "but I'm sworn to secrecy."

"Secrecy? What the bloody hell is going on? He's my boyfriend, and I want to know he's all right."

"Luke is fine. He's in a bit of a fankle, though, and I gave my word that I wouldn't tell anyone—not even you."

"Are you helping him?"

Magnus hesitates, then sighs. "Aye, I'm trying to help. That's all I can say. Please just stay home today."

Stay home? No, that statement doesn't make me feel any less anxious about the situation.

"Cannae promise to hide in my house," I say, "unless I know why I should do that."

"And I can't tell you. I'm asking you to please do as I say." Magnus lowers his voice to the growl that makes most people do whatever he says. "For once in your life, donnae be so stubborn."

"I will think about it."

"Have it your way. I tried, at least."

We say goodbye, and I ponder what Magnus said. I think he was both trying not to tell me exactly what's going on and also warning me, when he let slip that something is happening today. Something that must involve me. Why else would he suggest I should stay home?

I can't do that, though. I have a business to run.

On the drive to the shop, I don't see anything that warrants the dire tone of everything Magnus had said to me. Everything seems normal today. I park behind the shop building, as usual, in my car. Luke had taken the Jaguar. Not sure how Rory will feel about that, but then, he did say we could use the Jaguar for as long as we wanted.

Why did Luke run away before I woke up? What happened this morning?

I'm still wondering about all of that as I unlock the shop's back door and head inside. I do my usual routine to get ready for a day of peddling my wares to tourists and the locals who appreciate my shop. Then I unlock the front door, turn the sign that hangs on the door so it says "open," and carry the sandwich board sign out to place it on the pavement.

Luke would call it the sidewalk. Where is he?

I sit on the high stool behind the counter and open up my laptop computer so I can do some bookkeeping while I wait for customers. Half an hour goes by before the first person enters the shop, but that's not unusual. It's always slow first thing in the morning and things pick up later. But the state of my first customer is unusual—frantic, in fact.

My Aunt Glenna, Iain's mother, bursts through the door and races up to the counter. Her cheeks are flushed, and she's breathing hard as if she's been running for quite a ways.

"Glenna, my goodness," I say. "What's the bother?"

She holds a hand to her chest and shakes her head. "You shouldn't be in here, love."

"What? I don't understand." I grab the unopened water bottle I'd stowed under the counter and hand it to her. "You look like you need a drink."

Glenna unscrews the cap and guzzles water. "You need to go home, Kirsty, now. They're coming."

"Who's coming?"

My aunt hurries around the counter, tugging my arm hard several times in an apparent attempt to make me get off the stool. "Hurry, *gràidh*. Magnus and Logan can't hold them off for long."

"Hold who off? I'm not going anywhere unless you tell me what's happening."

The flush of exertion has left her face, replaced by a slight pallor. Her eyes have gone wide too.

"Who are Logan and Magnus trying to stop?" I ask.

Glenna clutches my hands. "The mob is coming for you."

Another person bursts through the door, but it's not a customer. My cousin Evan is breathing as hard as Glenna had been a moment ago, and his glasses have fogged up. "Get out of here, Kirsty. Glenna and I can lock up for you. Go out the back way—*now*."

Two of my family members have run here so fast they're almost out of breath, and both have urged me to leave in a tone that tells me they are genuinely worried for me.

I grab my purse, toss the spare shop key to Evan, and hurry out the back door. I should have minded Evan and Glenna's warnings sooner, but it's too late now.

The second I exit the shop, a camera flash goes off in my face, blinding me for a moment. I throw my hand up instinctively, shielding my eyes.

"Miss MacTaggart," a male voice says, "how does it feel to have your secret exposed to the world?"

As my vision clears, I see the person talking is a man in his thirties who has the strap of his large, professional-quality camera slung over one shoulder. He holds the camera with one hand while he thrusts his mobile in my face.

I can see he has a sound recorder app on the screen. He wants to record me answering his question, I gather, but I have no clue what he's talking about. "Excuse me?"

"Your secret has been exposed," the man says. "The international press will arrive soon, but the Scots got first chance to interview you. I'm with *The Loch Fairbairn World News*."

"That's Graham Oliver's paper, but he left the village years ago."

"I bought the paper six months ago. This will be my first big scoop." He snaps another picture of me, then lets his camera dangle from his shoulder. "Come on, Miss MacTaggart, tell everyone why you did it."

"Why I did what?"

"Conned the entire Highlands with your 'witchy powers' bollocks."

Voices shout and footfalls pound behind this man, then a swarm of people descends.

Chapter Twenty-Eight

Luke

Here's how it happened. If I'd known things would spiral so far out of control so fast, I would never have left Kirsty alone in her house. But it's hard to see the tsunami coming until it's practically right on top of you. Since this entire calamity is my fault, and Kirsty will despise me when she learns I did this to her, I guess it doesn't matter that I wasn't there for her when the tidal wave inundated her world.

The morning had started out peaceful. I woke up with Kirsty lying beside me, her hair tousled and her lips curled in the faintest of smiles. She looked so sweet that I didn't want to get out of bed, but I needed to make a call. That was the only reason I forced myself to crawl out of bed, then got dressed and went into the living room to avoid disturbing Kirsty. After our big day of researching Kieran MacTaggart, she needed to sleep late. I could've used more sleep too, but my conscience kept waking me up until I decided to bite the bullet.

I dialed Melvin's number.

"Have you done it?" he asked instead of saying hello like a normal person would.

"No," I said. "And I'm not going to. It's over, Melvin. I quit."

"You can't resign."

"I can, and I have. Check your email. My letter of resignation is waiting in your inbox."

He huffed. "I refuse to accept it."

"Face it, Melvin. I'm gone, and you will never get your grimy hands on the research I've conducted here in the Highlands."

"Your computer and all your equipment belong to me. Your research belongs to me." His voice dropped to a low snarl. "I own you, Mr. Turner. If you try to keep that research from me, I will have you arrested for theft."

"Can't. I destroyed everything. Good luck proving I stole 'your' research. I wiped the hard drive too, and just for good measure, I smashed the computer."

I hadn't done that, not yet, but I'd planned to do it right after I informed Melvin. I needed to find a sledgehammer or something, anyway, before I could destroy that shit. Last night, I had installed software on my computer that would erase every file on the hard drive, permanently, and started the program running. When I got up this morning, the deed had been done. All that was left was to trash the computer.

"Did you hear me, Melvin?" I said. "You will never get what you want. I finally stopped thinking of myself as your lackey and did what I should've done a long time ago. I grew a pair and stood up to you. Go on and tell Kirsty about my big mistake, the one that gave you leverage over me. I don't care anymore. It's over."

Silence followed for several seconds.

I'd just about decided we got disconnected when Melvin spoke again. He had that sneaky, slimy-bastard tone in his voice. "You might have wiped the hard drive, but I had installed spyware on your computer. Everything was copied to my machine. I just checked, and it's all there. Thank you, Mr. Turner, for so diligently documenting your experiments."

"But the results are the opposite of what you wanted."

"On the contrary. This is more proof that Kirsty MacTaggart is a cunning con artist. She brainwashed you, after all. Not hard to do to a weak-willed lapdog."

"Do you seriously think anyone will believe I was brainwashed? And who cares about what a woman who owns a little shop in a little village does with her life? This isn't exactly hot news around the world."

He chuckled, but it sounded nasty instead of cheerful. "I have reshaped the situation to suit my needs. I had a feeling you would be swayed by a pretty face, and I took action to ensure I would get the desired result."

Was Melvin saying he falsified the data? Changed what I gave him and turned it into something else? Even if that were true, I didn't understand what he thought he could gain from doing that. Nobody in the wider world knows where Loch Fairbairn is, much less who Kirsty is or what she does for a living—or that she believes she might have second sight.

"You're an idiot, Melvin," I said. "You won't get that grant you've been lusting after based on sketchy data and the fact Kirsty owns a metaphysical shop. And what kind of foundation gives money for something like that? It's garbage, and you know it."

"There is no foundation. I invented one strictly to convince you to do what I wanted. If I'd said I wanted to sell your girlfriend to the international media, you would never have gone along with my plan."

Sell her? Yeah, the bastard said that. But it didn't make any sense. Melvin might've been a complete jackass and possibly a nutjob too, but he wasn't stupid.

"What have you done?" I asked.

"If I want to become the most famous debunker of pseudoscience, I need to make a splash." He paused, then spoke in that slimy-bastard voice again. "A sweet girl who lives in a sleepy little village in the Highlands but secretly fleeces innocent people with her mind-reading nonsense? Exposing her will bring me international fame."

So that was his game. He craved fame and fortune at any cost.

But Kirsty might be the one to pay for it.

"The wheels are already in motion," he said. "You can either jump on the train with me or be crushed under its weight."

"Go to hell, Melvin. One way or another, I'll stop you from ruining Kirsty's life."

I hung up. Couldn't slam the phone down, though, since it's a cell phone. After thirty seconds of standing in the living room, not moving, while I racked my brain for a solution, I grabbed the keys to the Jag and took off. I had Logan's phone number—yeah, he voluntarily gave it to me—so I called him. Time to bring in the reinforcements. Maybe Kirsty's family isn't my family, and maybe some of them dislike me intensely, but I know they'll do anything for her.

When I explained the situation to Logan, he chuckled in that dark, I'm-a-deadly-spy way. "Ye donnae know the MacTaggarts if ye think that *bod ceann* will succeed. Kirsty rang me a few minutes ago, so I know something's going on. She sounded very worried because she doesn't know where you are."

"Didn't want to wake her up. I honestly thought I could fix things without her ever needing to know about the mess I've caused."

"Go to Magnus's house. I'll meet you there, and then you can explain what the bloody hell you've done to my sister."

He gave me the address, and I sped to Magnus's place on the outskirts of Loch Fairbairn. It was a modest-size house with no adornments, meaning no flowering bushes or decorative elements in the architecture, just a plain but well-kept house with a well-mown lawn.

I parked at the curb, then raced up the concrete walkway to the front door and knocked.

The door swung open, and Magnus raked his squinty gaze over me from head to toe. "What do you want, *cacan*?"

"Guess Logan didn't call you. Kirsty is in trouble."

"Aye, Logan rang me. But I wanted to see you squirm before I admitted to that."

"I didn't squirm."

"No, ye didn't. I'm impressed. Now, come inside so we can plot our revenge on that *bod ceann*."

We sat in armchairs in the living room while I explained the situation to Magnus. If I'd expected him to beat me up, I was wrong. The demon biker didn't get angry—not at me, anyway. He snarled a string of what I took for Gaelic curses when I told him about Melvin, and he stated his intention to "skelp the living hell" out of my former boss. But he didn't try to "skelp" me.

I'd just finished my story when Magnus's phone rang. I could hear only his side of the conversation, but I knew he was talking to Kirsty.

"I know where he is," Magnus told her. "But I'm sworn to secrecy."

Yeah, I'd asked him not to tell Kirsty anything about this debacle. I held out hope that I could straighten it all out before she ever knew a thing about it.

Magnus told Kirsty I was "in a bit of a fankle," which I thought meant I was in a mess. Understatement of the century. Finally, Magnus tried to convince Kirsty to stay home today, but I could tell from his responses that she wasn't having any of that.

I love her feisty side, but that stubbornness won't do her any good today.

Magnus hangs up the call and looks at me. "Once Logan and the others get here, we will come up with an action plan."

"Others? I thought it was just Logan coming."

"Ye donnae get it yet, do ye? MacTaggarts always step up when there's trouble, and we will die for each other if necessary."

"I'd rather not turn this into a death match."

"Aye, and I doubt violence will be required."

Yeah, all we need is the demon biker and the deadly spy to glare at whoever Melvin has wrangled to harass Kirsty.

So that's how I wind up in the alley behind Kirsty's store with Magnus, Logan, and several other MacTaggarts. We push past the crowd of morons who are shouting questions at Kirsty.

"How long have you been fleecing residents of this town?"

"Will you pay compensation to the people you've conned?"

"Does your family know what you are?"

Kirsty tries to turn around and rush back into the store, but one jackass gets between her and the door. Then another jerk—a woman, no less—blocks her way too. Kirsty glances around, seeming almost panicked.

Until her gaze collides with mine.

The panic melts away, and she almost smiles.

Does she think I've come to rescue her? Maybe I have, but I don't think she'll be grateful when she finds out the truth about this disaster.

Logan and Magnus wrangle the rest of the crowd while I barge through them to shove the two jerks away from the door. I pull Kirsty into my arms, thrust the door inward, and drag her through it with me, shutting the door and locking it before anybody else can try to storm inside. An older woman stands behind the counter beside a man who's probably my age. I recognize them both from the wedding reception, but I don't know their names.

Kirsty tells me, "My cousin Evan and my Aunt Glenna came by to check on me."

Her cousin adjusts his glasses and looks straight at me. "What's going on here?"

"It's a lot to explain, and I need to talk to Kirsty first."

She gives me a strange look. "We can go into my office."

While Evan and Glenna stay by the counter, I follow Kirsty into her office. I'd never noticed it before, but that's not surprising since a tall display case hides it.

Once we get inside the small room, Kirsty shuts the door. "I want to know why this is happening, and I have a strange feeling you know the answer."

"I do, but…" I shove my hands into my jeans pockets. "First, I need you to understand that I never meant for any of this to happen. I didn't expect to fall in love with you all over again, but I couldn't help it. Even after twelve years, I still loved you, and now my feelings are even stronger than before. You mean everything to me, Kirsty."

"There's a 'but' coming, isn't there?"

"Yes." I gesture toward the chair behind the desk. "Maybe you should sit down."

"Donnae want to sit. I need you to explain what the bloody hell is going on."

As much as I don't want to tell her, I know I need to do it. But I can't look her in the eye while I confess, so I bow my head. "Right after Alex called to tell me you needed my help, I went to my boss to beg him for time off so I could come to Scotland. Melvin Prickett isn't exactly the kind-hearted type of scientist. He's more like a hyena. Anyway, he said I could have the time off, but only if I turned it into a working holiday."

When I glance up, without lifting my head, I see Kirsty strapping her arms around herself. She rubs her arms too like she's cold. It's not a chill, though. I think she senses I'm about to tell her something awful.

"Melvin ordered me to do those experiments," I say. "He wanted me to debunk your second sight."

"How did he even know about me?"

"I, uh, kind of told him. Guess I was excited about seeing you again, and Melvin used that as a way to get me to tell him all about you." I shove a hand through my hair, staring down at my feet. "He's good at manipulating people. I wound up telling him about you, about how you believe you have supernatural powers."

"You did what he wanted. You tried to debunk me."

The tone of her voice has changed. Not quite anger. More like sharp disappointment.

Christ, it's about to happen. She's going to tell me to go to hell. And she should do that, but I don't want her to say the words.

"Yes, I did what Melvin wanted," I say. "Even after I realized the tests suggested you might have some kind of latent parapsychological abilities, I didn't want to believe it. Science has been my life and my refuge for so long that I couldn't accept what the data told me."

"So you kept trying to prove I'm a fraud."

"No." I thrust both hands into my hair and raise my face to her. "I tried to put Melvin off the idea, but he wouldn't let it go. I delayed. Thought I could come up with a solution to the problem, but I had no idea how far Melvin would go. He told me he needed to debunk a psychic so that some foundation would give him a grant. I agreed to do what he wanted, but when I tried to back out, he went ballistic."

"When did you try to back out?"

"This morning. I called Melvin—"

"You only wanted to back out this morning?" Tears pool in her eyes, and her lips quiver. "For days, you've been acting as if you're an objective scientist doing experiments. I helped you. Got my brother to help you too. But the whole time, you were trying to prove I'm a charlatan who takes advantage of tourists?"

"No, that's not—I wanted to back out earlier, but I couldn't figure out how to protect you from whatever Melvin might do once I—"

"Haud yer wheesht!" she shouts, even while tears stream down her cheeks. "Ye lied to me, for days. Said you loved me, said your experiments showed something you couldn't explain. You seduced me several times, even helped me research Kieran, but it was all an act."

"Please listen to me, Kirsty. That's not how it was at all." I pace in front of her desk because I can't sit still anymore. "Yes, I said I'd debunk you. But I couldn't do it. Not only because the test results weren't what I expected. It was mostly because I do love you."

"But you let your boss make me the center of some sort of tawdry scandal so he could get money."

"No, there isn't any foundation. Melvin just wants to become a famous debunker. The data I collected doesn't support what he wants everyone to believe, so he made up...I don't know what. He had a backup plan in place before I ever started these experiments."

Tears keep running down her cheeks, and her eyes have turned red. She sniffles. "Do you believe that I have second sight?"

"I don't know what I believe anymore."

"Do you believe me?"

"What are you asking? I can't say I subscribe to your Wiccan beliefs, but I trust you completely. If you say you've got witchy powers... I don't know."

"You trust me, but you don't believe me."

"I won't lie to you, Kirsty. I have no idea what to believe anymore."

She drops her face into her hands and cries, her shoulders shaking as soft sobs rack her body.

This is the moment I've dreaded for days. And I don't need to be psychic to know what she'll say next.

Kirsty lowers her hands and looks at me. She sucks in a breath, no longer sobbing. "I can't ever see you again, Luke. Go home. Leave me be."

And she walks out the door.

Chapter Twenty-Nine

Kirsty

I told Luke to go away, but he can't do that. The cretins out in the alley prevent any of us from leaving, unless we want to be accosted and pinned down like criminals on the run. Just as I return to the sales counter, I see more people have gathered out front. All I want to do is go home, draw all the curtains, and hide in my bedroom until next year. By then, maybe all these vultures will have gone somewhere else to gnaw on another innocent person's bloody carcass.

Bod an Donais. I feel like they've already gnawed the flesh off my bones.

Glenna drapes an arm around my shoulders and gives me a light squeeze. "Donnae worry, love. We will find a way to get you home."

"She will not be going home."

That's Logan speaking. I hadn't noticed he and Magnus were here until my brother spoke. Though I'd stopped crying before I left the office, I hadn't been in a good state of mind to notice much of anything.

Luke shuffles out of the office, head down, shoulders hunched. He stops at the other end of the counter, lifting his head, though he avoids looking at me. "Where will you take her?"

Though he spoke to Logan, he peeks at me out of the corner of his eye.

"Dùndubhan," my brother says. "It will be much harder for these bastards to harass her there. The castle is surrounded by a hundred acres of woodland, and there's a gate along the drive that requires a code to open it. We can also shut the gates of the compound itself."

He wants to close the massive wooden gates? I don't think anyone has tried that since…the Middle Ages, I think. Certainly, it has never happened since Rory bought the castle. He might know whether anyone has shut the gates in recent memory, but it hardly matters now.

I need to be locked inside a fortress. What has my life become?

Though I'd sobbed briefly in the office a few minutes ago, an inexplicable calmness has come over me now, as if my emotions have shut down. Maybe they have. The only man I've ever loved betrayed me, again, and I can't deal with the consequences of that right now.

Magnus ambles over to the windows and peers out at the street. "Looks like the bastards are relocating. I see them coming around the end of the building, heading this way. There aren't as many as it seemed like back in the alley. I see six or seven of them at most."

I hug myself, but the chill inside me won't melt away. "Felt like an army of rampaging Visigoths to me."

"Check the alley," Magnus tells Logan.

My brother hurries to the back door and yanks it open, peering through the narrow opening.

Voices shout, and cameras flash.

Logan shuts and locks the door, then turns toward us. "Still five of them out there."

"A dozen total, at most," Magnus says, "including the ones out front. We can distract them long enough for Evan and Glenna to get Kirsty out of the building."

"The alley seems like the best option," Logan says. "But we need to get a car into the alley without anyone noticing."

"Maybe what we need isn't stealth, but speed."

I pull away from Glenna, glancing back and forth between Magnus and Logan. "What are you two talking about? Speed instead of stealth?"

Luke chuckles, but it's a rueful sound. "I get it. They want to use the Jag like a rocket to get into the alley fast and grab you."

"That doesn't sound safe. You lot might run into a pedestrian or another car."

Magnus lifts one brow. "Not if I'm behind the wheel. I took a course in stunt driving."

"Why in the world would you do that?"

"To improve my chances of catching fugitives. They never see me coming."

Logan marches up to the counter beside me. He lays a hand on my shoulder. "Trust Magnus. He won't do anything that might hurt you. If anyone can get you out of this building and to Dùndubhan without those scunners out there seeing, it's Magnus."

What else can I do? Staying here does not appeal to me. Aye, a mob of scunners has chased me away from my shop and my home. Maybe I can figure out how to reclaim my life once I've recovered from the shock of this day.

My gaze travels to Luke, without my permission, and my throat constricts. I still love him. Can't help it. But I can never forgive him for lying to me. I gave him how many chances to tell me everything? He knows how much I despise secrets, yet he continued to hide the truth from me.

I still feel like there's another truth he hasn't told me yet. Doesnae matter. We are over, for good.

"How do we distract the crowds out front and in the alley?" Logan asks.

Magnus grins, but it's the sort of expression that conveys menace rather than happiness. "I know exactly how, but we'll need someone to bring the gear."

Gear? What on earth is he planning?

"I'll ring Jack," Logan says. "He lives in the village, so he could get here the fastest. What do you need?"

"He can retrieve the items from my house." Magnus brings out his mobile. "I'd better ring him to explain how to handle the gear. Donnae want Jack to injure himself accidentally."

Injure himself? I don't think I want to know what Magnus is plotting, but I have no doubt I will find out soon enough.

Magnus retreats into a far corner of the shop to make his call. A moment later, he approaches the counter. "It's set. Jack should be here in fifteen minutes at the outside."

Not sure if I can stand to wait that long, but I have no choice.

The so-called reporters are still shouting questions. The displays in the front windows block most of their view, and with only the lights in the back switched on, they shouldn't be able to spy on us very well at all. I hadn't shut off the front lights. I assume one of my cousins did that, or my brother.

Luke starts to walk toward me, but I raise a hand to stop him.

He backs away, hands stuffed into his trouser pockets.

What else can we do? The lot of us wait for Jack to arrive with whatever dangerous "gear" Magnus asked him to bring. So we stand here in silence, listening to the ticking of the wall clock and the hissing of the ventilation system.

A mobile rings.

Magnus pulls his out and answers it. "Jack? Where are you? Good. I'm coming out."

He returns his mobile to his pocket.

"Is everything ready?" Logan asks.

"Aye. Jack couldn't get closer than a block away, so I'll run down there to get the gear."

Wonderful. More waiting while the vultures circle us.

Magnus goes out the front door, shoving through the crowd with ease. They start to scatter as he strides past them, but soon, they swarm the storefront again.

Luke is gazing at me with a pleading expression.

I know he wants to talk to me, but I can't handle that right now. Maybe I never will be able to handle it.

A thunderous bang explodes out front, then another one erupts in the alley. I jump, my heart suddenly racing. What is Magnus doing out there? He must have Jack helping him, and those noises must be their doing. Have they set off explosives? That's illegal. Isn't it?

People shout and scream—and the crowd out front scatters as everyone scrambles to escape the apparent danger.

"Flash-bangs," Logan tells us. "They make a lot of noise and a blinding flash of light, but no one will be harmed. It's the most expedient way to disperse the crowd."

"Won't Magnus and Jack be arrested for setting off explosives?" I ask.

"I know the blokes at the Loch Fairbairn Police Station. They'll understand and look the other way."

That doesn't make me feel better. I'm still the object of that mob's harassment. Considering how determined they seemed, I can't help wondering how long the flash-bangs will keep them away, especially once they realize it wasn't an actual explosion.

Tires squeal outside.

Logan seizes my arm and hauls me toward the back door. He opens it a sliver, just enough to peek out into the alley. "It's clear."

He keeps hold of my arm as we hurry outside.

The Jaguar comes roaring around the corner into the alley, barreling toward us.

My heart races so fast I feel lightheaded. Magnus must be behind the wheel, but he doesn't seem to be slowing down at all. Though I feel a strong urge to leap out of the way of the car that's barreling toward us, Logan's hand on my arm stops me from moving.

Mowed down in a horrific crash? With my cousin behind the wheel of the car that crushes me? Aye, that will be the perfect end to this day.

Like a demonic beast, the Jaguar roars closer and closer.

I can't breathe, can't move, not even to squeeze my eyes shut.

Tires squeal as Magnus brakes abruptly, so hard I swear I see smoke curling up from the wheels. The Jaguar angles sideways, coming to a halt mere feet from where Logan and I stand.

My brother seems unfazed, as usual.

But I feel nauseous and ready to pass out from the shock.

Logan drags me toward the car and yanks the passenger door open. "Get in. Quick."

"What about Luke?"

"Donnae worry. We'll take care of him."

I leap into the Jaguar and strap myself in, then Magnus rockets back up the alley and swerves onto the street with more squealing of tires.

Maybe I've escaped from the vultures. But for how long?

Chapter Thirty

Luke

Kirsty got to escape in style, inside a Jaguar driven by her demonic biker cousin who apparently doubles as a stunt driver. Damn, that man is cool. But I only think about that for two seconds after the Jag disappears down the alley. Since the back door was unlocked, I held it open just enough that I could watch Magnus and Kirsty make their daring escape. It was like something out of a James Bond movie. The demon biker used flash-bangs too, and those evil jerks who came to harass Kirsty got out of Magnus's way faster than I've ever seen a crowd break up.

Yeah, maybe I've developed a slight man-crush on that guy. He's even tougher than Logan, I think, and he relishes any chance to show off his badass persona. I will never admit out loud that I admire Magnus, though. That wouldn't be cool. Not that anyone has ever accused of me being cool. No, I was the shy geek in college, then the science-obsessed psychophysicist after that. I got plenty of dates, but not because girls dig my career choice.

I bet women throw themselves at Magnus.

The only woman I want to throw herself at me is Kirsty, but I don't see that ever happening. The way she'd looked at me when I told her what I'd done… Maybe I should've explained the rest, but it wouldn't have made a difference. I screwed up so badly that nothing can fix it.

At least she'll be safe at Dùndubhan. I know her family will take good care of her.

I shut the back door and turn around to slump against it. Maybe I can't erase what I've done, but I'm not completely useless. Right? I can still do…something. To protect Kirsty. Don't care what happens to me.

Kirsty's aunt, Glenna, stares out the front windows.

Logan and Evan are standing on this side of the sales counter, both eying me with curiosity.

"What should we do with the *cacan*?" Logan asks his cousin.

Evan tips his head to the side like he's seriously considering the options. "Dump him in Loch Fairbairn? It's not as deep as Loch Ness, but it should do in a pinch."

"No, that's not punishment enough. He needs to suffer first."

"You may have a point."

It's bizarre to listen while a man wearing glasses who dresses like a businessman discusses how to punish me. Sure, I expect that from Logan and Magnus. But I thought Evan was a billionaire tech mogul, not a member of the MacTaggart Family Assassination Guild.

"You guys are hilarious," I say, without any humor whatsoever. "Don't need you two to remind me of how horribly I screwed up."

But suddenly, I know what I need to do.

"Maybe we should lock you up in the police station," Evan says. "Give you time to think on what you've done."

"I'm well aware of what I've done." I push away from the door. "And I know what I have to do to set things right."

Logan's brows hike up. "Do ye now?"

"Yes." I approach them, halting an arm's length away, and force myself to stand up straight as I fix my gaze on Logan. "I need to go back to England to confront my ex-boss. I might've gone along with Melvin's plan at first, but he's the one who sicced the sleazoid pseudo-journalists on Kirsty. Let me fix this. Please."

"Do what you want." Logan leans forward, staring into my eyes with unnerving intensity. "But I'm watching you, laddie."

"Fine, whatever. Not even your deadly spy stare will make me shit my pants." I glance at the windows and see a few of the sleazoids have come back. "Do any of you MacTaggarts have a private jet? It would be the quickest way for me to fly back to England and do what I need to do. Then I'll come right back."

"Come back?" Logan says. "Why?"

"For Kirsty. I'm sure you hate my guts, and that's cool. But I am not giving up on her, not this time around."

Both men observe me for several seconds, though I can't figure out what their narrowed gazes mean.

"You can take my jet," Evan says. "But I will need it back tomorrow. My wife and I are flying home to Utah."

"I'll bring the jet back before then. You have my word."

"Then you can borrow it."

A long sigh blusters out of me, though I hadn't realized I was holding my breath. "Thank you. I really appreciate this."

"Donnae be grateful yet," Logan says. "Ahm coming with ye."

"That's not necessary."

"Aye, it is."

What's the point of arguing? This trip will be the most un-fun excursion ever, whether or not Logan accompanies me. "Fine, we'll go together."

Evan glances at the front windows. "How will we get out of here?"

"I'll distract them," I say, "while you and Glenna go out the back."

"How do you mean to distract them?" Logan asks.

"Not with as much style as Magnus did, but I'll manage. I'm part of the story, after all, so the sleazoids ought to love to jump on me."

"Sleazoids?" Logan says. "And you Americans think Scots have a strange way of speaking."

"Let's call it a draw."

Logan squints at me for a moment, then sighs. "Go on, distract them. I'll meet you at the police station. That ought to discourage the 'sleazoids' from following you."

"Good idea. I'll meet you there." I skirt around the counter, heading for the front door. Then I glance over my shoulder at the others. "Ready?"

Logan leads Glenna and Evan toward the back door. "Aye, we're ready."

"Here goes nothing."

I swing the door open and step outside. The lock engages behind me with a click.

Half a dozen reporters have gathered on the sidewalk, and the instant they see me, they rush forward to surround me and shout questions.

Phase one, complete. On to phase two.

I spin away from the group and bolt down the sidewalk, aiming for the police station that I'd seen the other day when Kirsty took me to her house. I think the station is about three blocks away. Can I run full speed for that long? I'm about to test my physical fitness.

The sleazoids pursue me, just like I'd hoped they would.

Down the sidewalk I run, faster than I ever have in my life before today, keeping one thought in my mind to bolster me. *This is for Kirsty*. I dodge unsuspecting bystanders and pray the jerks chasing me will do the same, but I can't worry about that right now. My leg muscles start to burn from the exertion, and I'm breathing so hard my ears start to ring, but I don't stop or even slow down, despite my heart pounding and sweat streaming down my face. *This is for Kirsty.*

I reach the police station and bang through the door, skidding to a halt inches from the main desk, which is more like a counter than a real desk. Nobody is there to man the counter-desk whatsit.

"Took ye long enough."

Leaning against the counter, I turn sideways to look at Logan. "I'm not an Olympic sprinter."

I sound as breathless as I feel, but I am regaining the feeling in my face. Apparently, running flat-out for three blocks will make a person's face numb. I learn something new every day.

"What happened to Glenna and Evan?" I ask.

"Evan is driving our aunt home." Logan gets up from the plastic chair he'd been sitting in and approaches me. "Getting to the Inverness airport will be simple once we acquire transportation."

"You planning to steal a car?"

"No. Our transportation will be here any minute."

Tires squeal outside.

Magnus couldn't have gotten back to town so fast. He'd been driving Kirsty all the way out to Dùndubhan.

Iain saunters through the doors. "You two ready to go? The Land Rover is waiting."

Am I ready for what's next? Doubtful. But I'll do what I have to do.

The drive to Inverness takes three freaking hours, but finally, I'm climbing the stairs to board Evan's jet with Logan right behind me. Shortly after that, we're in the air, flying to London. The trip doesn't take long in a fast, fancy jet like this one, but it feels like forever to me. Yeah, okay, I can admit I'm nervous about what will happen when I confront Melvin in person. It's easy for the toad to ream me via the cellular network, but I doubt he'll have the balls to confront me that way in person. Before I left for Scotland, he'd never been as nasty as he has been lately. The jerk knows I can't punch his lights out long distance.

I've never been a violent person, but Melvin has pushed the one button he shouldn't have touched. The button labeled Kirsty MacTaggart.

Her face appears in my mind, like a mirage or wishful thinking. Her smile. Her lips. Her beautiful, shiny hair and those gorgeous, shimmering eyes. She said she loves me, but now I've made a mess of everything.

"Don't do that," Logan says.

He's sitting across the aisle from me, his chair rotated so he faces me since I've got my seat turned too. Logan, naturally, watches me with squinted eyes and an indecipherable expression.

"What are you talking about?" I ask.

"Don't think about Kirsty and whether she'll forgive you. Right now, you need to focus on what you want to say to Melvin Prickett."

"I want to tell him to shove a cactus up his ass."

Logan lifts a single brow. "You might try something more instructive."

"Do you mean constructive?"

"No. I meant what I said. Teach that *bod ceann* a lesson in whatever way seems appropriate to you."

It's my turn to lift my brows at him. "You want me to beat up Melvin?"

"Did I say that? Listen to my words and don't reinterpret them."

"Uh-huh. I'll have to think about that for a while."

Logan checks his watch. "Don't think for too long. We're landing in ten minutes. Evan arranged for a car to pick us up at the airport and take us directly to the British Institute for Psychophysics."

Just like Logan said, our jet lands ten minutes later and we're whisked away in a waiting car—a limousine, no less—headed for the institute. At least I get to ride in style instead of turning up in my old beater like I have every day since I started working with Melvin. He loves to make snide comments about my car, my clothes, basically everything about me, including the fact I'm American. He harasses anybody who's not British, so it's not just me. He also insults other Brits who don't meet his snobby standards.

The security guard at the entrance to the building doesn't want to let me or Logan go inside. I'm no longer an employee here, and Logan doesn't have a visitor's badge, so the guard tries to order us to go away. He sucks at being tough, though. Logan insists, in that deadly calm way he has, that the guard should allow us inside or he'll regret it. I swear the guy cringes, then he calls upstairs to get permission for us to enter the building. But of course, the person who responds is Melvin—and he says no.

Like that will stop us.

I glance at Logan, who smirks.

And we push right past the guard to board the elevator. The rent-a-cop wannabe runs after us, but he clearly hasn't exercised in the past ten years and can't get to the elevator before the doors close behind us.

Up to the fourth floor, we go.

And that's the actual fourth floor, not the fourth level above the ground floor. This ain't no castle. Yeah, I get Southern when I'm about to confront my jackass boss.

The secretary who occupies a desk outside Melvin's office tries to stop us too, but Logan and I burst through the doors and march straight up to Melvin's desk. He's sitting there frowning at his computer screen. When we barrel into his domain, he jerks his head up. His eyes go wide, and I swear his face turns a paler shade of sallow.

"You do not work here anymore," Melvin says, trying to sound tough, but it comes off as whiny instead. "You have no right to enter the building, much less—"

"Shut it, Melvin," I say. And yeah, I actually sound tough. "It's time we had a real conversation, man to man. Oh wait, what am I saying? You're not a man, you're a slimy rat in a designer suit."

"If you don't leave immediately, I will ring the police and inform them of what you did."

"Gimme a break, Melvin. It wasn't illegal. It was an honest mistake that you perverted into a crime by falsifying evidence. I let you hold that manufactured crime over my head and use my guilt and fear as leverage. That's over. I don't care who you tell."

Dr. Melvin Prickett leaps out of his chair, which sends it reeling backward. It thumps into the wall.

Logan just stands there, slightly behind and to the side of me, wearing his usual "I could kill you with my pinky finger, but you're not worth the effort" expression. His posture is apparently relaxed, but somehow gives off a deadly vibe too.

Damn. I wish I could do that.

"As far as anyone else will know," Melvin says, "you stole two million pounds from the institute. Unless you finish what you started in Scotland, I will make certain you go to prison."

"Go on, you slimy, spineless worm. Call the cops. I don't care anymore."

Logan chuckles softly, the sound laced with a kind of subdued menace I doubt anyone else except Magnus could pull off. "You think you're a clever sod, but you have no idea who you're talking to."

"Of course not," Melvin snaps. "You are a complete stranger who has no right to be here."

"Throw me in jail, if that makes you feel like a man," I tell Melvin. "But call your dogs off Kirsty. Do it now."

"Why should I?"

"Because if you don't"—I slant over the desk to grab the knot on his tie and yank him toward me—"I will beat you until you're covered in your own blood and your teeth are lying on your desk like a modern-art installation."

His lips quiver, but he juts his chin up. "You wouldn't. A mild-mannered researcher—"

"I'm not like that anymore." I shake him hard. "Even after I go back to Scotland, you won't be safe. I can fly back here on my buddy's private jet just to hunt you down and toss you into a shark tank. I'll come back as many times as it takes and stalk you until you're too terrified to pee in a public restroom, much less get any sleep, because I might be right there behind you in the shadows."

"Aye," Logan says, "and I'll help him. My years in MI6 taught me every method for dealing with uncooperative subjects. I also have a large family that's full of men who love to exercise their fists by skiting them on the faces of scunners like you."

I raise *my* fist. "Last chance, Melvin. Call off your dogs."

"All right," he says, cringing when I pull my fist back like I'm about to wallop him. "I'll do it. Let go of me and I'll make the call."

"Uh-uh. You do it while I've still got you in my grip."

Melvin picks up the phone on his desk, his hands shaking, and dials a number.

"Speakerphone," I snarl. "Let us hear it."

He punches the speakerphone button, and we hear the call ringing on the other end.

A Scottish male voice picks up with a gruff hello.

"It's Melvin Prickett," my former employer says. "There's been a change of plans."

"What now?"

"Cancel all of it. Leave the girl alone and stop everything we had planned. It's over."

"Are you sure? We went to a bloody lot of trouble—"

"Just do it." Despite Melvin's harsh tone, tears have pooled in his now-bloodshot eyes. "Stop everything."

"It's your decision. We'll cancel it all."

"Good." Melvin hangs up. "Happy?"

No, I won't be happy unless Kirsty forgives me and comes back to me, but that seems unlikely. Then again, I did just browbeat my ex-boss into doing the right thing, even if he didn't want to do it. Maybe the spine I've suddenly grown means there is hope for me and Kirsty after all.

I release Melvin and start to back away from his desk. But I change my mind, slanting forward instead.

And I slug him in the jaw.

Melvin staggers backward. He starts to sit down, then stumbles as he remembers his chair isn't there.

Damn, it felt good to punch that prick.

"Sayonara, Melvin," I say, and turn to walk away. "The bruise you're going to have will remind you not to mess me with me ever again."

Logan aims his glare at the slimy worm. "Remember, Dr. Prickett, we have eyes and ears everywhere."

We both stride out of the office.

Chapter Thirty-One

Kirsty

I try to sleep that night, but I don't have any luck at all. Tossing and turning segues into pacing inside my room in the dark, until I give up and go downstairs to the sitting room. Though it's not cold enough for a fire, I turn on the gas flames in the fireplace anyway. Watching them flicker and dance relaxes me, but I still can't sleep.

At dawn, I go into the kitchen to make myself breakfast, though I don't taste any of the food I eat. Might as well be cardboard.

Magnus had brought me to Dùndubhan yesterday, but he left immediately after that, saying he wanted to make sure the tabloid reporters had gone away. I haven't seen him since. My cousin Evan drove out here not long after Magnus left and vowed to keep me company until Logan returns from England. I find Evan in the dining room, where he's eating his breakfast while working on his laptop computer.

"Aren't you meant to be flying back to Carrefour with Keely and Joy?" I ask. His wife and baby daughter go with him everywhere, but a small town in Utah has become their home.

"We delayed our departure a wee bit," Evan says, shutting his laptop. "Logan called late last night and asked me to stay with you until everything is settled."

"How long will that take?"

"Your brother seemed to think it would be done this morning."

"What will be done?"

Evan shrugs. "Logan wasn't specific. But I think Magnus is involved in whatever it is, possibly Iain too."

What on earth are my brother and my cousins doing? I know they won't tell me until they feel like it. And where is Luke? I shouldn't care, not when he lied to me, but I can't help worrying about him after the debacle yesterday with the so-called journalists. Logan had rung me shortly after Magnus brought me to Dùndubhan to let me know he and Luke were flying to England, but I have no idea why or if they've come back to Scotland yet.

Since Evan seems to be out of the loop too, I leave him be and go upstairs to the tower bedroom. Why am I here? I could claim I don't know, but that would be a lie. I came to this room because it's where Luke made love to me like he meant it, not as if it were a casual shag. That had been the most intimate and meaningful sexual experience of my life, and I will never believe it meant nothing to him.

Had I pushed too far when I demanded he tell me whether he believes I have supernatural abilities? I shouldn't expect him to change his mind overnight, or at all. Maybe we could be a couple again, even with our diverging viewpoints on how the world works. Couldn't we? Luke had been confused yesterday, and I never gave him the chance to finish explaining.

I don't know if that would've helped. And I have no idea if I want to reconcile with him. All right, I want to do that. But I'm afraid of letting him in again only to have him walk away like he did before. He swears he loves me, but I can't shake the fear.

The long table still sits in the middle of the room, near the bed, where Luke had put it. I wander over to the table and run my fingers over the smooth wood surface. Have I been too rigid? Demanding Luke admit his tests showed something unexplainable? I've accused him of being unwilling to believe, but I might've done the same thing in reverse by expecting him to accept the supernatural.

"What are you doing up here?"

The sound of Luke's voice pulls me out of my thoughts, and I raise my head to look at him. "You're here."

"So are you." He shoves his hands into his trouser pockets. "But why are you in this room? I would've thought it's the last place you'd want to be, but Evan said he thought you were heading up here."

I might've mumbled something to Evan about going up to the tower bedroom, but I didn't think he'd heard me. "Why are you here? I told you to go away and never come back."

"Yeah, but I couldn't leave things the way they were. I need to tell you the rest, so at least you'll have all the facts before you kick me to the curb."

"All right." I shuffle over to the bed and sit on its edge, my feet hanging several inches off the floor. "I'm listening."

Why did I sit on the bed? That might imply I want to have sex with him again. I stifle a groan. I'm turning into a bampot for sure. Seeing me sitting here will not convince Luke that I want him to tear my clothes off.

He settles onto the chair he'd sat in during our experiments, his posture slumped. "Six months ago, I made a big mistake. Melvin tasked me with submitting a grant application to a foundation that's known for giving big bucks to scientific studies. But I screwed up. Thought the deadline was still a week away, and I missed it. It looked like the institute had lost out on two million pounds of juicy grant money."

"That's awful, but you didn't do it on purpose. And I don't see how this relates to what happened yesterday."

"I'm getting there." He rubs his forehead, slumping further in his chair. "Melvin managed to sweet-talk the foundation into giving us another chance, and the institute got the money after all. But Melvin threatened to fire me for my screw-up unless I promised to owe him a favor that he could call in anytime he wanted. Whatever he asked me to do, I would do it without questioning him. Honestly, I never could've imagined what he would do with that IOU. Took six months before he saw his opportunity."

"Why didn't you just quit your job?"

"Tried to find another position, anywhere, but I couldn't. Other organizations always wanted references, and of course, Melvin made sure to tank that for me. He liked having me under his thumb."

I slide off the bed and walk over to him, leaning my hip against the table. "Is that why you agreed to help him debunk me? Because he held that one mistake over your head and made sure you couldn't get another job? I don't quite understand why that gave him so much power over you, though."

"Neither did I, until the day I left for Scotland." Luke stares down at his lap, rubbing his palms on his thighs. "That's when Melvin announced he'd fabricated evidence that I stole the two million pounds the institute got from that foundation. He paid some hacker to do it since Melvin isn't exactly a computer genius. Together, they made it look like I'm an embezzler. The money did disappear, apparently. I'm guessing Melvin took it, though I can't prove that."

Suddenly, I'm beginning to see the whole picture. Luke, the lonely orphan boy, might have grown into an intelligent and strong man, but those old fears creep back in now and then. Melvin's blackmail and the incident yesterday had upset Luke more than he probably realizes. The events at my shop had affected me too, leaving me shaken and confused. But I have my family to support me—my large extended family, not just my brother, my sisters, and my parents. Luke has no one. Logan and Magnus seem to have taken him under their collective wing, but I don't think Luke feels completely at ease with the MacTaggarts, not yet.

Given his past, I shouldn't be surprised that he let Melvin Prickett use him. Luke doesn't want to be alone, though I doubt he would ever admit to that. And I kept saying I hated him.

He needs reassurance, not recriminations.

But I don't know if I should be the one to give him that. Aye, my own fears are getting in the way too.

"I understand why you lied to me," I say. "But I think we both need time to think about things, about us, about whether what we feel for each other is real."

"Think? I've done too much of that lately. It's time for action."

"Let's not make any decisions about us until things have settled down. I'll be here for you as a friend to help you through the fallout from the Melvin rubbish, but I can't say how I'll feel about things after that."

"No, I didn't think you'd jump into my arms and say you love me." Luke levers himself out of the chair and pushes it away. "But here's the thing you need to know about me, Kirsty. I'm not afraid anymore. Yesterday, I slugged Melvin and told him I don't care if he gets me sent to jail because I will not be his stooge anymore. Rory, Evan, and Logan are working on finding proof Melvin faked those files that showed I embezzled the money. I trust them. They'll get it done."

"Aye, they will. All the MacTaggarts will help, I'm sure."

He clasps my hands. "Listen to me, Kirsty. I am not leaving. Magnus has offered to let me stay with him until I get things sorted out."

"Magnus? I didn't know you two were mates."

"Not sure if we are, but he invited me to stay at his house. That's where I'll be." Luke raises our hands between us. "I love you, Kirsty, and I am never leaving, not unless you're with me. If I have to knock on your door every day for ten years, I'll do it. You can have me arrested for stalking, and still, I won't go away. No more running and hiding. Whatever it takes, I will show you how much you mean to me."

"Luke, I don't know—"

"I believe in you, Kirsty." He moves closer, holding our hands to his chest. "Sorry I didn't say that yesterday. I wanted to, but everything was so confusing then. Today, it's crystal clear. I love you, and I will do anything to prove that to you. Can't say if I'll ever believe in the things you do, but I will always respect your beliefs from this moment on. That's what love is, right? Respect and commitment—and understanding."

Luke has never spoken with such conviction before. The look on his face convinces me he means every word.

But when I open my mouth to say that, he silences me with two fingers on my lips. "Not yet. Take your time thinking about it. But I will be back, every day, wherever you are, until I can prove my commitment to you."

"That's not necessary."

"Yes, it is." He kisses my forehead. "I have to go now. Got some stuff to take care of. I promise I'll be back soon to tell you about everything."

Luke turns away, aiming for the door.

Just as he reaches the threshold, I say, "I'll be waiting."

He flashes me the sweetest smile I've ever seen and walks out the door.

Chapter Thirty-Two

Luke

Let me get this straight," I say. "In the space of six hours, you guys managed to not only find the proof that Melvin falsified those computer files, but you also managed to get the cops down in England to arrest him for embezzlement. You've got to be pulling my leg. Nobody could pull that off so fast."

I'm sitting in Magnus's kitchen with the demon biker and his two cousins, Logan and Evan. After a sleepless night and an entire morning of waiting, I'm finally hearing the news I've waited for.

Logan chuckles. "Havenae ye learned anything in the past few days? We're the MacTaggarts. When we see a problem that needs fixing, we get to work."

"Yeah, but six hours? That's impossible."

"Very little is impossible if you're willing to spend obscene amounts of money to get it done." Logan nods toward Evan. "Having a billionaire on hand doesn't hurt."

Magnus grunts, which I think might be his way of laughing. "Neither does having a former MI6 operative."

"Or a bounty hunter," Logan says. "Your connections played a large part in our success today, though it was Evan's computer skills that clinched it."

"Are you guys done patting each other on the back?" I ask. "Because I need to know that I am definitely not ever going to prison."

"You aren't," Evan says. "Relax, Luke. Melvin has been arrested, and based on the evidence we all provided, he will be convicted for sure."

Magnus pulls out his cell phone, taps the screen a few times, and rotates it toward me. "Here's the proof, laddie."

The image on the screen shows Dr. Melvin Prickett, in handcuffs, his head down, being escorted to a police car. Reporters encircle my former boss and his new best buddies as they hurry to the car that will take dear old Mel to his new digs—the kind with metal bars. Now that's poetic justice. Melvin sicced sleazoid reporters on Kirsty, and now he's being hounded by the same sort of scumbags.

Magnus scrolls the screen up. "You'll like this."

At the top of the web page that included the photo, I see a headline: "British scientist arrested for embezzlement."

Oh yeah, that's poetic justice all right.

"Don't know how to thank you guys," I say. "You stepped up to help in a big way, though I know you did it for Kirsty."

"We did it for both of you," Logan says. "My sister is in love with you, and I'm not completely opposed to the idea anymore. In fact, I doubt I'll skelp you anytime soon."

"Gee, thanks. I guess that's high praise coming from you."

Maybe I've sort of bonded with these weird guys. After what they've done for me today, I know I can trust them with my life—and Kirsty's. Strange as they are, MacTaggarts really do get the job done by whatever means necessary, though they never hurt anyone who didn't have it coming. Melvin sure deserved it.

I'm not going to be a felon. Awesome. But my most important task still lies ahead of me.

I clear my throat. "So, Evan, have you thought about what I asked you this morning?"

"Aye, and I made a decision." He pulls an envelope out of his back pocket and offers it to me. "Here it is."

"Here what is? I asked if you could buy Efrica MacTaggart's diary from Mungo, but that envelope isn't big enough to hold a book."

Evan tosses the envelope to me. "I spoke to Iain earlier, and he believes Mungo will sell the book—if you make the offer. I just gave you a check for five thousand pounds, made out to Mungo Gunn."

"Five thousand?"

"That's the amount Iain and I decided on. The diary might not be worth that much at auction, but if you want to be sure Mungo will sell, we recommend offering a high price."

"Guess that makes sense." I remember what Evan said a minute ago and have to ask, "Why did you say that I need to make the offer?"

"Mungo won't talk to MacTaggarts anymore. You stand the best chance of accomplishing the mission."

"Aye," Logan says. "Unless you're afraid to visit the barmy bloke on your own."

"Hey, I slugged my old boss and let a crowd of sleazoids chase me through Loch Fairbairn. Mungo doesn't scare me."

"We'll see."

Magnus tosses me a keyring that has one key attached to it. "Take my car. It's faster than Logan's or Evan's."

"Thanks. What kind of car is it?"

"You'll see. I parked it out front when I got back from Dùndubhan."

"How is Kirsty?"

"She's fine." Magnus waves a hand. "Go, laddie, before that bampot destroys Efrica's diary."

I rush outside to Magnus's car and almost trip over my own feet when I see what kind of wheels the demon biker owns. I guess I expected something super cool, the kind of car that might show up in a Bond movie. But no, that's not what Magnus has. It's a normal, boring four-door sedan with a boring gray paint job. It looks relatively new, though, and capable of getting me where I need to go.

Someone chuckles behind me. "Not what you expected, eh?"

"Not exactly." I glance back at Magnus. "This is seriously what you drive."

"Aye, when I'm at home. Which isn't often. That's why I bought an inexpensive car. I upgraded the engine, though, so it can get you where you need to be as fast as you need to get there."

"Thanks for lending me your wheels." I climb into the car and start up the engine, then roll down the window. "Keep your fingers crossed that Mungo will sell me the diary."

"Donnae ever cross my fingers. That implies I believe in luck, which I don't."

"Yeah, neither do I." Or maybe I'm starting to believe in it, but I don't want to tell Magnus that.

He opens the garage door for me, and I'm on my way. The app on my phone that gives directions tells me exactly how to find Mungo's house again. It's not as far outside the village of Loch Fairbairn as I thought it was the first time we came here. Kirsty had driven then, and I hadn't paid much attention to the path we took.

With Evan's check in my pocket, I knock on Mungo's door.

Nothing happens.

I don't see a doorbell, so I knock again—harder this time.

Still nothing.

The smell of smoke wafts over me, faint but distinct, and I hear soft crackling noises that seem to be coming from behind the house. I make my way around the structure, and the closer I get to the backyard, the stronger the smoke smell gets and the louder the crackling becomes. By the time I round the back corner of the house into the yard, I can see

Mungo. He's standing in front of a small bonfire, tossing sticks into the flames with one hand.

And he's holding the diary in his other hand.

"Hey, Mungo," I say, trying to sound cheerful and friendly. "How's it going?"

The Scot swerves his head to stare at me without blinking. "Who are you? Why have you invaded my home?"

"We've met before. Don't you remember? I'm Luke Turner. My friends Iain and Kirsty came with me to see Efrica MacTaggart's diary."

He relaxes visibly and faces the bonfire again. "Oh aye, you. What do ye want?"

"To make you an offer. For the diary."

Mungo huffs. "Too late. Ahm doing what I should've done ages ago. I'm burning the bloody thing."

"Please don't. I can pay you five thousand pounds for the diary."

He glowers at me. "Ye think money can break the hex? Away and boil yer head, Sassenach."

I know Sassenach is a derogatory term for a Brit, but I'm American. Still, pointing that out seems like a bad idea right now. I need this nutjob to sell me the book. How can I convince him when he thinks the diary is cursed? I don't like the idea of manipulating him, but it's not manipulation if I don't lie. Right? Everything I'm about to say could be true. Nobody knows if it is or not.

"Did you ever think," I tell him, "that maybe you don't need to destroy the diary to end the hex? It was written by a MacTaggart, so maybe giving it back to them will do the trick. I'll still pay you for the diary. Then I'll give it to Kirsty MacTaggart, who's a good witch. She would know how to remove the hex, I'm sure. She's very smart and knowledgeable about magic."

"Ahmno sure," Mungo says cautiously. "How do I know I can trust you?"

"Tell you what, I'll give you the check right now." I walk toward him, holding out the envelope. "If Kirsty can't remove the curse, you can destroy the book and keep the check."

Can't believe I just said that. I'm placing all my faith in things I don't believe in, like witchcraft and this guy's sanity. It's my only play. If this goes sideways... Well, Kirsty would probably have dumped me again anyway.

"Donnae know," Mungo says, narrowing his gaze on me. "You are a stranger, one who's joined the MacTaggart side."

I step a little closer and thrust the envelope at him. "Take the check. Then maybe we can sit down and talk about things."

He studies my hand for a moment, then takes the envelope.

Thank goodness. The crazy guy accepted my offer.

Mungo bends down to pick up a half-empty bottle of booze. Straightening, he takes a swig and stuffs the envelope into his pants pocket.

Is he drunk? It's hard to tell since he'd acted this way the first time we met too. Maybe he'd been drunk and high on pot then.

He raises the diary over the nearest flames. "No MacTaggart will ever touch this devil's bible!"

Mungo hurls the whiskey bottle into the fire, making it surge higher, and he throws the diary at the flames.

I don't think about it. Consumed by the need to save Kirsty's family history, I rush forward to snag the book before the fire touches it and come so close to the blaze that the heat scorches my face. My foot bumps into a thick chunk of burning wood. I stumble, stagger sideways, and careen out of the way just as the flames lick out toward me. But I lose my balance and tumble to the ground, rolling away from the bonfire.

"Shit, Mungo," I holler at him. "I almost got toasted Cajun style. Didn't anybody ever tell you not to play with fire?"

Jumping up, I brush myself off—and realize I've still got the diary in my hand. Thank goodness.

Mungo's eyes have gone wide, and he gapes at the fire. "Didnae mean to—I should put that out."

He jogs into the house.

I slip the diary into my shirt pocket for safekeeping. Though I'd love to take a peek at its contents, I won't do that until I've given the book to Kirsty. It's her family history, not mine.

Mungo returns carrying a wooden box filled with bottles of clear liquid. He sets the box down and pulls out several bottles, holding two in each hand, then hurls them into the fire. The glass shatters when it hits the pieces of wood that make up the blaze, splashing liquid onto the flames.

The fire erupts higher.

"What the hell are you doing?" I demand.

Mungo shakes his head. "No, water is meant to douse the fire."

I race over to him and snatch away the two bottles he just picked up, clearly intending to toss them onto the blaze too. But the sudden eruption of higher flames seems to have stunned him to the point of paralysis. I look at the labels on the bottles. "This is vodka, you idiot, not water. It's a hundred and fifty proof. You could've flambéed us both."

He stares blankly at the flames. "Oh."

"Yeah, 'oh.' Do you have a hose or a fire extinguisher?"

Mungo just stares at the flames.

I grasp his shoulders and shake. "We need to douse the bonfire, Mungo. Where's the hose?"

"Over there." He gestures vaguely toward the other end of the backyard.

A few minutes later, I've tamped down the fire until it's just some glowing embers and a lot of charcoal. Don't feel like I should leave Mungo here alone with the still-smoldering embers, so I call Logan for help. He says Magnus and their cousin Callum can get here faster than the fire brigade since the nearest station is at someplace called Kinlochleven, about half an hour from Loch Fairbairn. Besides, this isn't exactly an emergency. Since it's not a raging bonfire anymore, and I just need somebody to babysit Mungo the arsonist, sending two men seems a bit excessive. Logan told me Callum, who's Jack's brother, used to be a firefighter. He ought to know how to manage the remnants of Mungo's inferno.

Logan also told me I'd know when Magnus and Callum arrived "because of the noise."

I have no idea what that means—until I hear a sound reminiscent of a jet engine, drawing closer and growing louder every second. The ruckus sputters out just as it sounds like whatever vehicle made the noise has arrived. I jog around the house to the driveway.

Two men are dismounting a large, black motorcycle and removing their full-face helmets, revealing their faces. Magnus had been in front with Callum seated behind him.

As the two men approach me, I give Magnus a wry smile. "Thought you didn't own a motorcycle."

"I don't." He nods toward the other Scot. "This is Callum's machine, but he let me drive."

The other man steps up to me and offers his hand. "Callum MacTaggart. It's nice to finally meet you, Luke, since I've heard all sorts of blethering about you."

"Uh-huh," I say as I shake his hand. "Nice to meet you too. Is that a Harley?"

"Aye, it is. My cousin Evan gave it to me last year after an American mate suggested the idea. It was a birthday present." He grins. "Always wanted a Harley."

"That's one hot machine you've got."

"Did ye get the diary?" Magnus asks.

I pat my shirt pocket. "Right here. I want to get this to Kirsty right away. You guys mind if I split? Mungo's out back with his fire safety demonstration."

"Go on. We'll take care of the bampot."

"Thanks, guys. I appreciate this."

"Kirsty is at her house now."

I jump in the car and head for Kirsty's place. Whatever happens next, at least I will have kept my promise and helped her find information related to Kieran.

Chapter Thirty-Three

Kirsty

I've been home for fifteen minutes when the doorbell rings. It's probably Jack and Autumn coming to cheer me up or some such rubbish. I don't need anyone to make me feel better. All I need is for Luke to come back so I can tell him I never wanted him to leave. I said all that bollocks back in the shop because I was in shock. Since then, I've realized why he kept secrets from me. The man who has never had a family and got bounced from one foster home to another doesn't want to risk being abandoned again.

But I will never do that to him. And I know he will never leave me either. I don't think Luke realizes, consciously, how much his past still affects him.

When I hear the doorbell, I rush out of the kitchen and fling the door open.

Luke gives me a guarded smile. "Hey, Kirsty. I, uh, got something for you."

He thrusts a hand out, offering me a small book.

"The diary?" I say, hardly able to believe it. "Mungo gave it to you?"

"Not exactly. Evan ponied up five thousand pounds to buy the diary from Mungo. We had a mini-disaster involving a bonfire, but everything worked out in the end."

"Bonfire?"

"I'll tell you the whole story later." He thrusts the book toward me again. "This is yours. We all agreed the diary should go to you, as its guardian, though it belongs to the whole family."

"Aye, it does."

Though Luke still holds the diary, I reach a hand out to skim my finger over the worn leather cover.

A visible spark snaps across the cover and jolts us both.

"What was that?" Luke asks, eying the book warily. "Static electricity?"

"Maybe." I take the book from him. "Or maybe it was magic. The spirit of Efrica MacTaggart giving us her blessing."

"By trying to electrocute us?"

"No, silly. That was a spark." I wink. "Like the one we've always had sizzling between us."

He raises his brows.

I skim my fingers over the book again. "I'm almost afraid to read this. What if Kieran *was* an evil witch?"

"No way. You MacTaggarts are the best people on earth." He hunches his shoulders and averts his gaze. "Should I go?"

"Of course not." I grasp his shirt and drag him across the threshold, our bodies almost touching. "I love you, Luke. I want to be with you, only you, from this day on."

His gaze flicks to me. "I hope you mean that, because I want to be with you too. I'm completely in love with you, Kirsty."

"We should read this book together."

"You want me to see it too? Wouldn't you rather have one of your sisters here with you when you read the diary?"

I strap an arm around him, pulling his body snugly against mine. "No, Luke, I want you to read it with me. After all, I would never have found this diary or researched Kieran at all if not for you. Maybe the book sparked because we were both touching it, and the spirit of Efrica wants us to do this together."

"Not sure about the hocus-pocus angle, but I'd be honored to experience the diary with you."

We go into the living room and sit on the sofa side by side. I lean my head against his shoulder while we lay the book on our laps with half of it on my thigh and half on his. Luke turns each page gently as we begin our perusal of the sixteenth-century diary of my ancestor, who was a witch in her own right. At first, the entries have no bearing on the mystery of Kieran, but the slant of the narrative gradually shifts as events in the wider world become more and more relevant to Efrica's life in a remote part of the Highlands. The fervor driving the witch trials elsewhere in Great Britain hasn't reached the Highlands at this point, but I sense the danger approaching.

In fifteen ninety-four, Kieran comes to live with his three aunts in the abandoned castle they have inhabited for ten years. Their nephew was banished from his clan because someone framed him for stealing from other family members, though Kieran says, and Efrica believes him, that he did not commit the crimes. His father had no choice but to banish Kieran to avoid strife within the clan. Not much happens for a few years after that—until fifteen ninety-eight. That's when Simidh Gunn accuses Kieran of witchcraft. By then, the witch-trial insanity has crept into the Highlands, though the fervor never reached the catastrophic proportions seen in England.

But it's enough. A witchfinder is called in, and Kieran is convicted.

Despite the horrific events around her, Efrica keeps writing in her diary. She shares her fears for Kieran and her grief when he is executed. I feel like I'm reliving the past through Efrica's eyes, and I can envision every horrific thing she witnessed. The terrible truth of it all affects me more strongly than I would've expected, making tears gather in my eyes.

Luke folds an arm around me and kisses my temple. "I know it's a sad story, but you shouldn't cry. This happened a long time ago."

"I know. But I feel a connection with Efrica and Kieran. Can't explain why. It's like we're kindred spirits, but I'm sure you think that's nonsense."

"No, I think it's nice that you have a long family history. I can't understand what that feels like, but I'm glad you have it. The MacTaggarts are something else."

I lift my gaze from the book to his face. "You have a family, Luke. You're an honorary MacTaggart, and when we get married, you'll be an official one."

"Get married? Are you proposing?"

"No, that's your job. But I have *da-shealladh*, and I've foreseen when and where you will ask the question." I touch my lips to his. "The answer will be yes."

"Is that your standard prediction? You said the same thing to Logan."

"Don't get too cheeky with me. I might decide to flout my *da-shealladh* and say no."

"Hmm." He cups my cheek and kisses me, though he keeps it soft and tender. "So, my sexy little witch-kitten, what exactly did you foresee? Where and when will I beg you to marry me?"

"I'll tell Logan, and he can tell you after it's done. Wouldn't prove I have witchy powers if I told you in advance, now would it?"

"Good point." He kisses me again, then focuses on the diary. "Guess Kieran's story is over, but the diary goes on after that."

"Aye. Let's see what Efrica says next." I turn the page, and a tingle sweeps over me. "Luke, do you see this? Efrica says Kieran's daughter was born six months after his execution. The mother's name isn't mentioned. But then she says..."

Luke leans forward to squint at the text. "She says he's not dead. But we saw his grave, and she said he was executed."

"I know. It doesn't make sense." I turn to the next page, but it's blank. Flipping through the rest of the diary, I find all of it is blank except for the last ten pages. "This is a genealogy of the MacTaggart family, starting in the thirteenth century and continuing until the Highland clearances began."

"Highland clearances?"

"That's when the British forced many of the Highlanders out of their homes." I browse the family tree, which traces Kieran's bloodline down through the centuries and ends with a name I recognize. "This is my ancestor, Niall, who my Uncle Niall is named after. According to this information, I'm a direct descendant of Kieran MacTaggart."

"Maybe that's the real reason you and your sisters became Wiccans. It's in your blood."

"Are you implying it might've been fate?"

"Let's not go overboard. I'm not riding the Wicca train just yet. All I'm saying is... I don't know." He smirks. "Maybe being a kook is a family trait."

"Donnae tease me. I might cast a spell over you."

"Baby, you did that on the day we met. I've been spellbound ever since."

As I consider the mystery of Kieran's apparent rebirth, an idea hits me. "We should ring Iain and get his help in looking inside Kieran's grave. Iain told me once that ground-penetrating radar can detect what's under the earth."

"Let's discuss that later, kitten." Luke sets the diary on the coffee table and eases me down to lie on the sofa. "We need to have some serious make-up sex."

"Aye. We can worry about my ancestor later. But maybe we should start looking into your family."

"I don't need to do that. Knowing who provided the genes that created me doesn't change who I am. And you MacTaggarts are becoming like family to me."

Aye, even my brother has accepted Luke. He will join the clan soon enough, I'm certain of that.

The next morning, we get a surprising call from Iain.

"It's about Mungo," he says, sounding stunned, which isn't like Iain at all. He's the calm one, the cousin we all refer to as Buddha MacTaggart.

"What about him?" I ask.

"Is Luke there? If he is, I think you should put me on speaker."

"Aye, he's here." I switch to the speakerphone. "We can both hear you."

"Good." Iain hesitates, then sighs. "I don't know how to explain it, but Mungo is normal."

"I don't understand."

"He's not a nutter anymore. Mungo rang me early this morning because he wanted to tell me that giving you the diary lifted the Gunn curse. He's in his right mind again."

Luke and I glance at each other, both shaking our heads, too confused to say anything for several seconds.

"Have you talked to him in person?" Luke finally asks.

"Aye, I'm in his house right now. Mungo is fine. He's like he used to be until he turned twenty-eight. That was seven years ago. But now…" Iain makes a huffing sound, as if he can't believe his own words. "Today, Mungo Gunn is his old self again."

"I'm so happy for him," I say. "Please tell Mungo we wish him well."

"Aye, I will."

Iain says goodbye, and Luke and I just stare at each other in befuddlement for a minute or two.

Did returning the diary to the MacTaggart clan save Mungo from his mental illness? We will never know for certain. Luke doesn't even try to explain away Mungo's recovery. His response reveals how much he has changed, from a closed-minded scientist to a man who realizes the world is full of both facts and mysteries.

"I guess it's a miracle," Luke says. "Not sure I believe in that, but I can't offer any alternative explanation. And I don't want to, not anymore."

Aye, everything has changed.

Chapter Thirty-Four

Luke

Two days later, we gather around Kieran's grave with Iain, Magnus, Logan, Isla, and Elspeth. Lots of other MacTaggarts wanted to join the graveside party, but we decided to keep it informal and small. This is a solemn occasion, but also an exciting one. Did Kieran die? If not, how did he survive his execution? At least we can find out if Kieran is buried here or not.

Iain borrowed a ground-penetrating radar device from a colleague at the university where he works. The thing looks kind of like a lawn mower with a computer screen attached to the handle. Iain rolls the machine over the grave slowly, making several parallel passes to ensure he doesn't miss anything important. Once he's done, we wait while he uses a laptop to process the data.

At first, he focuses on the screen with a grim expression that I take for intense concentration. Finally, his lips curve into a self-satisfied smile and he looks at Kirsty. "There are no human remains in that grave."

Kirsty and I both whoop and jump up and down, though I have no idea why. Her ancestor isn't buried in the grave that supposedly belongs to him, which means we still have no clue what happened to him. Why are we happy? I guess it's joy that we found evidence of…nothing. Another mystery to solve. Yeah, that's a reason to celebrate. I've discovered I love hunting for clues with Kirsty.

That's right. The guy who doesn't believe in magic and who cherishes facts loves uncovering another riddle in need of solving.

"Why are ye so happy?" Logan asks. "Your search resulted in nothing."

"No," I say, as I finally stop laughing. "It resulted in proof that Kieran was not buried here, which means Efrica might've been right that he didn't die."

"But you said he was executed."

"Apparently." I pull Kirsty against my side and look down at her. "Now we have more mysteries to solve."

She smiles sweetly. "Thought you hated those, but now you're looking forward to exploring the enigma of Kieran MacTaggart."

"That's right." To everyone else, I say, "Kirsty and I have some personal stuff to talk about. We'll see you later at the party."

"It's a ceilidh," Logan says.

"Which is a big party with dancing and drinks. Right?"

"Aye," Magnus says. "Scottish dancing. That means ye need to wear a kilt."

"Oh, I know that. Logan already loaned me one to wear for the par—the ceilidh."

Logan scoffs. "I didn't loan you anything. It was a gift."

"Really? Thanks, Logan."

"You're a MacTaggart now, or ye soon will be, so ye needed the proper attire."

We all wander back to our cars, and Kirsty and I split away from the others. I drive us away, toward a secret destination. After all, I can't find out for sure if she genuinely knows when and where I'm going to do this if I tell her where we're going. Maybe it's silly to drive four hours away just to propose to my girlfriend, but I wanted to make this special, something we'll both remember for the rest of our lives. Besides, the site I have in mind seems like exactly the kind of thing Kirsty will appreciate.

Halfway to our destination, we stop to have a picnic in a scenic spot. Kirsty tries to seduce information out of me, but I don't tell her a thing, not even after we have sex in a heather-covered meadow. Then we get back on the road. We stop once more, to gas up the car, and I insist on blindfolding her for the rest of the journey just to make sure she can't figure out where we're going via mundane means. She'll have to use her second sight, if she really has that, to divine our destination. It's only about fifteen minutes away now, according to the map software on my phone.

"You know I love a mystery," Kirsty says, "but I'm starting to get motion sickness from being blindfolded while you swerve every which way. I might sick up my breakfast."

"Guess that means 'throw up,' hey?"

"Aye."

"We're almost there, promise."

The narrow road that skirts our destination also passes close by a loch, but we aren't going there. I don't see any actual parking lot, just a section where the road gets a bit wider, so I assume that's where visitors park. Once I've pulled over and shut off the engine, Kirsty tries to remove the blindfold.

I stop her by batting her hand away from her face. "Not yet, kitten. We're so close you could smell it, if this place had a smell. We need to walk from here, but I won't let you fall. Do you trust me?"

"Completely."

"Then relax and let me lead the way."

I climb out of the car—the Jaguar, naturally, which Rory and Emery let us borrow again—and open Kirsty's door for her. Then I take her hand to help her get out. I've got a backpack slung over one shoulder, but I won't tell her about that yet. It's a surprise. We take it slow, since getting to where we're going requires navigating a boardwalk that accesses the marshy site. I hadn't realized how far we'd need to go to reach our destination, but I know it will be worth the effort. I keep my arm around Kirsty's waist to guide her down the boardwalk, but soon we've reached the end. I help her step off the wood planks, and as we approach the structure before us, I turn her to face what we came here to see.

"Before I take off the blindfold," I say, "tell me where you think we are."

She pulls in a deep breath, releasing it slowly, and a slight smile tugs at her lips. "The Grey Cairns of Camster. The Long Cairn, to be precise."

"Holy shit. How did you know? Did Logan tell you?"

"Did you tell him where we were going?"

"Uh, no. I didn't tell anybody."

Her smile broadens. "I wrote down my prediction and put the sheet of paper in an envelope, which I sealed with wax. Call Logan and ask him to open the envelope so he can tell you what I wrote."

I remove the blindfold first, then dial Logan's number.

"You're wanting the proof, aye?" Logan declares before I can say hello.

"That's right. Kirsty said you have the sealed envelope with her prediction in it."

"I do." A ripping sound ensues, which suggests he's tearing open that envelope. "Here it is. Kirsty wrote that you'd be taking her to the Grey Cairns of Camster, today, and the pair of you would be standing in front of the Long Cairn at two thirty-eight p.m."

A quick glance at my watch confirms it's now two thirty-nine. Since it took a minute or so to call Logan and get his response, Kirsty's time prediction was amazingly accurate.

"Thanks, Logan," I say. "See you later at the ceilidh."

"Donnae forget your kilt. Cheers, Luke."

Logan MacTaggart just said goodbye to me in a way that did not imply he wants to murder me. That might just qualify as genuine acceptance of me.

Now it's time to do what I came here for.

I drop to one knee in front of Kirsty, pull out a velvet box, and flip it open so I can hold it up for her to see the diamond ring nestled inside it. "I love you, Kirsty, and I couldn't think of a more appropriate place to do this. After all, you are a sexy witch, and this is a mystical, ancient site where pagans probably conducted rituals. Even if I never believe in second sight or any of that other mystical stuff, I will always love and respect you. Can't imagine spending my life with anyone else."

She bites her lip while tears glisten in her pale blue eyes.

I lift the ring box higher, near her left hand. "Will you marry me, Kirsty?"

"Aye, of course I will, ye dafty." She wiggles the third finger of her left hand. "Put the bloody ring on there already."

The fact she's crying and smiling tells me her insults are affectionate, but I would've known that anyway. She has a right to tease me about this, after the way I'd behaved twelve years ago and again when we were first reunited.

I slip the ring onto her finger. "No more secrets, no more running away. I'm in this for life."

"So am I."

Rising, I pull her into my arms and kiss her.

When we finally peel our lips apart, she asks, "What next? You must have a plan, maybe for another experiment."

"How did you know? Either you do have second sight, or you just know me better than anyone else."

"A bit of both."

"I can accept that."

Her brows rise, then she smiles. "You've opened your mind to the wider world, haven't you? I don't expect you will ever become a Wiccan, but I'm glad you've found a way to accept my beliefs."

"Science is about facts, but I've learned lately that it's also about being open to new possibilities." I clasp Kirsty's hand to lead her closer to the cairn. It's composed of gray stones that don't seem to have any mortar between them, and I see two entrances that look too small to accommodate a full-grown man—or a full-grown woman. "If you're game, I'd like to conduct another experiment."

"Here?"

"Yes." I drop my backpack on the ground. "I brought my equipment."

"What sort of experiment did you have in mind this time?"

"I want to measure your neural activity while you do a Wiccan ritual."

She laughs, but it sounds affectionate rather than sarcastic. "More electrodes? All right, if that's what you want. But since I'm cooperating with your experiments, I think you should cooperate with my magic."

"Anything you want, kitten."

We sit down near one of the entrances to the Long Cairn, which is called that because the structure stretches out lengthwise across the landscape. Not far away, I can see the Round Cairn. Its name is fairly obvious too.

Kirsty sits cross-legged, hands on her knees, with her palms turned up. She touches her thumbs to her forefingers in the way I've seen people do when they meditate.

I bring out my gear and place an electrode cap on her head, then secure the strap under her chin. "This is basically an EEG. It measures neural activity through the sensors in the cap."

As I hook the digitizer up to the cap, Kirsty watches me with faint amusement.

"You think this is funny?" I ask while I plug the digitizer into my laptop.

"No, I think it's adorable." She slides a hand up my thigh. "And sexy."

"Please control your lust, kitten. This is a scientific experiment, not hot sex in front of an ancient burial mound."

"The ancients were clearly pagans, which means they must've worshiped the Sacred Feminine. Sex is an important part of that concept."

"Ah, so being a Wiccan is just an excuse to get naked with your fiancé. I knew it."

She slides her hand higher until it brushes my dick. "Do I need an excuse?"

"Never. Just give me that sexy smile again, and I'll strip you naked."

"Don't you want to do your experiment first? I'm ready to meditate for you."

I chuckle. "Got a better idea. And I'd much rather watch you come for me." While Kirsty observes, I finish setting up the equipment. "Time to get naked. Unless you're worried about someone seeing us."

"Donnae care."

She wriggles out of her clothes while staying seated on the ground, but I stand up to shed mine.

Now that we're both au naturel, I kneel beside her. "Ready to show me how a witchy sex ritual affects your neural activity?"

"Oh aye, please."

I grab my pants and dig out one of the condom packets I'd stashed in there.

Kirsty stays my hand with hers. "We're getting married, and I'm taking birth control pills, so why don't we skip the condom?"

"Love the way you think, baby."

She lies down on her back while I stretch out alongside her, and I begin my kind of worship. I pay homage to every inch of her body, kissing and licking my way down her skin, from her lips to her toes. I capture her nipples and suck on them until she gasps, then tease her navel with my tongue. She grips my head when I dip it between her thighs to feast on her cream, and when I suckle her clit, she writhes beneath me. When I sense she's on the verge of orgasm, I pull my mouth away and plunge my cock into her silky sheath.

"Oh Luke," she says, "I love the way you feel inside me."

I thrust in a slow rhythm, taking my time to experience every sensation, from her cream coating my cock to the hairs on her mound tickling my balls. Every moment with Kirsty brings a new revelation and opens me up in ways I never imagined were possible. Maybe she does have witchy powers because I've never enjoyed sex with any other woman as intensely as I love being with Kirsty.

She grips my biceps and rolls her hips into my thrusts, her moans escalating into cries that echo off the cairn. I push harder and faster as the need to come inside her body grows too powerful to resist. But I need her to jump off that cliff with me. So I reach down to part her folds and rub her clit until she's thrashing and crying out even louder. We come at the same time, like our bodies are in perfect sync, and we shout each other's names while her muscles grip my cock in rhythmic waves. Once she's done, I pound into her one more time, groaning as I release everything I have, like a ritual offering to the woman I adore. Then I drop onto the ground beside her.

Kirsty rolls over to lie half on top of me, her cheek on my chest.

I skate a hand down her back, but lift it when I notice something. "We're both dirty, kitten."

"That's what happens when you shag me on the ground."

"Not complaining. I love getting dirty with you." I palm her ass. "Let's do that again, but up against the cairn this time."

She grins, and I know we both want the same thing. Sex, yes. But more than that, we want to explore mysteries together. Answers? Don't need those. After all, the future is nothing but one big unsolved riddle.

After our long journey home, to the house we'll share from this day forward, it's time to change into our party outfits. The ceilidh will begin in less than an hour, which gives us just enough time to reach Dùndubhan. It's the only place to hold a proper Scottish party.

Kirsty helps me get my kilt on, since I've never worn one before. Then she takes two steps backward to admire my plaid skirt. "Donnae tell anyone

I said this, but you look better in the MacTaggart tartan than any man in my family does."

"Yeah, we should keep that to ourselves."

She moves closer to finger the buckle on the belt that holds up my kilt. "I wish Magnus could've stayed for the ceilidh, but I understand he has a job to do."

"He promised he'd be back for our wedding. And I have no doubt Magnus always keeps his word."

"Aye." She grasps my belt and tugs me closer. "Should we have a quick poke before the ceilidh?"

"Hell yes."

What have I learned since coming to Scotland? Kirsty is the only woman for me, second chances do happen, MacTaggarts are weird in a good way, and not every riddle requires a solution. I won't give up science, but I no longer need to unravel every enigma until the last thread disintegrates. Instead, I'll spend the rest of my life exploring the most enchanting mystery of all.

Love.

Epilogue

Magnus
Montijo, Portugal
One Week Later

I ease the door inward and peer into the dimly lit hotel room, just to make sure my quarry hasn't returned ahead of schedule. The laddie at the front desk informed me the guest staying in this room had asked for directions to a nearby clothing shop, which means the unit should be empty, and he also gave me a key to this room. Aye, all I had to do was slip some euros into his palm. I learned a long time ago that a bounty hunter needs the freedom to use whatever means necessary to capture a dangerous fugitive. The people who hire me don't care how I trap my quarry provided nothing I do blows back on them.

As I steal into the room and shut the door, careful not to make a sound, I survey the space. One bed. A nightstand. A cramped bathroom. The occupant's belongings lie inside an open suitcase, though a few items are strewn across the bed. Someone slept here, as evidenced by the rumpled sheets. I conduct a quick search of the premises but find nothing of interest. The fugitive didn't leave behind anything incriminating, but then, only a dunderhead would make that mistake. Since I know my quarry went to a store not far from the hotel, I shouldn't have long to wait.

I position myself along the wall adjacent to the door. When it swings open, I'll be hidden from my quarry.

Footsteps clap on the concrete walkway.

My body tightens as anticipation awakens all my senses.

The footfalls cease, replaced by the distinctive sound of a key being inserted into the lock.

I curl my fingers into a loose fist, every muscle taut. This is it. As the door swings open, I flatten myself against the wall.

Someone walks into the room, and a shadow distends past the doorway. The familiar scent of vanilla perfume wafts over me.

My quarry steps into the room, shuffling past the door.

I slam the door shut.

The fugitive whirls around, eyes wide, jaw slack. "How—"

"How do ye think? You're clever, but not as clever as I am." I pull out my handcuffs. "Piper Lang, you are coming with me."

"Like hell I am." She stumbles backward, shaking her head, her coppery hair flapping around her face. She stares at me with her caramel eyes widening even more. "I'm not going anywhere with you."

"Did I suggest you have a choice?"

The shock fades as her expression hardens. Her gaze narrows.

And she pulls a small revolver out of her waistband, behind her back, raising it in front of her. "Get out of my way, MacTaggart."

Her hand is shaking. The tough act is just that—an act.

I take one large step toward her. The gun almost brushes my chest. "Last chance. Come willingly, or I'll do it by force."

Her lips tighten, and she pokes the gun into my chest. "Get out of my way, or I'll shoot you."

"Been shot before. Stabbed too." I lean into the gun's muzzle. "A wee lassie doesnae scare me."

"I got away from you once, I'll do it again."

Aye, only one fugitive ever got the better of me—Piper Lang. I won't let her wriggle away from me again.

I snatch the gun from her grasp and drop it on the floor. Then I snare her wrist and spin her around before she realizes what I mean to do, cuffing both her hands behind her back with one of mine. Tugging her into my body, I lash my other arm around her waist. "Willnae get away this time."

With her body pinned to mine, I have a clear view down her shirt where the low neckline reveals the mounds of her breasts. Not all of them, but enough to inflame my lust. The last time I saw Piper, she escaped by using her feminine wiles. For the first time in my entire career, my entire life, a lass got the better of me. Never again.

But I can't resist sliding my hand up her belly until it grazes her breasts.

She sucks in a breath. "Let me go, please."

Her voice is huskier now, and her nipples have gone hard, their peaks visible through her shirt.

"I don't let murderers go," I growl into her ear. "Ye should've considered the consequences before ye poisoned your boss so you could get a promotion."

"That's insane. I was an archivist at a museum, not next in line to be CEO of a mega-corporation."

"Greed is universal. And you should've wiped your fingerprints off the glass after you gave the man champagne laced with strychnine. But ye aren't that clever, are ye?"

"Outsmarted you, didn't I? The great Magnus MacTaggart screwed up."

The vanilla scent of her perfume surrounds me, the erotic aroma arousing more than my senses. My cock is getting hard too.

"I'm innocent," she says, her breasts rising and falling. "Someone framed me. I had to run because the cops wouldn't believe me. Please, you can't take me back to the UK. Everyone there thinks like you do, that I'm an American slut who tried to advance her career by seducing and killing her boss."

"Not my problem. I bring in fugitives, I don't try their cases in court."

"Just listen. Let me explain—"

"Donnae give a damn if you're guilty or innocent. I'm doing my job, full stop."

"But—"

I drag her to the bed and toss her onto it, reclaiming her wrists before she can process the action. I restrain her hands over her belly. She squirms and glowers at me. I hook one handcuff around her right wrist, then slide the other cuff through the rails in the headboard so I can snap it tight around her left wrist. "No slithering away from me this time."

"What are you going to do?"

I hadn't considered my next move, concerned only with detaining her. Capturing her. Winning the game. Aye, it's a dangerous game to play, but that's what makes it exciting. The thrill of the chase always gets me wound up, and often, I need a release after a particularly rough assignment. Never had I fucked a fugitive, though. Never until I caught Piper Lang seventeen months ago. Then I made the cardinal mistake.

I fell asleep after we shagged. The hunter let his guard down.

And my quarry ran away.

The last thing I should do is have another poke with her. But she's at my mercy now...

I crawl onto the bed, straddling her legs, and lean forward to brace my palms on the mattress at either side of her shoulders. "Ye want me to fuck ye."

"Ugh. I hate you."

"Donnae care if ye like me." I mold one hand to her breast, and her breath hitches. "But we both know you want me inside you."

"You are evil."

I chuckle. "Aye, but you like that. Wouldn't have seduced me last time if ye didn't."

"Maybe I…kind of like it. But I still hate you."

"Good." I drag my tongue up her throat. "Then ye'll be wanting me to take ye now."

Breathing hard, she bites down on her bottom lip.

"Say it," I growl. "Tell me what you want—really want—right here, right now."

The lass arches her back when I squeeze her tit. "Just hurry the hell up and do it, MacTaggart."

"Not until you beg for it."

She glares at me. "Told you to do it already."

I pinch her nipple and rub my erection into her groin.

Her hips thrust up. "Please, you bastard, fuck me."

I pull out my switchblade and grip the neckline of her shirt, slicing it open, the halves gaping away from her tits. This time, I won't give her a chance to escape. She can't, not with her hands cuffed. But for reasons I don't understand, this woman always drives me insane with lust, and I need to come inside her body one more time before I haul her back to the UK.

What happens to her after that is not my concern.

I shove the knife back into my pocket and yank her trousers and underwear down to her ankles. I leave them there, so they shackle her feet. Then I allow myself a moment to admire her body while I stroke my *slat* through my jeans and imagine all the ways I want to make her scream.

"Please let me touch you," she says.

"No." I unzip my jeans, freeing my cock, and I close my fist around it to skim my palm up and down my length. "You're at my mercy, and I mean to keep it that way."

She writhes, grasping the headboard rails.

This is a mistake. I know, but I donnnae care, not with her lying beneath me and the scent of her desire shattering my self-control.

I push her legs apart and plunge inside her body.

Aye, I'll pay for this later. But not yet. Not until I've slaked my lust. Even if she finds a way to escape again, I will hunt her to the ends of the earth.

Piper Lang is my obsession.

Magnus MacTaggart returns in *Relentless in a Kilt*.

*A*nna Durand is a bestselling, multi-award-winning author of contemporary and paranormal romance. Her books have earned bestseller status on every major retailer and wonderful reviews from readers around the world. But that's the boring spiel. Here are the really cool things you want to know about Anna!

Born on Lackland Air Force Base in Texas, Anna grew up moving here, there, and everywhere thanks to her dad's job as an instructor pilot. She's lived in Texas (twice), Mississippi, California (twice), Michigan (twice), and Alaska—and now Ohio.

As for her writing, Anna has always made up stories in her head, but she didn't write them down until her teen years. Those first awful books went into the trash can a few years later, though she learned a lot from those stories. Eventually, she would pen her first romance novel, the paranormal romance *Willpower*, and she's never looked back since.

Want even more details about Anna? Get access to her extended bio when you subscribe to her newsletter and download the free bonus ebook, *Hot Scots Confidential*. You'll also get hot deleted scenes, character interviews, fun facts, and more! Plus you'll receive audio bonus content narrated by Shane East, Vanessa Edwin, and Ava Lucas.

Visit AnnaDurand.com to sign up.